WHISKEY

A Reed Security Romance

GIULIA LAGOMARSINO

Cover Design courtesy of T.E. Black Designs

www.teblackdesigns.com

❀ Created with Vellum

To Katy and your brother. Thank you for helping me with this book while serving our country.

CAST OF CHARACTERS

Sebastian "Cap" Reed- owner
    Maggie "Freckles" Reed
    Caitlin Reed
    Clara Reed
    Gunner Reed
    Tucker Reed
    Lily Reed
    Carter Reed
    Julia Reed

Team 1:

Derek "Irish" Cortell- team leader and part owner
    Claire Cortell
    Janie Cortell

Hunter "Pappy" Papacosta
    Lucy Papacosta
    Rylee Papacosta
    Colt Papacosta

Rocco Turner
   Brooke
   Evelyn Rose Turner

Team 2:

Sam "Cazzo" Galmacci- team leader and part owner
   Vanessa Galmacci
   Sofia Galmacci
   Leo Galmacci
   Max Galmacci

Mark "Sinner" Sinn
   Cara Sinn
   Violet Sinn
   Asher Sinn

Blake "Burg" Reasenburg
   Emma Reasenburg
   Ryker Reasenburg
   Beatrix (Bea)

Team 3:

John "Ice" Peters- team leader and part owner
   Lindsey Peters
   Zoe Peters
   Cade Peters
   Willow Peters

Julian "Jules" Siegrist
   Ivy Siegrist
   John Christopher Hudson Siegrist
   Katie Siegrist

Chris "Jack" McKay

Alison (Ali) McKay
Axel McKay
Elizabeth (Lizzie) McKay

Team 4:

Chance "Sniper" Hendrix
  Morgan James (Shyla)
  Payton James

Jackson Lewis
  Raegan Cartwright
  Annie Lewis
  Parents: Susan and Robert Cartwright

Gabe Moore
  Isabella (Isa) Moore
  Vittoria
  Lorenzo (Enzo)
  Grayson Moore

Team 5:

Alec Wesley
  Florrie Younge
  Reid

Craig Devereux
  Reese Pearson
  Grant Devereux

Training:

Hudson Knight- formerly known as Garrick Knight
  Kate Knight
  Raven Knight

Griffin Knight
Cade Knight

Lola "Brave" Pruitt
Ryan Jackson
James Jackson (Cassandra Jackson- mother)
Piper Jackson
Ryder Jackson
Paige Jackson

Team 6:

Storm Hart
Jessica Finley

Daniel "Coop" Cooper
Becky Harding
Kayla Cooper (daughter)

Tony "Tacos" Russo
Molly Erickson
Marcello Russo

IT Department:

Robert "Rob" Markum

Chapter One

CHRIS

17 years ago...

"Ali, I have to do this. My brother joined the Blood Devils and he got into some bad shit. I have to get him out."

"You can't get him out, Chris. Once you join, there's no leaving. There's nothing you can do for Will."

I grabbed the gun Will had given me and put it in the back of my pants. He had always told me that he was going to take me and teach me to shoot. He hadn't had the opportunity yet and now I wished he had. I was going to need to know if I joined the Blood Devils and sold my soul. The initiation was to kill someone. I had never even fired a gun before and now I was expected to kill another person. I had already met with Slasher, the man that initiated my brother into the gang. He had informed me that if I failed, I would be killed and so would my brother. There was no going back once I walked onto their turf.

"I can't just leave him, Ali. He's my brother, the only family I have left."

"I thought...you said that we were going to get married. You said you wanted to start a life with me."

"I wanted that, but it's not going to happen now." My dad left us and my mom wasted away. There was no one to watch out for us. Will made sure that I didn't starve. He did things that no one should have to do to make sure that I didn't get taken away from him. "I won't abandon him now. I have to do this."

She took a step back from me, tears streaming down her face. "I can't do this with you. I won't be a part of that life."

"I'm not asking you to. I've made my choice. It's time for you to move on."

"I can't believe that you're choosing a gang over me. We've been together for two years. We've known each other since we were kids."

"I'm not choosing the gang. I'm choosing my brother and I always will. Ali, let's face it. We're seventeen years old. You'll forget about me in a month and move on to some college kid that will bring you to parties and show you a great time. Then you'll meet the love of your life and get married."

It killed me to say that. I was the love of her life. I was the one that was supposed to marry her. I was the one that was supposed to give her the world.

"This was never going to work anyway. I have nothing to offer you, Ali. I'm just the kid from the wrong side of the tracks." I huffed out a laugh and looked away. "Your parents will be happy to be proven right."

"This isn't you. You're doing this out of some kind of loyalty to your brother and I get that, but he wouldn't want you to join that life. He only did it so that you had a chance."

"And I won't leave him behind."

The tears were pouring down her face, but I couldn't let it get to me. I had to get to my brother and try to help him out of the trouble he was in. I didn't know how I would do that yet, but I'd do everything I could to get him out.

"Goodbye, Ali. Don't contact me again."

I turned and walked away, leaving her in my mom's trailer, sobbing and crying out for me. It broke my fucking heart to do that to her, but

I couldn't see a way out. I was fucking seventeen. What could I give her?

I went to the meet up and immediately felt on edge. My brother was standing between Slasher and another member I hadn't met yet. Will was beaten badly and looked like he could barely stand. Why weren't they doing something for him?

"Looks like you got here just in time, Chris." Slasher pulled out a gun and let it dangle at his side. I eyed it warily, not wanting to give him a reason to use it. I felt my own gun pressed against my back, but since I didn't even know how to use it, it didn't seem wise to pull it out and threaten him with it.

"In time for what?" I asked.

"To see what happens to those who betray us. Your brother has been stealing from us. He says that he needed the money to feed your sorry ass."

I glanced at my brother, but he wouldn't meet my eyes. I knew he had done some terrible things, but to cross the Blood Devils was a death sentence if caught. I couldn't believe he had done that.

"If you want to join us, you have one job." He held out the gun to me, but I just stared at it. I couldn't kill my brother. There was no way I could ever do that. I looked at him and saw him shake his head slightly. He wouldn't want this for me, even though he knew they would make it ten times as worse for him if I didn't do it. They were hoping I would show him mercy and shoot him myself, and then I would be a part of their gang. But my feet wouldn't move. I wouldn't kill the one person that was always on my side. I couldn't.

"Do it!" Slasher barked, but still I stood there. An evil look crossed over his face. I watched as the other man delivered blow after blow to my brother until he was a bloody mess on the ground. He was no longer moving or even opening his eyes. There was so much blood that I had to look away to keep from vomiting everywhere, but I had to stay and make sure they put that bullet in his head. I had to make sure that he wasn't suffering anymore.

After what seemed like an interminable amount of time, they finally racked the slide on the gun and held it to his head. "This is what happens to people that cross us. You go to the cops or even think of saying anything to anyone, I'll come after you, your sorry excuse for a mother, and that little girlfriend of yours. I'll make sure no one will ever recognize you. You feel me?"

I nodded, unsure what else to do. The gun fired and my eyes slid closed as memories of my brother and I washed over me. He had always been there for me and I had failed the one time he needed me. I opened my eyes and stared into the dead eyes of Slasher. He jerked his head in a signal for me to leave. I didn't want to leave my brother there, but I knew this was my only chance to leave. If I stayed, they'd put a bullet in me and my brother's sacrifice would have been for nothing.

I turned and ran as fast as I could, determined to get away from this life and everything that reminded me of it. I briefly thought of Ali and considered taking her with me, but I was a coward. I had just watched as my brother was beaten and executed and I did nothing. I had a gun and I didn't even try to defend him. What kind of man would I be to take Ali with me when I couldn't even protect her? I didn't go back to my trailer that night. I walked the streets, trying to think of how I would escape this life when I walked past a recruiting office for the USMC. I could learn to fight. I could learn to defend myself and never be vulnerable again. I sat outside on the sidewalk until the next morning when the office opened.

"I'm Sergeant Mills. What can I do for you today, son?"

"I'm here to enlist."

He sat down behind his desk and leaned back in his chair, steepling his fingers as he assessed me. I was a tall, lanky kid. I didn't look like much, but then, I never had regular meals either.

"What's your name, son?"

"Chris McKay."

"And why do you want to join?"

I ran through all the answers in my head. There were so many reasons and I didn't know which one he wanted to hear, so I told him all of them.

"I don't have a home. My dad left a long time ago and my mother is a waste of a human being. My brother joined the Blood Devils to try and put food on the table and take care of me. I saw him murdered last night when they caught him." I shook my head and looked down. "I don't have anywhere else to go, and I don't want to end up dead like him."

Sergeant Mills was quiet for a moment before he leaned forward and gathered some paperwork. "When do you turn eighteen?"

"Six months."

"Do you think your mother would sign a paper letting you join?"

"Not likely. She's always stuck in a bottle."

He nodded, leaning back in his seat. "I'm sorry, but you can't join until you're eighteen. You need a guardian's consent to join at seventeen. You'll have to wait."

"I can forge it. No one would ever know," I said desperately.

"There are other things too. You're malnourished and I'm sure you won't meet the weight requirements, not to mention you'll have to pass a physical, which I doubt you would. Have you graduated high school?"

I shook my head dejectedly. This was it. I wasn't going to get in. I wouldn't be getting away from this life. I would end up like my brother, dead on the streets before my eighteenth birthday.

"I'm sorry. You wouldn't be accepted."

I stood and made my way to the door, wondering if I could steal some food to eat.

"Wait," Sergeant Mills commanded. I turned and looked at him, lost and completely alone. "I have a proposition for you. You can come home with me. My wife, Cheryl, is an excellent cook. We'll get you healthy and you'll study for your GED. While you stay with me, I'll teach you everything you could ever want to know about the Marines. We'll train every day and I'll prepare you for boot camp. You'll also have to pass the ASVAB, it's the military entrance exam. I'll help you study for it. If in six months, when you turn eighteen, you still want to join, I'll get you signed up. If you don't want to, you can get a job to support yourself. Until then, your job will be to get healthy and prepare for the next stage of your life. If that's something you're interested in, you'll come home with me tonight. If you don't want to, I'll give you $20 and you can go get yourself a hot meal. What's it going to be?"

"I'll go home with you." It wasn't even a difficult decision to make. This man had just saved my life and I wouldn't waste it. I would do everything possible to ensure that his faith in me didn't go to waste.

Chapter Two

ALISON

Tennessee-present day

I walked out of the hospital like I did every night to see Gimpy waiting for me on his bike. I threw my messenger bag over my shoulder and climbed on back. I hardly ever touched him if I didn't have to. He was a disgusting man who smelled like he never showered and his teeth were yellow and falling out. When he first started taking me to work and picking me up, I clung to him because I had no other choice. I had never been on a bike and I didn't have much of a choice in whether or not I got on. Slasher made sure that I was watched around the clock. I was lucky that I got the freedom to go to work. Not that I kept any of my money. Slasher took everything from me and used my skills to fix up his guys when they came back bloodied. I was only a nurse, but he seemed to think that was the same as having a medical degree.

When we got back to the rundown house I called home, I hopped off the bike and ran inside. The only good part about coming back to this place was seeing my son. Every day I walked out the door, I wondered what Slasher would do to him when I was gone. I had tried to run in the past, but it had never worked. When Axel was younger, it was too hard to get away with him. He wasn't fast enough and I would always get caught. As he got older, Slasher kept a tighter rein on me and threatened me daily with killing my son if I ever tried to run again. I had taken enough beatings, and so had Axel, for me to know that he wasn't bluffing. But Axel was sixteen now and I was almost ready.

When I got to my room, I changed quickly and went to check on Axel. He was doing homework in his room and appeared fine. I home-schooled him because Slasher wouldn't allow him to attend public school. Probably because social services would be called on us if anyone ever saw him after a beating. At this point, there were days that I prayed someone would call DCFS on us just so that Axel could escape this life. Sadly, most people didn't actually care about their neighbors.

"Alison! Where the fuck is my food?"

So much for spending some time with my son. I quickly went downstairs and pulled out some things for dinner. Slasher was leaning against the counter, drinking a beer and staring at me. He was one of the ugliest men I knew. At one time, he hadn't been a bad looking guy, but years of smoking and doing drugs had aged him drastically. His brown hair was long and stringy and his brown eyes looked dead to me. His once muscular frame was now lanky with a pouch where he now had a beer belly. The worst part was his mouth. His teeth were rotting and his breath was always horrid.

I did my best not to make eye contact with him. I didn't want to see what he was thinking right now. As I stepped around him to take out some meat for dinner, he grabbed onto my arm and swung me around to face him.

"Why the fuck are you ignoring me?"

"I'm not," I said, refusing to meet his eyes.

"Don't fuck with me. What's going on with you?"

"I'm just making dinner," I said quietly. "Gimpy just brought me home. I went right upstairs to change and then I came down."

"Something's up with you."

I finally looked up at him and saw the questions in his eyes. There wasn't anything up with me, well, no more than there had been over the past two years. For some reason though, he was questioning me now. I blinked quickly, trying to hold back my panic. Had someone followed me? How had he found out? I took deep breaths trying to hold in the terror. He shoved me backwards, causing me to hit my head on the corner of a cabinet before I hit the ground.

"The problem is, you're not scared enough anymore. Why is that? Have I not given you enough lessons?"

I couldn't think of a good response. I wanted to tell him that I was plenty scared of him, but the truth was, I wasn't as scared of him as of getting caught. That would be a death sentence for me and then no one would be there to protect Axel.

He grabbed me by the hair, pulling hard as he jerked me closer to him. "Make my fucking dinner and don't forget who owns you. If I have to give you reminders, you won't be making it into work for a while."

He threw me backwards and stormed out of the room. I stood quickly and got to work on his dinner. By the time I finished, I was a nervous ball of energy. I wanted desperately to call Adam, my one true friend at the hospital, and check on him, but I had no way of doing that without giving myself away. I would have to wait and talk to him tomorrow.

Slasher left me alone that night and I helped Axel with his homework. He was a really smart kid and if he had actual teachers, he would probably be further along with his classes. I had been a good student too, but I wasn't a teacher. There was only so much I felt I could bring to the table for him. I just needed a little more time and then I could get us both out of there. I was close to being ready, but I had to be sure that I could succeed.

When I was able to get through my morning without being stopped by Slasher or any of his men, I really started to worry that I had been caught. Gimpy gave me a ride as usual, but he was quiet the whole way. Usually, he tried to flirt with me or something, but he was preoccupied this morning. I got off his bike and looked back at him warily, but he was already roaring out of the parking lot. I ran inside and to the locker room, quickly stashing my stuff. I had just five minutes before I had to clock in and I was determined to find Adam. I didn't want to page him in case one of Slasher's guys was in the hospital watching me. I raced down to the physical therapy wing and pushed through the doors to see Adam sitting at his desk going over paperwork. I took a deep breath and sighed in relief.

"Ali? What's wrong?"

He stood and walked over to me, placing his hands on my arms and rubbing them lightly.

"Nothing. I was just worried."

"Is this about..." He looked around to make sure no one could over hear us. "Is this about Slasher? Did he do something?"

"No," I said with a shake of my head. "I thought he suspected something last night and I was worried that he knew that we had been meeting."

Adam's jaw clenched and he took a step back. "I wish you would go to the police. They could help you."

"I can't. He'll kill my son."

"He'll kill you if he finds out that you're taking self-defense classes."

"The only way he'll find out is if someone tells him and since you and I are the only ones that know, that doesn't seem very likely."

"How many more times are you going to let him smack you around before you decide you're ready to leave?"

"Adam, if I'm not ready and I can't get away, I'll get myself killed. Who would protect Axel? I have to be sure about this."

He nodded and ran a hand over the back of his head. "I know. I just wish there was more I could do."

"You're doing plenty. Do you know how much you're risking by helping me? The Blood Devils don't mess around. If they found out about you, you'd be dead before me."

"I'm not worried about me. I can take care of myself."

I bit my lip and wondered if I should tell him my plan. It was probably safer if he didn't know, but I didn't want him to worry either. "There's going to be an initiation soon. Within the next few days. Slasher always throws big parties the night before. I think that might be my time to slip out. We might be able to get away if they're all wasted."

"If you get the chance, you run and you don't look back. Cash only."

"I know," I said, taking a deep breath. "I don't have much, but it's enough to get me where I need to go."

"Are you going to tell me where that is?" he asked.

I shook my head. "I'm sorry, but it's better if you don't know. If we make it there, we'll be safe."

"So, what? I shouldn't worry if you don't show up at work in a few days?"

"Just pray that I actually made it out and I'm not at the bottom of the lake," I said with tears in my eyes. Adam had been so good to me and I hated saying goodbye to him, but it was the only way. I would miss him so much when we left. He had been my rock over the past two years.

"I know I can't hug you or anything. Just be safe. Call me if you need me and I'll be there for you."

I nodded and took a step back. "I have to get to work. Be careful," I said as I spun around and ran back to clock in. I prayed like hell all day that nothing I did would ever touch Adam. He was a solid guy and had done more for me than I could ever have hoped for. One day, I would find a way to let him know that I was okay and that I appreciated all he had done for me. If I made it out.

———

"Tomorrow's the big day!" Gimpy said in excitement as I climbed on his bike.

"What are you talking about?"

"Tomorrow, your boy becomes a man. A real member of the Blood Devils. Slasher's pretty fucking excited."

My insides churned and I almost threw up right there. I knew that he was planning an initiation, I just didn't know it was for my own son. I couldn't let that happen. We would have to leave tonight. There was no other way. No matter what happened, I would get my son away from Slasher once and for all.

I was in a daze the whole way back to the house, trying to think of something that I could do. An idea struck me, but it was dangerous. If my plan worked, there was every chance for escape. There was also every chance that I wouldn't make it out of the house alive. I had to try. I had to pick a fight with Slasher and make sure that he beat me up. It was the only time that he left me unattended. If I was beaten too badly, he would get high with everyone else and forget about me. It was my last chance and I had to take it. One way or the other, I was leaving this place tonight, either on my own or in a body bag.

I walked in the house and immediately searched out Slasher. I had to do it while I was still good and pissed and had the nerve. I stomped into his office, flinging the door open. His eyes whipped up at me and he scowled.

"What the fuck do you think you're doing? You fucking know better."

"You can't do this. I won't let you. Axel is not joining your little gang of drug runners. He's going to college and he's going to make something of himself."

"He'll do what I say and that's final. How do you think it would look to the guys if all their sons joined and mine went off to be some pussy lawyer?"

"I don't care what they think. He won't be a part of this life anymore. You really want to force your son to kill someone?"

He stepped around the desk and was in front of me before I could even blink. His fist shot out and cracked me hard in the cheek. I fell to the floor, whimpering in pain. It hurt like a bitch, but this was what I needed. Slasher lived by his own set of rules and he did whatever he had to in order to keep people in line. I'd seen more people killed over the past seventeen years than anyone should have to. While I once was a naive seventeen year old girl, I now lived with the realities of the gang life.

"Bitch, you don't get a say in this. Unless you want to end up at the bottom of the river, you'll keep your fucking mouth shut."

I gathered up the bloody spit in my mouth and did the only thing I could think of. I spit in his face. His eyes turned molten as he grabbed me by the hair and yanked me off the floor, throwing me onto the desk. I scrambled to get away from him, but he was faster than me. I should be used to this by now, but it never got any easier to take.

His hands gripped my waist as he tore open my pants and pulled them from my body. I kicked and thrashed out at him, but it only angered him more. A backhand to the face sent me sprawling off the desk and across the floor. Before I could curl into myself, he kicked me in the stomach. I barely had time to register the pain before he kicked me again. I felt something crack and gasped for breath, hoping that I would live long enough to protect my son.

When his foot connected with my jaw, I was done fighting. I laid there like a limp rag as he punched me and kicked me a few more times. I could hardly breathe and my whole body ached. When he dragged me across the floor, I whimpered and tried to beg, but nothing would come out of my swollen mouth.

I felt my panties torn from my body and his erection pressing at my entrance. I let my mind drift as he roughly shoved himself inside me and remembered better days when Chris had been mine and we were planning a future together. His rough thrusts brought me back to the present and reminded me that Chris was no longer a part of my life. It didn't matter. I would see him soon if I could get through this.

"You're a dried up whore," he said, slapping my face. "You ever wonder why I didn't want you anymore?"

I didn't care why he had stopped coming to me so often. I was just glad to not be assaulted repeatedly by him.

"I should just fucking kill you," he hissed as he shoved himself inside me one final time. "You're not worth the fuck."

He pulled out and shoved himself back in his jeans, stomping out the door. I laid on the floor, bleeding and broken. When Slasher had first taken me, I had thought that our son would always keep me protected from the worst of his anger, but I was wrong. He didn't seem to care at all that I was his son's mother. In fact, it seemed to anger him that I was attached to him at all. If it weren't for my son, I would pray for death. I was close to it at this point. Being in the medical field, I knew that he had just beaten me badly, but that was what I had planned on and it would save me in the end.

I laid there on the floor for a good half hour until I finally decided that I had to drag myself upstairs and try to clean myself up. It would be painful and getting away wouldn't be easy, but I had to get Axel out of here. I had to be sure that he didn't turn into a murderer, and there was only one man I knew that could stop this train wreck.

———

By the time I was able to drag myself off the floor and back to my room, I almost passed out on the bed. I had been living with Slasher since he grabbed me from my home the day after Chris left. My parents had assumed that I had run off with Chris and when I tried to see them, they took one look at my burgeoning baby bump and turned me away.

I hadn't wanted to be with Slasher, but he wasn't someone that you walked away from. The few times I had tried to run, he beat me so bad that I couldn't move for weeks. So, I stopped trying to run and focused on a way to make myself useful to him. I convinced him to let me go to nursing school, telling him that I would be able to help out more when his men were injured and I would be bringing in income for him.

It had worked and I focused on that as much as possible. I thought that I would be able to stash at least some money away, but he had quickly rid me of all my money. He knew what I was trying to accom- plish and made it very clear that he would kill Axel if I attempted anything. I had done my best over the years to stay away from him, but there were still times that just my presence angered him and he would take it out on my body. At least a few times a year, he would beat on Axel, just to prove to me that he would do it.

Moving off the bed as gingerly as possible, I knelt down on the floor and cringed as my bruised knees pressed into the wooden floor. I took out the loose floorboard and pulled my life savings from it, stuffing the $500 in my pockets. It was all I could collect over the years. I took a few dollars here and there when Slasher would leave money in his pockets. It wasn't much, but it was enough to get Axel and I to Chris in Pennsylvania. A few weeks ago, I had done a search on him and found out that he was working for a security company and that he was a retired Marine. I knew that Slasher wouldn't wait long for Axel's initiation, but I hadn't realized it would happen tomorrow. Now, I would have to get to Chris as fast as I could. I had been putting it off because Slasher had been watching me closely, but now that he had given me a good beating, he wouldn't bother with me for days, assuming that I was too weak to do anything. I had counted on this. I had prayed for this. It was my one chance to get help.

Slasher's crew was having a party and by midnight, they would all be passed out downstairs, completely unaware of anything going on around them. I soaked in the tub, trying to ease the pain in my muscles before I ran. It helped a little and allowed me to at least move without intense pain. I popped as many pain pills as I could and put together a small backpack with a change of clothes and grabbed the burner phone that Adam had given me a few weeks ago. By the time it got quiet downstairs, I was ready to go. I crept downstairs and saw everyone was passed out or too high to give a shit what was going on. A few of them had needles sticking out of their arms. This life was the worst and it was time to get away.

I went back to Axel's room and knocked lightly. When he swung the door open, I could see the way his eyes flicked to the bag over my shoulder and then the disappointment. He didn't comment on my battered body. He'd seen it enough to know what had happened.

He looked so much like Chris when he was sixteen. He had the same dark eyes and the same stern expression when he was angry. It made me wonder how closely he resembled him now.

"So, you're finally leaving?"

"We're leaving."

He shook his head and walked back to his bed, plopping down. "There's no leaving this life and you know it."

"I have some money set aside and I know someone that can help us, but we need to leave tonight before Slasher wakes up."

"Mom, you know that Slasher will kill you if you try to leave. It's not worth it."

"Slasher wants you to be initiated into the gang tomorrow." His eyes flicked up to mine and I saw the terror in them. He knew exactly what it took to be initiated into the gang. He also knew the consequences if he failed. "I won't let that happen. Now's our chance to run. Please," I begged him. "I won't leave without you."

He looked defeated, but there was a spark of hope underneath that. Axel never wanted this life. He never liked Slasher and the beatings he had taken since he was a little kid had trained him to obey Slasher without question. But the idea of getting away from it all and starting over was one that I didn't think he would resist.

"If they find us, they'll kill us. Are you sure you want to do this?"

"I would rather die trying to get away than stay one more minute under this roof," I said fiercely.

He didn't waste another minute arguing. He grabbed a bag and threw some spare clothes inside, leaving everything else behind. We didn't have much as it was, so leaving it wasn't a hard decision. There was nothing that we wanted from this life.

I went downstairs first, making sure it was still clear. My heart thundered in my chest as I walked past each of the twenty members passed out downstairs. Usually, there were a few guys guarding the house, but on party nights, they sometimes joined in after the others were too wasted to care. Luckily, this was one of those nights. I waved Axel downstairs and together, we walked out of that house, not looking back once.

Anxiety crept over me with every step I took. If they realized we were gone before we made it out, I would be dead and Axel would have only one option. He would have to kill someone and become part of the gang. The further we got, the more my body tensed. It wouldn't abate until we made it out of this hellhole and were safely on our way. Even that wasn't a guarantee that we made it out.

We made it to the corner before my body hurt too much to go on. I handed the burner phone to Axel and had him call a cab as I sagged down on a bench. I hadn't wanted to waste the money on a cab, but we would never make it out of there if we didn't catch a ride. The cab arrived and took us to the bus station. The driver didn't mention my bruises or even look twice at me. Around here, it was perfectly normal to see people walking around looking half beaten.

We made it to the bus station and as we bought our tickets, I made sure Axel pulled his hoodie up over his head to hide from the cameras. I pulled on a baseball hat and pulled it low to cover as much of me as possible. As I handed over the money, I couldn't help but glance around to make sure no one had followed us. I bought tickets to Kansas, figuring it would be best if we zigzagged around the country first.

I didn't breathe normally until the bus finally pulled away. I sagged back against the seat and felt the first tears of relief finally slip free. I gripped onto Axel's hand in the seat next to me and squeezed tightly. It was finally over. We were going to get out of here and live life. We were going to be free.

It took us four days to get to Pittsburgh. That's where the last bus stopped. I didn't have enough money to get a cab to the town Chris lived in. I had only five dollars left to my name and we hadn't eaten yet today. It was closing in on night time and I didn't know anything about the city, but I knew I didn't want to stay the night here. I pulled out the burner phone and found the number I had stored for Reed Security and pressed send. As the phone rang, I sank down to the ground. My body was aching so badly and all I wanted to do was sleep, but I had to get to Chris. He was my last hope.

"Reed Security. This is Sebastian Reed speaking."

I almost started crying when I heard the voice. I was so close. I just had to hang on a little longer.

"I need to speak with Chris McKay please."

"May I ask who's calling?"

Did I tell him my name? Was it safe? I didn't know if I had a choice in the matter. He had told me never to contact him again, but he may not take my call otherwise.

My voice shook as I answered. "Ali. Just tell him Ali is calling."

The silence stretched for a moment before he finally asked me to wait a minute. I prayed that he would answer. I prayed that he wouldn't turn me away. I had no other options. If he didn't help, my son would fall back in the hands of the Blood Devils.

"Who is this?"

"Chris?"

"Yeah. Who's asking?"

I choked down a sob and took a deep breath. "Ali. I need your help."

Chapter Three

CHRIS

"Chris?"

"Yeah. Who's asking?"

"Ali. I need your help."

I'd recognize that voice anywhere. That was the voice of my angel that I hadn't spoken to in seventeen years. I thought about her every day, but I didn't allow myself to dwell on what she was up to. I was sure she had gotten married and was living the good life. When I left, I pushed her from my mind, but when the long nights got to me while I was stationed overseas, I let my mind drift to Ali and the life we could have had together.

"Ali," I croaked out. Sebastian stared at me from the other side of the office, obviously sensing my distress. "What's going on?"

"I need you to come get me and my son. We're in Pittsburgh and I need someplace to hide."

I tensed immediately. "Hide from what?"

"Slasher." My world bottomed out just like that. She was with Slasher? What the hell had happened? "Please, Chris, I'll explain everything when you get here. We're at the bus station on 11th St. Please. I need you, Chris."

I could hear the desperation in her voice, but I hadn't missed that she had a son. Was it Slasher's son? And why the hell had she gotten mixed up with him? It didn't matter why. I couldn't let her live in fear of Slasher. I wouldn't let another person fall prey to him.

"I'll be there in an hour. Stay out of sight and I'll call you back on this number when I get there."

"Okay," she said quietly.

I didn't say anything else before I hung up. It was on the tip of my tongue to tell her that I loved her. I always had and I always would, but that was seventeen years ago and I had no clue what she had been up to since then or if she even felt the same way. All I knew was that I wouldn't let her down.

"Everything okay?" Sebastian asked as he walked toward me.

"A girl I used to know needs a place to hide out. She's in Pittsburgh, so I'm gonna go get her and her son."

"Who's she running from?"

My jaw clenched, hating that I had to tell Sebastian this. "The Blood Devils."

"Fuck," he whispered. He ran a hand across his jaw and picked up the phone. "Ice, get Jules and meet us downstairs in ten."

He hung up without another word, motioning for me to follow him.

"I can take care of this, Cap."

"I know you can, but if the Blood Devils are involved, we're not taking any chances. You have no idea if they followed her or not. You could be walking into a trap."

I followed him out to the elevator and we headed down to the level where all the guns were stored. Five minutes later, Ice and Jules walked in, seeing us gearing up and did the same.

"I want to take two vehicles. Let's load up both and get on the road. I want everyone wearing vests and bring one for her."

"She has her son with her."

He nodded and tossed an extra at me. He picked up several handguns, magazines, and pulled on his shoulder holster. I did the same and attached my ankle holster. I had no idea if she had taken the proper precautions when coming here, but I wasn't about to show up unprepared. It took us another five minutes to load up the SUVs. Most of them were already stocked, so it was a matter of making sure we had everything we needed. I rode with Cap while Jules and Ice rode in the other vehicle.

We hadn't even made it five minutes down the road before Cap started in.

"So, you gonna tell me the story finally?"

I shrugged. "I'm not sure this has anything to do with it."

"How could it not? It's the Blood Devils."

I sighed and ran a hand across my jaw. "I was dating Ali when I was seventeen. She was the one, I knew it from the moment I met her. I was going to take her away from our crappy town and start over, but then my brother got involved with the Blood Devils and I couldn't leave. I knew that he was doing some nasty shit to make sure that I had food and clothes. I wanted to join and help him get out."

"You don't get out of a gang like that," Cap said, glancing over at me.

"I know that now, but I was seventeen and I wanted to help my brother. Anyway, when I decided to join, I told her that it was over, that I never wanted to see her again. Then I went to meet with Slasher. He was waiting with my brother and another guy. My brother had been stealing from them and they wanted me to kill him. That was supposed to be my initiation."

"Did you do it?"

"No. There was no way I could kill him. He was all I had left. I watched as they beat the shit out of him and then put a bullet in his head. They told me that was what would happen to me and Ali if I ever told. I walked away and that was the last I ever heard from Slasher."

"Slasher is the leader?"

"At the time he wasn't. He was just an enforcer. I have no idea what he is now."

"How the hell did she get wrapped up in their shit?"

"I don't know, but she has a son. I hope to God he's not Slasher's kid."

My mind drifted to the first time I met Ali. We were just little kids, but I knew right away that she was the sweetest little girl I would ever meet.

I walked into school, embarrassed because Mom had forgotten to do laundry for the past two weeks. My already too short pants were filthy with grass stains and they hung loose on my lanky frame. I was tall, but way too skinny. Mom didn't care if my pants didn't fit. My dad had left us a few months back and she ceased to care about anything to do with my brother or me.

Kids shoved me and laughed at me as I made my way to my locker. All I had for a backpack was a plastic bag I used from the grocery store. I unloaded the few school items I had been able to scrounge up and debated hiding out in the bathroom for the rest of the day. There was a pretty strawberry smell drifting toward me and when I shut my locker, I saw a pretty girl standing next to me, smiling at me. At first, I thought maybe she was smiling because she was laughing at me, but then she held out her hand and introduced herself.

"Hi, I'm Alison. What's your name?"

I stared at her hand and then glanced down at my filthy one. She didn't seem to care, though. She slipped her fingers through my hand and grasped my hand tightly.

"Chris," I said quietly.

"It's nice to meet you. I'm new to this school. Do you think you could show me around?"

"Sure," I said hesitantly. She would learn soon enough that I wasn't the kid to be seen with. But as we walked around the school, she just talked to me, telling me about where she was from and how excited she was to start at this new school. Being in the seventh grade, now was really the time for her to make friends with the right crowds. I was not in any of those crowds.

"Look, you seem really nice, but if you keep walking around with me, kids are going to make fun of you."

She looked at me strangely. "Do you not want me around you?"

"It's not that. You seem nice, but all the kids make fun of me. I just don't want you to get picked on."

"Well, you're the first person that's been nice to me, so I think I'd like you as a friend."

From that day on, we were inseparable. She ignored all the people that made fun of her and acted like it didn't bother her. She would pack extra food in her lunches to share with me. She had noticed that I never really had a lunch. We would usually start walking home together, but I went to the trailer park and she went to a nice subdivision on the other side of town. I never wanted to leave her side, but no matter how many times she asked me if I wanted to go to her house to play, I always turned her down. I was too embarrassed to show up at her house looking the way I did.

Ali became my best friend over the years. My only friend, really. And by the time we made it to high school, I hoped that one day she could be more than my friend. I was sure that I didn't deserve her, but when I finally worked up the courage to ask her to go steady with me, I was relieved when she said yes. For so many years, she had been my whole world, and I had just walked away from her one day.

We drove the rest of the way in silence and when we got close, I gave Ali a call and let her know we were almost there. We drove around for a few minutes, checking to see if there was anything suspicious. When we didn't see anything, Cap parked and Ice pulled up alongside him, rolling down the window.

"Jules and Chris will go get Ali and her son. We'll stay here on standby. Keep your eyes open."

Ice nodded and I got out of the SUV, joining Jules on the sidewalk. We walked down to the edge of the building where they were hiding beside the dumpster and what I saw nearly killed me. Ali was on the ground, curled up in pain. Her face looked like it had been bashed in with a baseball bat and her son was hovering over her protectively.

"Ali," I said, kneeling down beside her. "What the fuck happened?"

"We need to get out of here," she gasped in pain. "I think I saw one of them."

Jules immediately straightened and pulled out his phone, calling Cap and letting him know.

"I'm gonna pick you up, okay? Try not to make any noise." I turned to the kid, who looked about fifteen or sixteen. "Stay with Jules and do exactly as he tells you."

The kid nodded and reluctantly stepped away from his mother. I put my arms under her and cradled her gently against my body. She whimpered softly, but didn't cry out in pain. Jules pulled out his weapon and guided us back toward the SUVs. I watched the shadows as best I could, but if we were attacked, I was fucked. I couldn't carry her like this and shoot a weapon.

We were about half way there when we heard the voice.

"There's the kid!"

I spun around to see where the hell they were and that's when I saw four of them with guns aimed in our direction. Jules was already shoving the kid on the ground and aiming at the group of Blood Devils. The first shot hit a little too close for my liking, but they obviously weren't very good shots. Still any gun being fired was dangerous. I set Ali down, none too gently, and pulled my own weapon, hovering over her. I fired off a few shots, hitting one before the others took cover. Jules got in a better position and took out another.

Cap came screeching up in the SUV along the curb and opened fire to give us cover. I hauled Ali up over my shoulder and took off for the SUV. Jules was running behind, dragging the kid with him. I flung open the door and shoved Ali inside, climbing in behind her. The kid came in behind me and Jules slammed the door, running for the other vehicle. I lowered the back window and fired at the last two guys, hitting one while Cap took out the other.

Cap threw the truck in drive and we peeled out of the deserted bus station and headed for Reed Security. I knelt over Ali on the seat, hearing that she was wheezing badly and gasping for air.

"Shit. Shit, shit, shit. Cap, get Pappy on the phone. I think I punctured Ali's lung!"

Cap dialed Pappy quickly, barking at him that we had an emergency.

"Alright, Chris, get the med kit out. Inside is a chest tube insertion kit with everything you'll need."

"You want me to stick a chest tube in her?" I asked incredulously.

"Just shut the fuck up and listen or she's gonna die from lack of oxygen or her heart will give out from the pressure."

I was shaking, but I took a deep breath and pulled myself together, grabbing the kit and opening it up. Cap pulled over in an empty parking lot and got out, sliding the front seats forward for more space. I laid out all the equipment and wiped the sweat from my forehead.

"Alright, grab the hand sanitizer and wash your hands as best you can. Then put on a pair of gloves." I did as he said and snapped the gloves in place.

"What's next?" Cap stood outside the door, having done the same thing and waited for instructions.

"Use the wipes to sanitize the side of her body by her ribs. Cap, there's a syringe and a bottle with the local anesthetic. Get it ready for him. Chris, you need to pull up her shirt and locate the 4th or 5th intercostal space. That's below either the fourth or fifth rib. That first rib is hard to find, so it'll be about nipple high. You want to aim for the lower end of the space along the anterior axillary line."

"What the fuck does that mean, Pappy? I'm not a fucking doctor," I yelled as vomit rose in my throat.

"Calm down, Chris. I'll walk you through it. Follow the edge of the front of her shoulder down to the side of her breast. That's the anterior axillary line. Don't go too far back toward the midline, which will be the line right down the middle of her armpit. Got it?"

I counted her ribs, not sure if I had gotten the first or not, but I went with the fourth one down and felt the inside space. "Okay, I think I found it."

"Alright, you're going to want to give her the local anesthetic. Don't be stingy. You don't want her in pain."

Cap handed me the syringe he had filled and I inserted the needle, hoping to God that I didn't hurt her even more. "Okay, done."

"Good. Now, Cap, you need to find the tubing. One end is flared and gets gradually bigger. The other end connects to a Heimlich valve, which is a plastic piece that looks like a pencil point on both ends. One end is blue. That blue end connects to the bigger end of the tube. There should be an arrow directing you. Get that ready. Chris, you need to grab the catheter with the cannula inside, which is the tubing with a needle covered in plastic. The cannula isn't sharp, but inside that is a stylet. That's the needle. It's sharp and pointy."

"Got it." I grabbed the tubing and made sure I had everything.

"Okay, grab the surgical blade and make a skin nick where you're going to insert the tube."

I picked up the blade and squeezed my fist tight before putting the blade against her skin. I saw her kid staring at me out of the corner of my eye, which only made this more difficult. I pressed the blade lightly to her skin, only applying enough pressure so that I could insert the tube.

"Okay. What's next?"

"Put the needle inside the tube that fits tightly over it and then put that inside the catheter. You want to hold the tube in your left hand by the ribs, stabilizing the chest tube, and hold the needle with your right hand with your thumb pushing at the back of it. This is very important," he said urgently, "because if you don't press the needle into the tubing, you're going to be trying to shove that inside her without a sharp end."

That kind of flew over my head, but I got the gist. Hold the sharp stick inside the blunt stick.

"Now, you want to hold it perpendicular to the space. It's not going to slide right in, but as soon as you feel it give, stop pushing."

I took a deep breath and held the needle against her skin, saying a quick prayer that I didn't kill her. I pushed, feeling the needle tearing through and then the moment it was inside, I stopped pushing immediately. "I'm in."

"Okay, pull out the needle and put it aside. Make sure you don't stab yourself."

I pulled it out and set it aside.

"Now, push the needle covering tube in just a centimeter or so. You need to confirm that you're in the plura. Take a syringe and attach it to the end of the tube and you should be able to aspirate air easily."

I nodded and took the syringe that Cap handed to me, hooking it up to the tube and pulling it back, relieved when I was able to get air. "We're good!"

"Okay, push the catheter in a few more inches and then remove the tube." I did as he said. "Cap, hand him the tubing with the Heimlich valve. You want to attach it and make sure the stop cock valve is open. It's a little port looking thing that has a lever to open and close it."

I attached it and made sure the valve was open. "Done."

"Okay, look at the Heimlich valve. You should see some fluttering in there when she's breathing."

I looked at it, not seeing what he was talking about. Fuck, I had screwed it up. "I don't see it," I said urgently.

"It should be when she's breathing out."

I looked again and there it was. I blew out a breath and nodded, then realized Pappy couldn't see me. "I see it."

"Good. You need to secure that line. Put the petroleum gauze over it and tape it down."

When it was done, I sat back for a moment staring at Ali. Suddenly, I didn't feel so good. I shoved the kid out of the way and jumped from the SUV, emptying the contents of my stomach onto the pavement. My whole body shook and I wasn't sure if I was going to pass out or not.

"Stick your head between your legs," Jules said as he walked over to me. I did as he said and felt myself slowly starting to breath normal again. He handed me a water as he continued to keep an eye on our surroundings. When I felt like I wouldn't throw up anymore, I went back to the vehicle, noting that Cap had cleaned up and gotten her secure in the back seat.

"What's your name, kid?"

"Axel."

I instantly hated it. It was exactly something Slasher would name his kid. "You're riding in the back of the other SUV with Ice and Jules. We have to get your mom to the hospital."

He nodded reluctantly and followed Jules back to the other vehicle. I took a seat in the front with Cap and leaned my head back against the seat, closing my eyes. That had been a little too intense for today. I could handle bullets and I could handle being the one that was almost killed, but to watch the woman I still loved struggling for air and having to try and save her life was more than I could take.

Since Ali was stable, we took her to Kate's clinic where she could get x-rays. Hunter met us there so that Kate had another pair of hands if necessary. I stayed in the waiting area with Ice, Cap, Jules, and Axel as we waited to find out how she was. It took longer than I expected and I was getting impatient, waiting around for them to tell us anything. I didn't even give Axel a second thought after Ali was taken back. All I could think about was how she had suddenly come back into my life.

When Kate finally came out, I rushed over to her, eager to know how Ali was.

"You did a good job placing the chest tube," she smiled. "It looks like she'll be fine without surgery. A large portion of her lung collapsed, though, so she'll need to keep the chest tube in for a few days to allow her lung tissue to expand again. She should be fine within a few weeks. I'll have her do some breathing exercises to make sure she's expanding her lungs enough in the meantime. Where will she be staying?"

"With me," I said before I had a chance to think about it.

"Okay, I'll stop in regularly to make sure that she's doing okay. You can always call me with any questions and Hunter is also aware of what she needs."

"Thank you. When can I take her home?"

"Why don't you let her rest for a little longer and then you can take her."

"Thank you, Kate."

"You're welcome."

Kate went back toward the exam room and I sank down in a chair, finally able to breathe again.

"What do you want to do?" Cap asked as he sat down next to me.

"Aren't you supposed to tell me that?" I asked, shooting him a look.

"Look, I don't know what the hell this girl means to you now and how far you want to get involved. You know I don't like to see innocents wrapped up in shit, especially with scum like the Blood Devils. But you don't know what's happened over the last seventeen years. You don't know if she's innocent or if she got involved in something too deep and couldn't find a way out. So, I'm asking what you want to do."

I leaned forward, resting my head in my hands. I ground the heels of my hands into my eyes, trying to figure out what the hell I should do. He was right, I had no fucking clue what Ali had gotten herself into and I needed to find out before I got everyone at Reed Security involved.

"They can come home with me. I'll find out what's going on when she's better and we'll take it from there."

"Take Ice and Jules with you. They stay with you until we know more. If they found her in Pittsburgh, then they probably know that she was headed for you."

I shook my head. "I haven't had anything to do with her in almost twenty years. They wouldn't assume she would come to me."

"No, but they're going to want to know why she ran to Pittsburgh and it won't take them long to connect the dots. Be smart about this, Chris."

"You're right. It's been a long night. Let's just get everyone settled and figure shit out."

"You've got one hell of a source of information in that kid. I suggest you have a chat with him before Alison wakes up."

Once we got Ali settled at my house, I took Axel aside to have a chat. Jules and Ice were keeping watch outside.

"So, what can you tell me about what your mom has been up to the last seventeen years?" He looked at me warily, like he wasn't sure if he could trust me. "I was your mom's boyfriend a long time ago. I would never do anything to hurt her. I can understand that you don't know who to trust right now, but I'm trying to help and the more information I have, the more prepared I can be."

"As far as I know, she's always been with Slasher. I don't know why. He beats the shit out of her on a regular basis. He treats her like shit."

"Does he ever beat on you?"

He shrugged like it was no big deal. "Not as much as my mom."

There was a huge ache in my chest from hearing that she had been dealing with this shit for so long. Why hadn't she run sooner? Why hadn't I bothered to go back and check on her over the years?

"Is Slasher your dad?" He nodded. "Are you a part of the Blood Devils?"

"No, but Mom said that he was getting ready to initiate me. That's why we ran."

"Why didn't she run sooner?"

"She tried," he said, staring me down. The ache in my chest grew to a painful stabbing feeling. If she had tried to run before, that meant that this was a last ditch effort.

"Is the initiation still the same?"

"Killing someone? Yeah. How did you know?" he asked me warily.

"My brother was a Blood Devil. He didn't want to join, but he didn't think he had a choice."

"I didn't want to join either. I just didn't think I had a choice. It'd be pretty disappointing if the leader's son couldn't pass the initiation."

"So, Slasher's in charge now?"

"Yeah, he killed Bullet five years ago and took over."

I studied him for a moment, not believing that he turned out so normal. This kid didn't look like a killer. He didn't have gang tattoos and he didn't talk like a thug.

"How did you turn out so normal? You don't look like a gang member's son."

"Around Slasher, I had to talk like he wanted me to, but Mom always made sure that I knew how I was supposed to behave. I just don't get it. I've never understood why she was with him. She seems to despise his life."

The kid looked exhausted and I didn't think I was going to get too much more information out of him tonight. Well, I wasn't going to get the answers I needed, which seemed to be aligned with Axel's questions. He was right, nothing about this made sense.

"Come on. I'll show you to your room."

He stood and followed me upstairs, taking his bag with him. I showed him his room and the bathroom and then told him where his mom was staying, which was in my room. I only had two bedrooms and I wanted to keep an eye on her. Or, at least, that's what I told myself.

When he was settled, I went into my bedroom and checked on

Ali's breathing. She seemed to be doing okay, so I grabbed my Jack Daniels and a glass and sat down in a chair that I had brought up earlier from the living room to watch her sleep. I couldn't help but think about all the things I had wanted for her and all the ways I had let her down.

"What do you want to do when we graduate?" I asked Ali as we laid out under the stars near my trailer.

"I think I want to be a doctor. What do you want to do?"

"I just want to get out of here. I don't want to live in this town near my mom anymore. I want a life for myself." I rolled onto my side and looked at Ali. "I want you to come with me. I know that'll make it harder for you to get your degree and if you decide you don't want to, I'll understand. But you're it for me, Ali. I want to marry you and spend the rest of my life making you happy. I'll work three jobs to get us by, whatever it takes."

"Chris, it doesn't matter if I become a doctor, as long as I have you. I can work my way through college. We could live in a crappy apartment and I would be happy as long as you were with me."

"What about your parents? You know if you left with me, they would never speak to you again. They don't like me."

"They don't like anyone that isn't like them. But I don't want to be like them, Chris. Ever since I met you, I feel like I've found someone that I really connected with. Someone that really understood me and cared to listen to me. Maybe my parents care enough to feed and clothe me, but they're just as bad as your mom because they don't really care about me."

"I'll always love you, Ali. I'll always be there for you."

Her life could have been totally different if I had taken her with me. But after my brother was murdered in front of me, the only thing I thought about was getting out. I had done that, but I had left her behind and it looked like that was almost a fatal mistake.

Chapter Four

SLASHER

"I want her and my kid back," I shouted at my second, T-Bone. "I don't care what the fuck you have to do to get them back here. No one walks away without my permission. When was the last time you heard from Crusher?"

"They were in Pittsburgh, but that was two fucking days ago and they ain't pickin' up now."

"Fuck!" I roared, flipping over the table in front of me. I started pacing around the house, running my fingers through my hair. I needed something to take the edge off. I tried not to dip too much into our supplies, but when things got too intense, I did what I had to. If I started losing my shit in front of my guys, nobody would think I could still do the job. That was how I took out Bullet five years ago. He was weak and I saw my opening. I couldn't afford to be weak now. I had to show everyone that the Blood Devils didn't let anyone walk all over them.

"I'll call Ruger. I'll have him send out some scouts, find out where they are and who's protecting them."

"You want to involve the Night Kings?" T-Bone asked incredulously.

"We don't have a fucking choice. You know as well as I do that if we go walking around on their turf, they'll fucking kill us. It was one thing to just go grab Alison and Axel, but it's another to start hanging around for days. We don't need a war right now with them."

"They're gonna want at least fifty grand."

I moved fast, wrapping my hand around his throat and shoving him up against the wall. "And I'll fucking pay every last penny of it. My kid isn't walking out of here with his bitch mother. That kid needs to learn his place and that's here or in the fucking ground."

T-Bone gave a slight nod and I released the pressure around his throat, taking a step back as he choked and gasped for air. "I'm making the call. Start getting the guys ready because as soon as we have some intel, we're moving in and we're getting them back."

"Dead or alive?" he asked.

"The kid comes back alive. The bitch can be in a fucking body bag."

Chapter Five

ALISON

I glanced around the unfamiliar room and tried to remember what had happened. The last thing I recalled was sitting at the bus station with Axel, waiting for Chris to arrive. This was a nice room, so chances were that Slasher hadn't found me. I tried to sit up, but pain shot through my side and I had to ease back down onto the bed.

"Don't try to move right now. You have a chest tube in."

Chris's deep voice rumbled across the room. I glanced to where he was sitting and saw him lounging in a chair and staring at me, holding a glass in his hand. There wasn't much light in the room, so I couldn't make out his features. I wanted desperately to see his face, to know what he looked like after all these years, but he just continued to sit in that chair and lazily sip his drink.

"What happened?" I asked.

"We got you and Axel out, but Slasher's men came after you. Do you want to tell me what the fuck you're doing with Slasher?"

His voice was low and menacing. I wasn't expecting this level of hostility from him. He was the one that left me. He was the one that walked away and left me to deal with the fallout of his decisions.

"I didn't choose to be with him," I croaked out. My throat felt dry and rough. I coughed slightly, but cringed when pain shot through my side. What was wrong with me? I thought back and remembered the beating I had taken from Slasher. Broken ribs. That's what the problem was.

Chris walked over to me and handed me a bottle of water, removing the cap first. I could see now that he had a cowboy hat on, but it hid the rest of his features. "Take small sips."

I did as he said and felt the roughness ease in my throat.

"What do you mean that you didn't choose to be with him? You have a son with him."

"He's not Slasher's son."

"Then why the fuck did you stay with him? Raise him with him?"

"I didn't exactly have a choice," I said, trying not to let the hostility into my voice. "He would have killed him if he knew who Axel's father was."

"Yeah? Who's his father?" he sneered.

"You are," I said quietly.

Chris stared at me, the rage on his face growing by the second. He shook his head slightly. "Don't fucking lie to me."

"I'm not lying. I found out that I was pregnant the day you left. I wanted to tell you, but you were so insistent on joining the Blood Devils to save your brother. I figured the baby was safer if you didn't know. You told me never to contact you again."

He stumbled back a step and then turned toward the window, staring out at the darkness. "How did you end up with Slasher?"

"He came for me the day after you left. I figured that you joined and he was bringing me to you. He wasn't. He took me and made me his. He said it was payment for you not joining."

He turned to me stone faced, his jaw clenched with uncontrollable rage. "What the fuck do you mean 'he made you his'?"

I just stared at him. I wasn't going to spell it out for him. I had lived through it. I didn't need to repeat it. "Exactly how it sounds." I shook my head, refusing to think of those days anymore. It was in the past and that's where it was going to stay. "I made him think that I was pregnant with his child," I said softly. Every word I said hurt. My breaths were short and painful, but I had to tell him. "It was the only way that he was safe. He was actually happy when he found out. I thought that maybe everything would be okay. That my life wasn't over."

"If you knew I hadn't joined, why didn't you try to find me? I would have taken care of you."

"I did try, but you were gone. I had no idea where you went." I tried to take a deep breath to calm myself, but it hurt too much and tears slipped down my face. Every breath hurt more and more and I tried to hold in the whimper of pain, but it slipped out and Chris was immediately by my side.

"What's wrong? Are you in pain?"

I couldn't answer, so I nodded slightly and closed my eyes, trying to focus on every breath. I felt the bed shift and then he was gone. I laid there for what seemed like forever, just trying to breathe through the pain, until finally a woman walked in with a kind smile.

"Hi, Alison. I'm Kate. I'm a doctor and I took care of you when Jack brought you in."

I looked at her strangely, not sure who Jack was. I shook my head in confusion.

"Sorry," she smiled kindly. "Chris. The guys call him Jack sometimes."

I looked over at Chris, not understanding why they would call him that. He held up his glass with the amber liquid inside and shook it slightly. "Jack Daniels. It's my drink of choice," he said roughly.

"The guys all have these nicknames for one another and I never know who to call what. It gets very confusing."

I gave a tentative smile as she sat on the edge of the bed and began examining me. Chris turned on the bedside lamp for her and I closed my eyes at the intruding light. She lifted my shirt and examined my side, where I saw a tube coming out. I glanced away, not wanting to see it, and met Chris's concerned eyes. He was staring at me with an intensity I had never seen before. Now that I could see him better, I took in his handsome face. He was harder than before and his eyes were so dark and terrifying, but he was just as striking as I remembered. Only now he was all grown up and filled out very nicely.

He glanced away when he saw that I was watching him also. Kate finished examining me and then gave me some pain meds.

"You'll need to start doing breathing exercises. It'll help your lungs expand and heal. I'll show you before I leave. You need to take it easy for a few days. Give your body a chance to heal. I'll check back on you every day and when you're doing better, we'll see about getting you up and moving around."

"Thank you."

I already knew how to do the breathing exercises, having worked in a hospital, but it was different when I was the patient. She showed me how to do the breathing exercises, which hurt like a bitch, but she assured me would get easier every time I did them. When she left, I felt completely drained, but I didn't want to go to sleep now that Chris was here. I felt safe for the first time in seventeen years and I was afraid if I went to sleep, I would wake up to find it had all been a dream.

Chris came to sit next to me and took my hand in his. He looked up at me from under his low riding cowboy hat, his dark eyes intense and full of questions. "Go to sleep. I'll stay here with you."

"I need to use the bathroom. Could you help me up?"

He pulled back the covers and slid his hands under my body, lifting me gently against him. The heat from his body warmed me instantly as he carried me into the bathroom and set me down on my feet. He held onto me for a minute, making sure that I could steady myself before walking to the door to give me privacy. When I was finished, I washed my hands and then slowly walked to the door, grimacing with every step. When he heard me, he turned around and glared at me.

"You should have told me you were done."

I ignored him as he picked me up and put me back in the bed, pulling the covers back over me.

"Promise me something." He nodded. "Don't let Slasher get his hands on my son."

His jaw hardened, but he nodded and went back to sit in his chair, picking up his glass and sipping from it as he watched me. I eventually slipped off to sleep, dreaming of dark, menacing eyes that used to bring me comfort. In my dreams, they were absolutely terrifying.

The next few days were a blur to me. I was so doped up on pain meds that I didn't really remember anything that was happening. The days seemed to fade into each other, but Chris was always there, sipping his drink in his chair as his eyes watched me. I vaguely recalled Axel stopping in, but I was too tired to talk. By the fourth day, I was awake enough to refuse the pain meds. Kate stopped by to check on me and deemed that it was now safe to remove the chest tube.

I still wasn't able to shower for another forty-eight hours and I was really beginning to stink. I sat up a little in bed after she left, refusing the high dose of pain meds she offered and settled for some over the counter pain meds instead. I was tired of feeling doped up all the time.

Chris walked in the room after she left and for the first time in days, I studied him with a clear head. He was a lot bigger than I remembered. He had a lean, muscular frame, but he was taller. His hair was slightly shaggy. His dirty blonde locks hanging slightly around his ears, sticking out from under his cowboy hat. He had always worn it shorter when we were younger.

"You look different," I said as I studied him. "You look huge."

"Yeah, well, some good meals and the military will do that to you."

"I heard your mom died a few years after you left. A drug overdose."

He nodded, but didn't say anything.

"Did you go home for her funeral?"

"I was overseas. Besides, she wasn't there for me when Will and I needed her. I didn't have anything to say to her."

She had been a worthless mother and the few times that I actually talked to her had been just horrible. She was not a nice person and she didn't care about anybody but herself.

"Can I get you anything?" he grumbled.

"Could I have a wet washcloth? I feel disgusting."

He nodded and left the room, walking into the en-suite bathroom. He returned with a bowl of steaming water and a washcloth. "Sit up."

"I can do it."

"Don't be fucking stupid. You can hardly move."

I didn't appreciate his tone, but I sat up as best I could. I was wearing a thin tank top that he gently pulled off me. If it weren't for his help, I wouldn't have been able to do that. He dipped the wash-cloth in the water and wrung out the excess water. I shivered as the warm cloth brushed against my skin. It felt so good to have the grime washed away. I was all too aware of the hair growing in my armpits and my legs, but it would have to wait until I could shower on my own.

"Axel said that Slasher beating you was a regular thing," he said quietly.

"Yeah." Oh, God. We weren't really going to have this talk right now, were we? I didn't want to discuss what my life had been like. I didn't want Chris to look at me with pity or disgust. I just wanted to move on with life, whether that meant Chris was there or not.

"How often did he…"

I knew what he was asking and I didn't really want to talk about it. "Not as often over the years. He lost interest in me pretty fast. He only kept me around because of Axel," I said, refusing to look at him. I was over that part of my life. The beatings were the worst of any of it because they came so frequently. It seemed like every time my body healed, Slasher was back at it again, pissed at me for something else I had done.

"Why did you choose the name Axel?"

"Slasher wanted something that sounded badass. I wanted some-thing normal. We compromised. You should have heard some of the names he wanted to give him."

He ran the washcloth around my breasts, gently washing them and running the cloth down my stomach. It wasn't sexual, but I also didn't miss the way he stared at my breasts. When he was finished, he cleared his throat and helped me get dressed again, tucking me back in.

"I need to know what he did to you," he said fiercely.

"No."

"Yes."

"Chris, that part of my life is over. It happened, but it didn't destroy me. There's nothing good that comes from rehashing shit that I can't change. I don't want to talk about it and I don't want to see the anger on your face. Don't ask me again. The answer will be the same."

His nostrils flared, but he nodded and walked toward the door. "Does Axel know I'm his father?"

"No. I always thought it was safer if he didn't know."

He nodded and left, leaving me to stew in my room. I needed to talk to Chris about what would happen from here. I didn't know if it was safe here and I didn't know if he wanted to get to know Axel. There were so many unanswered questions and I didn't even know where to start with him. He wasn't the same person I remembered. The years had obviously changed him as they had me. I didn't even know who I was anymore. Where did I go from here? One thing was for certain, I had to keep Axel away from Slasher and I would do whatever it took.

As the day went on, I found myself getting bored. Usually, I was at work and kept my mind busy. Lying here, I had too much time to think about my life and what had become of me and my son. It was painful to think that I had allowed my son to go through his short life surrounded by drugs and murder.

I got up out of bed and sat in the chair Chris had been watching me from. It felt good to sit up, but I was still bored. I glanced around the room and took in everything. There wasn't much to it. It was a masculine room, but there wasn't anything that told me who Chris was now.

"Mom?"

I was so lost in my thoughts that I hadn't heard Axel knock on the door. He looked around and when he saw I was alone, he came in and closed the door.

"How are you feeling?"

"Better," I smiled. "Clearer. It's nice to not be on those drugs anymore."

He took a seat on the edge of the bed and glanced around the room. "So, what are we gonna do now?"

I sighed and chewed on my lip. "I wish I knew. For now, I just want to get better. We're safe as long as we're with Chris."

"How do you know?"

I saw the wariness in his eyes. He wasn't a stupid kid. He saw over the years how a man could tear someone apart. He didn't trust anyone.

"I know Chris. There's no way that he could ever do anything to hurt either one of us."

"You haven't seen him in years," he scoffed.

"He was my boyfriend. He was always a good person. I know that didn't change."

"If he was such a good person, why didn't you go to him sooner? Why did you stay with Slasher?"

"Axel, you know the way of the gang. It wouldn't have been as simple as calling up Chris and asking him to take us away. I didn't tell you this, but I had been working on a plan for the past two years. There was a man I worked with at the hospital. He knew that I was in a bad situation and he was teaching me to fight. I was going to make my move soon, but when I found out Slasher was going to initiate you into the gang, I knew I couldn't wait any longer."

"I just don't get it. I know how Slasher is, but I don't understand why you didn't leave."

I looked at him in confusion. "What do you mean?"

He ran his hand over the back of his neck and stood quickly, pacing the room. "You should have left a long time ago. You should have left me!"

"I would never leave you behind. What kind of mother would that make me? Do you really think I could ever just walk away from you?"

"But the things he did to you-I heard it. I saw the bruises all the time. I wouldn't have blamed you for leaving. He could have killed you any one of those times."

"Axel," I said softly. "You're my life. If I had left without you, I never would have been able to live with myself."

He sat down hard on the bed, his shoulders slumped. "I just feel like this is all my fault. Like you could have gotten away if it weren't for me. You wouldn't have had to deal with him all these years."

I leaned forward, ignoring the pain from the movement and grabbed his hand, squeezing it tight. "None of this is your fault. Slasher is the worst kind of human being and what that gang stood for-that's not something you just walk away from and live to tell about. Even if I had left without you, they would have come after me. They still will, but I'm ready for the fight now."

It was quiet for a while as we sat there together. I wanted to say something more reassuring, but there was really nothing I could say or do. It's not like I had given him any kind of hope that I could do more for him.

"One day, we're going to have a different life," he promised. "I swear, this is not going to be our life anymore."

I appreciated the sentiment behind his words. It was like he was vowing to protect us, but the truth was, he was still a kid and he was no more capable of taking care of himself against the Blood Devils than I was. He must have seen the disbelief on my face because his jaw hardened as he shook his head slightly.

"I know you think I'm just a kid, but I've seen more in my life than most kids my age. I'll do anything to make sure that we don't go back to him. We'll run, we'll hide, we'll fucking fight back." I scoffed at his language, but he just raised an eyebrow in challenge. "I'm not a kid anymore, Mom. Don't treat me like one. We'll beat this together."

I nodded, knowing that he was right. We were way beyond pretending that he was still in need of my protection. If we were going to come out on top, he needed me to treat him like the adult that he had become instead of the scared child I still thought of him as.

"Okay. We'll do this. Together."

Chapter Six

CHRIS

"What the fuck is going on, Chris? How is she wrapped up with the Blood Devils?" Ice asked as I joined him outside on the porch. I didn't know what to tell him. I had never really told anyone but Cap about my association with the Blood Devils. Jules was sitting in a chair, sipping a cup of coffee, acting like he didn't have a care in the world.

I leaned against the porch railing, facing the two men that I knew would always have my back no matter what. "There's this asshole, Slasher. He's now the leader of the Blood Devils, but seventeen years ago, he was the man who murdered my brother."

Ice's stare was ice cold, just like his nickname implied. Julius just raised an eyebrow at me, as if to tell me I had some explaining to do.

"My brother was trying to take care of me. I was just a teenage kid and he was looking for any way that he could take care of me. He knew what he was doing, but he couldn't see another way. I was going to join to have his back. I knew he was getting involved in some shit that he shouldn't be going near. I thought I could save him. Ali was my girl-friend. Apparently, after they killed my brother, Slasher took Ali as his own."

Jules stood, shoving his chair back in the process. "What the fuck do you mean?"

"Exactly how it sounds. Axel is her kid." I ran a hand over my scruff and sighed. "My kid. I didn't know. I didn't know shit about what was going on. After my brother was killed, I just walked away from everything. I went to a recruiting office to join the Marines, but I didn't meet the requirements. The sergeant could see that I was desperate. He and his wife took me in and made sure that I was ready when I turned eighteen. They gave me my life."

"Does the kid know?" Ice asked.

"That I'm his father?" I shook my head. "I just found out. That's something Ali has to be with me for. I don't know the first fucking thing about being a father, let alone to a kid that's almost an adult."

"Have you talked to the kid yet?" Jules gaze was penetrating, obviously wondering if I had tried to make a connection with the kid.

"A little. I talked to him before I knew he was mine. It doesn't sound like he liked his life much. Slasher beat Ali frequently. He said he didn't get it as much, but that's still too fucking much."

"I know this is fucking hard," Ice said, "but the sooner you tell that kid that you're his father, the sooner you'll have an idea about what to do next. One thing's for sure, the Blood Devils will come for them and we have to be ready. You need to be sure that Axel is on your side and he won't go back to Slasher."

I avoided Ali for days. I just didn't know what to say around her. I felt terrible that her life had turned out so shitty because of me. I had walked away from her and she suffered for it. How did I even begin to make that right? I knew I was being a pussy by not talking to her, but I figured that she probably needed the space too. At least, that's what I told myself.

I couldn't stay away from her forever though. We had to make a plan. The guys were getting irritated with me. It wasn't safe for us to stay at my house for much longer. The Blood Devils probably knew where she was now and every second that I delayed put us in danger. The fact was, if I was going to keep her and my son safe, I had to take them to a safe house where we could properly protect them.

I knocked on the bedroom door, but didn't hear anything. I cracked it open to see her staring out the window. She looked at peace for the first time in days. Even with her fading bruises, she was just as beautiful as I remembered. Her light brown hair was longer than when we were kids and right now, it was pulled out of her face on top of her head. Small wisps hung down and tickled her shoulders. Her blue eyes used to be so vibrant and full of life, but they seemed to have dulled over the years, which made sense. Anyone living the life she had would have all the joy sucked out of them. It would take some time, but eventually, the swelling would go down in her face and I would see her cute little button nose again with the small smattering of freckles spread across it.

"Can I come in?"

She shrugged, her tiny frame hardly moving as she took a shallow breath and blew it out.

"Ali, I'm sorry that I haven't been around. I fucked up when I walked away and I ruined your life. I'm so fucking ashamed and I just didn't know how to talk to you."

She turned and looked at me, questions written all over her face. "Why would you think that you ruined my life?"

"I left you and Slasher took you."

"That wasn't your fault, Chris. I don't blame you for getting out. I heard what happened with your brother. That would have messed anyone up."

"But I didn't even consider taking you with me. I just walked away. You were pregnant."

"You didn't know, so stop beating yourself up about it." She was letting me off the hook too easily. I didn't deserve her kindness or her forgiveness. "It wasn't completely terrible. I convinced him to let me go back to school for my nursing degree. I was working on a way out of there. And Axel turned out great despite his surroundings. He's really a great kid."

"I can see that. I wish I had known him all these years."

There wasn't anything to say to that. Nothing we said could change the past.

"So, what did you do with yourself after you left that day?" she asked after a few minutes.

I sat down on the window seat with her and took off my cowboy hat, running my fingers through my hair. "I went to a recruiting office. I was going to join right away, but I wasn't old enough. I had to wait six months unless I had parental consent."

"Fat chance of that happening," she smiled. Ali and I had grown up together. She knew my family better than anyone.

"The recruiter realized how desperate I was to escape. He gave me a choice. I could go home with him and he would help me get ready for the Marines, or he would give me $20 for food. Six months later, I was headed off to boot camp."

"Wow. I can't believe they did that for you."

"They were better than my own parents. I still keep in touch with them."

"How long were you in the military?"

"Ten years. I loved every damn day of it. It whipped my ass into shape and gave me something to live for." Her eyes dimmed as she looked back outside. I closed my eyes, feeling like a complete ass.

"Have you talked to Axel at all?" she asked as she stared out the window.

"Just a little. I didn't want to say anything unless you were there."

"Now's as good a time as any," she said with a hesitant smile. "Are you ready for this?"

"No, but I think it's time we got to know each other."

"Okay. Let's go talk to him."

We stood and I walked next to her and she gingerly made her way to the door. She was doing a lot better, but her ribs were still hurting her. Her breathing had gotten a lot better over the past few days. We went down the hall to the living room where Axel was watching TV. He flicked off the TV when he saw us enter the room.

"Hey, what's going on?"

Ali sat down across from him and took a deep breath. "Axel, I need to talk to you about something."

"Okay," he said, leaning forward on the couch so that his elbows rested on his knees.

"Axel, before you were born, Chris and I were a couple. We broke up and Chris left," she said, glancing over at me. I could tell she was trying to sugarcoat things because she didn't want to make me look like the asshole that walked away. "The day after he left was the day Slasher took me. I made him think that he was your father because I knew it would keep you safe. But he's not your father. Chris is."

Axel just stared at his mom for a few minutes, obviously taking in all that she was saying. Then he looked at me and a faint smile touched his lips. "So, I'm not that guy's kid?"

"No," Ali replied. "I'm sorry that I let you think he was, but if Slasher knew that Chris was your father, he would have killed you. It was the only way I could protect you."

Axel nodded slowly. "I know, Mom. It's okay. Just knowing that I don't actually have his DNA in my body is worth every year I spent with him."

I cleared my throat, wanting to ask him so many questions, but we didn't have time for that right now. "Axel, I know we have a lot to catch up on and I'm sure you have a lot of questions, but the fact is that the Blood Devils will be coming for both of you. They won't let you just walk away. You've been here now for over a week and we need to move. If they haven't connected Ali to me yet, it'll happen soon and they'll come at us full force."

Axel's eyes widened in panic. "I can't go back there."

"I won't let them take you back. We'll fight back against them, but we need to have a plan. I need to talk to my boss and figure out the best way to handle this. It's not something we can deal with on our own. But in the meantime, we need to get out of here and go to a safe house."

"Alright. Yeah, I'm good with whatever you tell me to do."

"Ali, you okay with that?"

"I trust you, Chris. We'll do whatever it takes to stay away from him."

"Alright, then let's grab our stuff and head out. I'll talk with my guys and we'll hit the road."

"Cap, we're heading to the safe house. We need to put a plan in place to protect Ali and Axel."

"Alright. Take her to the one outside of Pittsburgh. I'll meet you out there with the guys. We're going to have to strategize."

"Cap, I know that you have rules about being involved with someone you're protecting, but I can't walk away from her. Axel is my kid. I've missed out on so much time with them. I need to stay with them."

"I understand. We'll discuss it when we get to the safe house."

Cap hung up and I got into the SUV with Axel and Ali. Jules and Ice were in the other SUV, following us and watching our backs. This would most likely be the last time that I could ever go anywhere with Ali and Axel alone. Cap would pull me from their detail and I wouldn't be allowed to take them anywhere without someone else with us. I understood why. I had been there when Cazzo had been protecting Vanessa. He had been involved with her and he let his emotions get in the way of protecting her. Cap wouldn't allow that to happen ever again.

"So, you were in the military?" Axel asked.

"Yeah. I was in the Marines for ten years."

"What was it like?"

I glanced over at Ali, not sure how much detail she wanted me to go into, but she looked just as curious.

"It was the best fucking thing I could have ever done. It set the course for the rest of my life. I'll be honest with you, when your mom and I were together, I wanted to marry her before everything went south. But I don't know what kind of life I could have given her. I'm sure it would have been better than what the two of you have been through."

"But you liked it?" he asked.

"Hell yeah. Those were some of the best years of my life. I'm not gonna lie. It's tough as hell and they push you to your limits, but it really lets you know what you're made of."

"How did you know which branch you wanted to go into?"

"I was just walking down the street and saw the recruiting office. I knew it was my only chance of getting out of the life."

I felt so damn guilty for saying this shit to them. They had lived the life I had been destined for, but he was my kid and I had to be honest with him.

"You said you still keep in touch with the Sergeant?" Ali asked.

"Yeah. I still go see them whenever I get the chance. They're like family to me. Sergeant Mills and his wife saved my life," I said honestly. "I would have fucking died if they hadn't taken me in. Actually, he whooped my ass pretty good before I even went to boot camp," I said with a grin.

"What kind of stuff did he do?" Axel asked. I could tell that he wasn't angry, just truly interested in what had taken me to that point in my life.

"He trained me. He had me run every morning with him. I was tall, but I was a scrawny little shit back then. My brother provided what he could for me, but it really wasn't ever enough. I was always fucking hungry. Cheryl, his wife, made sure that I bulked up before I went off to train. The sergeant, Thad, he helped me study for my GED and taught me everything that I needed to know so that I could pass the tests. He taught me to fight so that I had the best chance possible. I stayed with them after boot camp until I was deployed. They never had children, but they treated me like their very own son. They sent me care packages when I was overseas and Cheryl wrote me letters. They treated me better than my own damn parents did."

"It's strange to know that you're my dad. I mean, you've had like this whole other life that's completely different from ours."

"I'm really sorry about that, kid. If I had known, I would have gotten you out a long time ago."

"I'm not blaming you," he said with a shrug. "I'm just saying it's weird."

I blamed me though. I had pushed Ali away and she and my kid had paid the price. All I could hope now was that I could keep them safe from the Blood Devils.

The ringing of my phone brought me out of my thoughts. "Yeah?"

"We've got a tail. I've got Alec and Cazzo's team headed to us. Alec and I will head them off and Cazzo will go with you to the safe house."

"How many vehicles?"

"One. We'll get what we can out of them and then meet you at the safe house."

"Watch your six."

He hung up and I tightened my grip on the wheel. It was starting already and I had a feeling we were in for the fight of our lives.

"Cap, this is Ali and my son, Axel."

Cap shook both their hands and a grin twisted his lips. "Welcome to the club, man."

"Cap," I shook my head in warning. "Don't."

He held up his hands and grinned. "Alright, alright. It's nice to meet both of you. Why don't you get settled upstairs while we discuss our next steps? When we have a plan in place, we'll let you know."

Ali looked a little uncomfortable with just walking away, but she nodded and her and Axel headed upstairs.

"What the hell?" Cap said. "You finally have a woman and a kid and you're not claiming them?"

"Claiming them? They're not fucking cattle, Cap."

"I'm just saying, I thought you would be all over this. You're the one always griping at the guys about respecting women and shit. I just assumed that you would be making sure everyone knew she was taken."

"First of all, it's because I respect her that I'm not claiming her. She's a grown woman and if she wants me, we'll discuss it like adults. Second, I just got her back a few days ago and found out that I had a kid. You can bet that I take my responsibilities seriously, but give me a fucking chance to catch up. And third, there's not a fucking guy on our teams that would dare touch them knowing that she was my girlfriend and he's my kid."

"Just checking, man. I'm happy for you, but it's gotta be hard to find out you have a kid that's sixteen years old. You doing okay with that?"

I shrugged. "I haven't gotten to know him all that much yet, but he seems like a good kid. But then, Ali always had a good head on her shoulders. She did a good job with him, especially considering the circumstances."

"I can't believe she was with the Blood Devils all these years. She seems so normal."

"She's fucking strong."

"Well, let's get a plan in place to end this."

The alarm on the front gate sounded and Cap and I walked over to the video feed. Alec and Ice were pulling up, but when they got out, they were dragging two guys with them. I looked over at Cap. Obviously, Ice didn't intend for them to leave here alive or he never would have brought them to our safe house.

We headed out back in the direction that Ice was dragging one of the guys. Cazzo, Sinner, and Burg were on first watch, so I didn't have to worry about Ali and Axel. Ice was dragging one of the guys into the woods and Alec had the other guy, dragging him to a different section of the woods. Cap and I split up and I headed for Alec.

"Who sent you?" Alec said as he threw the guy down on the ground against a tree. The guy had his hands tied behind his back and had a gash on his forehead.

"I'm not saying shit."

Alec nodded to Craig and Florrie, who were standing off to the side. They walked over to him with a length of rope, tossing it over a branch to make a noose. Florrie wrapped the rope around his neck, making sure it was tight.

"You gonna tie me up, mama? We gonna have some fun?"

"Oh, I'm definitely gonna have some fun," Florrie smirked. "I'm afraid the only screaming you'll hear is your own voice."

She yanked on the rope, jerking him up until his feet were just barely scraping the ground. He choked and spluttered as he tried to reach the ground. His hands were fisted behind his back as he struggled to breathe.

"Who sent you?" Alec asked again.

The guy was red and couldn't speak. Florrie lowered the rope just enough for him to rest his feet on the ground. He coughed as he gasped for air, but he only got a few seconds before Florrie had him dangling from the tree again. I had to hand it to her, the girl was fucking strong. Just when the guy was about to pass out, she let him back down, this time, dropping him to his knees on the ground.

"Who sent you?" Alec asked for a third time.

"Fuck, man. If I had known the bitch was this much trouble, I never would have come," he croaked out.

"Who were you sent after?"

"Bitch named Alison and her kid, Axel."

"Who asked you to look for them?"

"Fuck, man. I already said more than I should have."

A tortured scream in the distance had him whipping his head around.

"Looks like they already got something out of your buddy," Craig said. "Guess we don't have any use for you anymore."

"Wait! No. I can tell you anything you want to know."

Alec bent down, his face right in front of the gangbanger's. "Who sent you? Who are you with?"

"Night Kings," he said hastily.

"Prove it," Alec narrowed his eyes at him. The guy looked down at his stomach and then back up. Alec ripped his shirt up, showing a nasty burn that had never healed properly. It was probably only a year or two old, which meant this guy was a new member.

"What do the Night Kings want with them?" I asked, stepping forward.

"Man, I don't know. Ruger gave me orders and I follow them."

"Who would know?" I asked.

"Fuck, I don't know, man. He might have told Stones, but I'm new. He didn't tell me jack shit."

"Then why am I keeping you alive?" Alec asked darkly. The guy's eyes widened and he shook his head.

"No, I can...you can send me back. I can deliver a message for you."

"Believe me, you are." Alec whipped out a knife and slit the guy's throat before he even knew what was happening. I watched as the guy dropped to the ground, gurgling as his eyes grew dim. He was dead moments later.

"We'll handle clean up," Craig said. I nodded and headed off in Cap's direction. It was time to see what Stones knew. When I got over to them, he was bleeding from his ear. I watched as Ice talked to him quietly, the gleam in his eyes as deadly as ever. Ice was a straight shooter, most of the time. But these assholes wouldn't cut us any slack if they had one of us and we weren't about to show them any mercy now. They knew what they were doing when they decided to follow us.

"Please," the guy whimpered. "That's all I know."

"Then I don't need you anymore."

The guy was dead before he hit the ground and when Ice turned around, his face was lethal. "The Blood Devils."

I didn't really need him to confirm it. I already knew it. "Why did they involve the Night Kings?"

"The Blood Devils didn't want to step on any toes," Ice confirmed.

"Shit," Cap said. "Now we're going to have the Blood Devils *and* the Night Kings retaliating. We need a plan ASAP."

"That's not the only problem," I said grimly. "The Night Kings are known for going after families. I just put all of us and everyone we love in danger."

Cap, Ice, and Jules all looked at me in resignation. We all knew that there was a very good chance that we wouldn't all be walking away from this. Cap walked over to me and put his hand on my shoulder.

"This isn't your fault. They had your family first. Our advantage is that we're all highly trained and they don't realize who they just fucked with. Let's get back to the house. We have a lot of calls to make."

Half of Reed Security was already at the safe house, but there wasn't time to get everyone together. The rest of the teams were back at Reed Security, so Cap got everyone on a conference call to fill them in on the situation. When we were all gathered in the living room, Cap stood to fill everyone in. I pulled Ali into my side on the couch, needing to feel her close to me. Axel sat next to her and I saw her grip his hand.

"Here's the deal," Cap said, his voice pure steel. "Most of you already know that Ali and Axel escaped from the Blood Devils. Axel is Chris's son. That means that Ali and Axel have our full protection.

The problem is that the Blood Devils involved the Night Kings and we just took out two of their guys."

A round of curses filled the room and Ali shrank into my side. This wasn't her fault or Axel's. They were just trying to escape that life.

"I don't know how many of you are familiar with the Night Kings, but they aren't going to just walk away from us taking out their guys. And the Blood Devils aren't going to stop until Ali and Axel are back with them. From this moment on, everyone is on high alert and no one goes anywhere alone. Wives and girlfriends need to be brought in immediately. We don't have room for everyone at this location, so we're going to have to split up."

"I have room at my place," Cazzo said firmly. "I can fit a few people in the house and the guest house. I have all the security we could ever need and an arsenal to go with it."

"Good. Let's stick to teams," Cap said with a nod. "Sinner and Burg, you'll stay with Cazzo. Since Rob is already familiar with your system, he'll go with you. Chance, you're with Cazzo also. We'll bring Becky here to run things from here. We have six rooms here. Alec, your team will stay here, as will Derek's team. Hunter, you get on the phone and call Lola. Let her know what's going on and tell her to get her ass here now. If she gives you any shit, tell her we'll go get her and drag her here. That leaves Ice's team, Knight, and myself. It's gonna be crammed and we're going to have to take shifts, but it'll do for now. As for extended family, we can't protect them all. There's just not enough of us. We'll send them away if we have to until this is over. Make arrangements with your parents and siblings to be somewhere protected or out of the country."

There was a grave silence around the room as we all digested that information. We were going to war with two gangs and there was no question about whether or not blood would be spilled. It was kill or be killed. This would never end until they were dead.

"Our first priority is to make sure everyone is safe. When we're all secured, we'll make a plan to end this. Everyone clear?"

Everyone agreed and Cap ended the call. "Alec, I need your team to stay here on protection detail while Cazzo, Sinner, and I collect our families."

"No problem, Cap," Alec agreed.

"Chris, I think we both know that you're working on the detail, but you won't be on close protection."

I nodded. I already knew this was coming. "That's fine. As long as I can be here."

"Good. Alec, you're in charge. Ice and Jules, you're with us. Get what you need and we'll get back here."

Everyone was out the door within minutes and then it was just Ali, Axel, and I in the living room while Alec's team was watching the perimeter. Florrie was still inside working close protection, but was giving us some space.

"Chris, I'm so sorry I've brought this on you. I never imagined that us coming to you would be this bad."

"Don't. This is not your fault," I said fiercely.

"But it is. All of your friends and their families are in danger because we ran to you."

"And who else would you have run to? I'm Axel's father. I may not have been there for the last sixteen years, but I don't ever want you to doubt your decision to run to me. I'll always protect you."

Ali looked back at me with tears in her eyes and I knew that my words hadn't eased her conscience any. Axel stood and walked out of the room. I let him go because I needed to make some things clear with Ali. I lifted her chin so that I could look into her eyes.

"Hey, none of this is your fault. I'm the one that left you. You held on for way longer than you should have. I'm sorry I wasn't there for you and Axel, but I'm here now and I will do everything I can to keep you safe. As for my teammates, we would do the same for any of them that were in trouble, so don't start putting the weight of the world on your shoulders. This is what we do and we're damn good at it."

She nodded as the tears slipped down her face. "I've missed you, Chris."

"I've missed you, too." I rested my forehead against hers and let out a sigh. "There's not a day that went by that I didn't think of you and wonder how you were doing." I shook my head in disgust. "I wish I had never walked away, or that I had come back for you. I hate that I've missed out on all this time with you and Axel, but I swear to you,

we're going to figure this out and you'll never have to worry again." I
pulled back and looked into her beautiful eyes. "When this is over, I
want you and Axel to stay with me."

"Are you sure?"

"My life hasn't been the same without you in it," I said, feeling the
truth of the words as I spoke them. "I always thought you had found
someone better and were living the good life. It just didn't occur to me
that I had put you in danger."

She laughed sarcastically. "Let's face it. The area we grew up in?
There was no escaping that hell without something drastic happening.
I don't care about the past right now. I just want to move on and forget
that part of my life."

This woman amazed me. Her strength was something I had only
seen a few times in my life. What she had lived through the past seventeen years was more than any person should have to deal with, yet she
just wanted to move past it and get on with her life. There was no
crying and carrying on. It was over and that was that.

"Chris?" I looked up to see Axel standing a few feet from us,
looking at me with uncertainty. "Sorry, I'm not sure what to call you."

"Whatever makes you comfortable."

"Uh, I was thinking, with everything that's going on, I want you to
show me how to protect us."

I looked back at Ali, not sure if she was okay with this. "Are you
okay with me showing him how to use a gun?" She bit her lip and
lowered her eyes. "Hey, I know what you're thinking, but I'm going to
teach him the right way to use a gun. He won't be going out and killing
anyone unless it's to protect himself. But he's right. You should both
know how to handle a weapon."

"If you think that's best," she said sullenly.

"Hey, I will do everything to protect both of you, but if something
goes wrong, I need to know that you can at least handle a gun."

"Okay. You're right. Let's do this."

Chapter Seven

REED SECURITY

Knight

Becky ended the call with Cap and we all glanced around the room at each other. We all knew that we were in for one hell of a fight. I stood and headed for the door.

"I'm going for Kate."

"Wait," Derek yelled. "We should meet back here and drive out together. You heard Cap. No one does anything alone."

"I'm not waiting around to get Kate, but I'll get her and meet you back here."

"We'll grab Claire and Lucy. Let's meet back here in twenty minutes. Rob, take Becky to her place and grab whatever you need," Derek ordered.

I pulled out my phone, needing to know where Kate was.

"Hello?"

"Kate, where are you?"

"I just got home. Why?" I heard her heels drop to the floor and I could imagine her walking in the back door and slipping them off her feet as she grabbed a bottle of wine. I heard the cork pop and the rattle of the wine glass as she set it on the counter.

"Just stay there. I'm coming to get you. Pack a bag and be ready when I get there."

"Is everything okay?"

"Just do this for me. We have to leave right away."

"Alright. I'll-"

I heard a crash in the background and then heavy breathing. "Garrick!" That name only slipped out when Kate was nervous or scared. I put the phone on speaker and pulled up the app to show me what was happening at the house. Kate was running up the stairs and into our bedroom. She tried to slam the door shut, but a hand shot out and forced it open. I heard her scream echo through the room as the guy shoved his way into the bedroom and tackled her to the ground.

"Shit," I ran for the elevator, not stopping when Pappy and Derek yelled at me. I didn't have any time to waste. Kate was in danger and I wasn't close enough to protect her. I cursed that I had to take the elevator instead of stairs. It was one of the safety features in Reed Security so that no one could enter without permission. There were stairs in the back, but that would take twice as long. When the doors finally opened, I ran to the garage and hopped on my bike, released the clutch and twisted the throttle.

I roared out of Reed Security and onto the highway, heading for my house. I hit every light along the way, but I didn't slow down even once. I rode on the shoulder and burst through the traffic, not giving a fuck if someone got in an accident because of me. I was at the last light, driving along the shoulder when a car pulled over to the side, blocking my way. I wove through the traffic, driving around the cars that were at a stand still and sped through the light. A car was coming at me from each direction and I didn't have enough speed because of having to slow down. I wasn't going to make it across the intersection. At the last second, I turned the bike right and went down the crossroad. It would take me at least a few minutes out of the way and cost me precious minutes that I didn't have to get to Kate.

When I pulled down our street, my headlight flashed across the front of the house and I knew that I was already too late. The front door was hanging open and there was no sound coming from inside. I needed to be sure and ran inside, clearing each room as I went, faster than I should have. Images of Kate dying on the floor flashed through my head, but I refused to believe that they had killed her. They needed her for leverage; at least, that's what I would have done. I just hoped they thought along the same lines as me. The house was empty. The master bedroom was completely trashed and there were a few drops of blood on the carpet, but no other signs of whether she was injured or not.

"Fuck!" I shouted, punching a hole in the wall. I ran downstairs to my computer and quickly pulled up the security footage, getting any detail that would help me find her. I zeroed in the guy's wrist and saw the Night Kings tattoo. That didn't tell me shit about where she was. I pulled up the outside feed and got a license plate and the direction they headed.

"Cole," I barked into my phone as I headed for my bike. "Someone took Kate. I don't have time to explain right now. Is Alex safe?"

"She's with me now."

"Grab a bag and take her to Reed Security. I'm going after Kate."

I hung up and shoved the phone in my pocket as I took off in the direction the car had gone. But the further I drove, the more I knew that I was fucked. There was no sign of her or the car. I pulled over and yanked out my phone again.

"Knight, I really hoped I wouldn't be getting any calls from you," Sean Donnelly said into the phone.

"Someone took Kate. I have a plate number for you." I rattled it off quickly, repeating it and giving him the description of the car.

"What the fuck is going on?"

"Let's just say that we stepped in some deep shit and now everyone at Reed Security is in danger."

"Fuck. Let me make sure Lillian and Cara are safe and I'll meet you over there."

"Bring them with. Sinner should be making his way to you now to get Cara. Let him know when you have her."

"Alright. I'll see you over there."

Fuck. For the first time in years, I was fucking terrified. This was so much worse than the last time Kate was in danger because this time, she was already on her own. I needed information now and I wasn't going to get that sitting on the side of the road. I sped off to Reed Security, letting the anger leach through me. I needed rage on my side right now because it was the only thing keeping me from losing my shit. I was going to be breaking my promise to Sebastian because there was no way I was letting any of the fuckers that took Kate survive.

Becky

When Knight's alarm went off, so did several others on my computer. I quickly pulled up where the alarms were going off and switched into op mode. I pulled up the footage and my eyes went wide. We were being hit all around.

"Derek!" He ran into the conference room where I was working and looked over my shoulder. "Your house is being hit. Looks like Claire and Lucy are both there. There are two men shooting at your house."

Derek and Hunter were gone before I could finish my sentence and I moved on to the next location. I quickly put on my headphones and dialed Cap.

"What do you have?" he answered tersely.

"Cap, they're at your house now. They're hitting everyone."

"Pull up the feed," he demanded. I quickly pulled up the live video feed from his house. "I don't see Caitlin. Maggie's got her gun and she's shooting at someone."

"We're going over there," Chance said from behind me.

"Cap, Chance's team is heading to your house now."

"Fuck, I'm still twenty minutes out."

"Cap, I've got alarms going off everywhere. I need to check them all out. Everyone's meeting back here."

"I'll contact Chance. Don't go anywhere, Becky."

He hung up and I glanced over at Rob who was talking to Hunter about the video feed from his house. I went back to work, checking the next alarm. I got Sinner on the phone next.

"Becky, what's going on?" he asked urgently.

"Sinner, I don't see Cara on the footage, but your house is on fire."

"She's still over at Sean's. I'll get ahold of him now."

"Are Cazzo and Burg with you?"

"Yeah. We already got alarms on their houses. We're headed to Cazzo's place. Meghan's out of town."

I quickly pulled up the feed from Cazzo's place. I quickly scanned through the video feed, but she wasn't on any of the screens. "I don't see Vanessa in the house." And then I saw it. She was running outside toward the woods surrounding the house. Men were chasing her and I jumped with a squeak when I saw her fall to the ground. "Cazzo," I whispered.

"What? What the fuck happened?" Cazzo's terrified and angry voice roared through my headset. I pulled myself together. I had to be professional. They needed me right now.

"They have Vanessa. I think they shot her. They're taking her to their vehicle. Cazzo, Chance's team already left to get Maggie, and Hunter and Derek went for Claire and Lucy. We don't have anyone else here."

I could hear him swearing and yelling, but I was still trying to pull myself together. Reed Security was rapidly falling apart. Everyone's houses were being burned to the ground or shot up. These assholes weren't leaving anything to chance. They were sending a message.

———

Claire

"So, the other night, I was reading this book about a motorcycle club and usually I don't get into that kind of book," I said to Lucy as we sat drinking wine. I had already had two glasses and this was my third. I was well on my way to past tipsy since I hadn't had anything to eat since lunch.

"What made you decide to read it?"

"There was a really hot guy on the cover. I mean, smokin'. He had all these tattoos on his arms and a leather jacket flung over his shoulder. It was hot, and let me tell you, the sex scenes were even hotter."

"What kind of stuff are we talking?" Lucy asked as she guzzled down some more wine.

I leaned in close to her, almost afraid to say it out loud. "Voyeurism."

"Seriously? I never took you for the type to like that stuff."

"Neither did I, but Derek and I like to try different things and it just sounded so hot."

"What happened to all the Superman fantasies?"

I shrugged. "I haven't totally given up on them, but I saw that Knight got that motorcycle and then I read this book. It just got me thinking about bad boys and the appeal of the danger and everything."

"Derek's not enough of a bad boy?"

"Definitely. This is just a fantasy, Lucy. It's not like I want him to go out and become a killing machine who smokes and drinks all the time. I'm just looking for a little adventure."

Something loud cracked around the room and before I knew it, things were breaking all around me. Holy crap, someone was shooting at us! I dragged Lucy to the ground and started crawling for the safety of the other room. Before I got too far, I turned back and grabbed the bottle of wine.

"Really?" Lucy shouted. "You're going back for the wine?"

I army crawled into the other room until I got to the hallway that led to our bedrooms. "Hey, this wine is really good and it was expensive," I hissed. When we were both covered by the walls, I got up and ran for the bedroom. Derek had several guns in the wall safe and I went for them right away.

"Is this what you had in mind?" Lucy asked as she reached into the safe for one of the guns.

"Not exactly. I mean, if Derek and I had discussed this and planned it out, that would be different. But since I haven't talked to Derek about this particular fantasy, I'm guessing it's not him."

"Shouldn't we call Derek and Hunter?"

I walked to the doorway to look around into the hallway. It was quiet in the hallway, but I had a feeling that we should expect more. I shut the door quietly and pulled Lucy to the other side of my bed. We sat down on the ground, ducking down so that no one could see us. I took a deep breath and tried to think of what Derek would want me to do.

"The alarm alerts anyone at Reed Security as soon as it sounds. The alarm would have gone off as soon as the first bullet hit. We just have to wait here for them to show up."

"We're just going to sit here and wait for someone to rescue us?" Lucy asked incredulously. "Is that what the heroine in your books would do?"

"Okay, I admit that you can't always rely on what people do in books as reference. I know this is what Derek would tell me to do. We just need to keep our heads down until they get here."

The door slammed against the wall and Lucy and I both screamed, instantly giving away our location. I perked up just enough to see over the bed and verify that it wasn't Derek and then I started shooting. Lucy followed my lead and we took turns shooting at the door. It was all going great, until we ran out of bullets.

"Shit," I hissed. "I'm out."

Lucy raised her gun and fired, but nothing happened. "Me too. What do we do now?"

"Now you come with us," a voice said from the doorway.

Lucy and I slowly stood with our hands raised. My instincts were screaming to not go with him. The guy had tattoos all over his body and was wearing a leather jacket and a bandana.

"Well, this kills the fantasy," I mumbled to Lucy.

"What's wrong, Claire bear? Don't like the bad boy fantasy anymore?" she snarked.

"Let's go," the man shouted. Lucy and I walked around the bed slowly toward the man. I was waiting for it. Any second now, Hunter and Derek would break through the door and take down these guys. The man reached out and grabbed me, shoving me into the hallway. Lucy stumbled into me from behind, causing me to trip and fall. "Get up. Stop stalling."

I got up and slowly made my way into the living room. There were large bullet holes in the walls and the couch was in shreds. My wine glasses were shattered on the ground. I hadn't even finished the glass I was drinking. My heart started to pound harder when we stepped out of the house. There was only one vehicle in the driveway and it wasn't Derek's. I was starting to get a very bad feeling about this.

The man shoved us into the back of the car and Lucy gripped my hand tightly. This was starting to become very real and now I understood her fear. Derek wasn't here and we were about to be taken somewhere else. I swallowed down the wine that I was about to spew all over the back seat and took a deep breath.

"They'll come for us. We'll be fine," I whispered to Lucy.

The car started moving and I closed my eyes, not wanting to see us driving away from my home. The screeching of tires had my eyes flying open. I turned around in my seat, seeing Derek's truck come roaring up behind us. I quickly pulled the seat belt across my belly. Lucy was doing the same. I looked back one last time, just in time to see headlights right on our ass. I wrapped my hand around Lucy's as the truck crashed into the back of the car. We jolted forward, but the strap stopped us from going far.

The men up front were swearing and trying to get control of the car. The truck rammed us from behind again, sending us into a street light. Not wasting a second, I flung off my seat belt and swung the door open, dragging Lucy out behind me. Derek and Hunter ran past us, holding their weapons on the men in the front seat. They dragged them out of the car and cuffed them, leading them over to the truck.

"Claire," Derek barked at me. "Get your keys and go straight to Reed Security. You don't stop until you're parked in the garage, you got me?"

I nodded quickly and ran back in the house for my keys, opening the garage door, and pulling my car out. Lucy got in, slamming the door behind me and we sat there for a moment collecting ourselves. Derek honked the horn, signaling for me to get my ass moving and I put the car in reverse and followed his instructions.

"I bet that wasn't how you pictured your fantasy going," Lucy mumbled.

"Not exactly, but it wasn't bad."

"Claire, you need help."

I sighed, knowing it was true.

Cazzo

I drove like a bat out of hell onto my property. Becky had seen her being taken, but I had to be sure. Slamming the truck into park, I jumped out and ran to the back of the property where Becky had said Vanessa was running. The floodlights were on in the back yard and I could see almost everything. I scanned the tree line for any sign of her, my weapon held steady in front of me. But she wasn't anywhere around. It wasn't bright enough to look for clues back here. I ran back to the house just as Burg was coming out.

"She's gone, man."

"Fuck. This can't be happening. I can't fucking lose her."

"I know. Let's get back to Reed Security. We need information right now. We're not going to get her back by losing it out here."

I nodded, knowing that he was right. I couldn't think about what could be happening right now. I needed to work with the guys to get her back. We jumped back in the truck, Burg driving this time as I stared out the window. I swallowed hard as I remembered our conversation this morning.

"Sam, we need to talk about something."

"Can we talk later? I have to get to work."

"Um, this can't wait."

I stopped and stared at her. She looked nervous and my initial thought was that she didn't want to get married. We had been going back and forth about it for a while now. She wasn't sure if she wanted her mother there and I was getting tired of waiting. I had been patient so far, but now I wanted more with her. I didn't want to put it off any longer. I sat down on the couch, preparing myself for whatever she was going to tell me.

"I'm pregnant."

I was frozen. I hadn't been expecting that. I thought we would be married first. We had been careful. Now she was pregnant and all I could think about was that my mother was going to be thrilled. She had been waiting for Vanessa and I to get married and give her grandkids. When I realized that I was just staring at her, I wrapped her in my arms and kissed her silly.

"I can't believe this. I mean, I wanted to be married first, but hell, I don't care right now. We're gonna have a kid."

"You're really okay with this?" she asked hesitantly.

"Sweetheart, I'm over the fucking moon."

"Good. Because I would hate to have to leave you before we got married."

"We're getting married this weekend. We're not waiting another minute. We can have a big celebration later, but right now, I want to make you my wife."

"I want that too." She gave me a radiant smile. "We're having a baby!"

I had to get her back. The thought of losing her was too much to bear, but knowing that she was pregnant was even worse. And Becky said it looked like they had shot her. I closed my eyes and fought off the nausea that was building. Dark thoughts crept into my head, reminding me of the last time I thought I had lost her. I wouldn't go down that road again. I made a promise to her and there was no way I would let her down.

Maggie

I was just putting Caitlin down for the night when I heard what sounded like a window breaking. Stepping into the hallway, I peered around the corner and saw a shadow moving downstairs. I quickly shut Caitlin's door and crept across the hall to my bedroom, quickly grabbing Sebastian's gun that he kept in the nightstand. It was heavier than the one that I used at the range, but I didn't have time to get to the safe and get it out.

I crept down the hallway, my gun firmly gripped in my hand. I took a deep breath as I started down the stairs.

"Let's get the bitch and get out of here."

"What about the kid?"

"We only have a few minutes. We need to get out of here fast."

My pulse thundered against the skin of my neck. I looked back up in the direction of Caitlin's room. I didn't want to leave her here alone, but I definitely didn't want whoever this was to have her. If I could distract them long enough, maybe they would just take me. I wished that Sebastian was here with me right now. As much as I prided myself on being able to hold my own, this was totally different. My daughter was involved and I couldn't let them get their hands on her.

Taking a deep breath, I spun around the corner and fired at the first man, hitting him in the shoulder as the other man raised his gun. I barely had time to duck back behind the wall before the bullet flew past me. I took a few deep breaths and spun back around, firing as I went. The guys were hiding behind some furniture, but if I could keep them pinned down for just a few minutes, someone might get here in time to help. I was careful with my shots, not wanting to waste any bullets, but I was running out of time.

"Come on, Sebastian," I whispered to myself as I prepared to fire my last shot. I had to make it count. "I'm out. Don't shoot," I shouted.

"Come out with your hands up," one of them yelled.

I stepped out from behind the wall and prayed that they wouldn't shoot me. I bent down like I was going to put my gun down and watched as the men stepped closer to me. I took a deep breath and whipped the gun upright, firing my last shot into the man's chest. His gun went off, hitting far right in the wall and the other man stepped out, blood dripping from his arm. His gun was trained on me.

"Drop the gun right now or I'll shoot you."

I dropped the gun immediately and yelped when he yanked my arm behind my back. I wanted to fight back. Everything inside me screamed to fight, but if I didn't kill him, he might go after Caitlin and I couldn't let that happen. I stumbled along as he dragged me out of the house and flung me in the back seat. I went for his gun at the last second, but he was faster and pulled his arm back, hitting me hard in the head with the gun. I fell back against the seat and tried to keep my eyes open, but I couldn't fight the overwhelming desire to drift off.

Cap

Sinner and I crept through the darkness of my yard to the front door that was standing open. Sinner looked over at me, nodding that he was ready to enter and I nodded, ready to find out what happened to my family. Sinner entered first, gun drawn and ready to fire. I entered second, my back to his as we started to clear the first floor. I stepped on some broken glass that was scattered on the floor, the sound echoing throughout the house.

"Don't shoot, Cap." Sinner and I both spun toward the sound, but lowered our weapons when we saw Chance at the foot of the stairs. Just feet in front of him was a man lying on the ground giving the thousand yard stare. The blood pooling under him stained the floor red, but I didn't give a shit. I was just thankful it wasn't Maggie.

"Where are my girls?" I croaked out.

Jackson came walking down the stairs carrying Caitlin. Her head was resting on his shoulder and her thumb was popped in her mouth. Her unicorn doll was tucked tightly in the crook of her elbow. I walked over quickly, holstering my firearm before taking her gently from Jackson. I breathed in her scent and kissed the beautiful curls on the top of her head. She appeared completely fine, just a little grumpy from being woken up in the middle of the night.

"Maggie?" I asked hopefully.

Chance shook his head. "No sign of her Cap. I called Becky and had her pull up the footage. It looks like she was trying to get taken so they wouldn't go after Caitlin."

My eyes slid closed as I held my daughter tighter. For all that Maggie and I went through over our little peanut, I had no doubt that she loved her daughter unconditionally and would do anything for her. Even get taken on purpose.

I nodded and looked around the house. As I held my daughter in my arms, I suddenly found myself unable to make a decision to save my life. To save Maggie's life. I was at a complete loss right now, torn between needing to find Maggie and wanting to hold onto my child and make sure nothing ever happened to her.

"We should head back to Reed Security, Cap. We're all meeting back there to find out anything we can," Chance said persistently. I nodded, knowing that was the right thing to do.

"I'll grab a bag for Caitlin," Sinner mumbled as he ran upstairs. Chance, Jackson, and Gabe stood watching me, probably waiting for me to say something, anything. I was in some kind of haze though. When Sinner came back down, he pulled at my arm and motioned for the other guys to follow.

"Come on," Sinner said. "Let's get over to Reed Security. I'm sure Cara would be willing to watch Caitlin. Sean was taking her over there with Lillian. He's trying to track a plate that Hunter got."

I quickly strapped Caitlin in the back and got in the passenger seat, not even arguing when Sinner took over. I glanced back at the house and cursed myself for having left my family when they needed me most.

We were pulling into the garage of Reed Security in a flash and Sinner was out, unbuckling Caitlin before I even had a chance to unbuckle my own seat belt. He walked over to me and I reached for Caitlin, but he shook his head.

"You need to get your shit together. I'll take care of Caitlin."

"Sinner, hand over my child before I fire your ass."

He snorted and shook his head. "Yeah, like I haven't heard that one before."

"I'm serious. Give me Caitlin."

"I'm serious too, Cap. Freckles is waiting for you to get her away from those assholes. You're the fucking boss. Get your ass in gear."

"Hey, language," I snapped, glancing at Caitlin.

"Sorry. Get your derrière in gear."

I glowered at him as he strolled off with my daughter like he owned the fucking place. He was right though. I needed to pull my head out of my ass and figure out how to get Maggie back. Not to mention, I had no idea what was going on with everyone else's family. I took a long, deep breath and blew it out, then headed for the elevator where Sinner was waiting. I punched in the code and rode the elevator up to the main floor of the building. When we stepped off, I took an inventory of who was here.

Cara rushed over to Sinner and gave him a big hug, then held out her arms for Caitlin. Sinner mumbled something to her about watching over her and told her where I kept all of Caitlin's things for when she was here. I watched as Caitlin was carried off to the other room, with Lucy, Claire, Lillian, and Alex following, and then turned back to my men.

"Status report," I barked.

Cazzo cleared his throat and stepped forward. "Vanessa, Kate, and Maggie were taken. Everyone else is safe, but they hit everyone at Reed Security. So far, we have one license plate, but no hits on it yet. Sean's been coordinating with the police department to try and locate the vehicle. We've also reached out to several contacts in Pittsburgh, looking for information on where the gangs would take hostages. We haven't heard back yet, but it's still a little early."

"Cazzo, I assume your house is no longer safe?" He shook his head. "We can't stay here. Our location is too public. We need to head for the safe house and work out a plan."

"We need to find them," Knight growled.

"We're not going to do ourselves any favors by running out of here half cocked."

"I do things my own way," Knight said as he stepped toward me. This was the Knight that I knew from before. He was no longer the man that worked with us day in and day out, but the ruthless killer that would go to any lengths to achieve his goals.

"I'll gladly do things your way, but we need information. There are three lives at stake here and a helluva lot more if things don't go our way. Besides, the Night Kings would have gone someplace familiar, which is Pittsburgh. Our safe house will put us right outside the city. That's a much easier distance to deal with this situation."

Knight stared me down, but I refused to give in. This was my goddamned company and I had just as much at stake as him. If he went off on his own, this would end very badly for the rest of us. He finally nodded and stood down.

"Now, we need to load up as many vehicles as possible. There's no way this ends in any way other than a hail of bullets. We have the safe house fully stocked, but I want to be damn sure that we're fully prepared. Let's get loaded up and then we'll get out of here."

"Are we taking different routes?" Derek asked.

"It's a toss up. We're safer together, but if we all drive together, we're flashing a fucking signal in their faces if they're watching for us. They planned this attack early on. The two men we took earlier today were decoys. They wanted us to take them so that we would be split up. They know that we'll retaliate and hit them hard, so they'll be watching for us."

"They probably have lookouts on all roads leading into Pittsburgh," Cazzo said. "I say we stick together. With how many women we're guarding, we can't protect all of them and ourselves if we're split up. There's just not enough of us."

"I agree," I said with a nod. "Cole, can you stay at the safe house with the women?"

"Fuck no," he said fiercely. "They took my cousin. You can fucking bet that I'm going to get her back. I'm still in top shape. You don't have to worry about me."

"Never did," I grinned. I still wished that I could have talked him into working for me, but I knew that wouldn't happen.

"This is gonna be like driving in a fucking convoy in the desert," Burg grumbled.

"Did I miss the party?" I turned around to see Lola quirking an eyebrow at me. "I'm gone on vacation for a few months and you're already needing me to come back and clean up your mess."

"We have a situation that we need to take care of."

"I've heard. What did Maggie do this time?" she asked.

"Why does everyone always assume it's Maggie?" I asked Sinner.

"Well, come on, Cap. If she's not the cause, she's involved still."

"It's not Maggie. This time. Now that everyone's here, let's get on the road and get our women back."

We pulled out of Reed Security and headed for the safe house. I saw the motorcycles as soon as we reached the gates. They were waiting for us, hoping to tail us wherever we were going. I had Sinner in the SUV with me and his wife, Cara in the back with Lillian. Sean stayed back in town so he could coordinate with the police department and feed us any information he could. He had contacts in Pittsburgh that could get us information faster than our contacts could.

"Did you see them?"

"Yeah, I saw them," Sinner grinned. "They're really fucking stupid if they thought we wouldn't."

"Message the other guys. Let them know we're going to split up and try to lose them heading out of town. We'll meet up at Old Woody Bridge."

"Gotcha, Cap."

I split off from the other guys, weaving my way in and out of traffic. Only one motorcycle followed me and I planned to ditch his ass long before we reached the outskirts of town. I got in the left turn lane and waited for the light to turn red before gunning it through the intersection. The cross traffic had already picked up and the motorcycle didn't have time to cut across.

"That was too fucking easy," Sinner said.

"Well, we're not clear yet," I said as I turned back down another road, heading in the opposite direction. I had to weave my way through the city to make sure no one could tell where we were headed. Although, there was really only one direction we would go and that was towards Pittsburgh. We just had to keep all of the Night Kings from knowing which route we would be taking so that we could make it to the safe house unseen.

Sinner's phone rang and he answered it cheerily. "Sinner from Reed Security. How may I help you?...Sounds good, man. Thanks for the help." He hung up and grinned at me. "Sean spotted the motorcycles and called in a suspicious activity report. The cops are pulling the rest of them over now. We should be able to sneak out."

"They're still going to have scouts on all the roads leading out of town."

"Yeah, but at least we won't have their whole crew breathing down our necks." He tsked as he shook his head. "It's a shame. Freckles is gonna be pissed that she missed all the action."

"What action? We haven't done anything but slip a motorcycle."

"Aw, come on, Cap. Don't you want to try out our new toy?"

"You're not getting your hands on that gun."

"Don't be like that."

"We haven't been able to fully test it yet. You'll end up making a bigger mess than we're in now."

"You're no fun," he grumbled as he sank back in his seat.

We headed out of town toward Old Woody Bridge and saw the other SUVs headed toward us.

"Looks like everyone's arrived." Sinner was counting vehicles and then sighed as he sat back. "That wasn't nearly as thrilling as I thought it would be."

I rolled my eyes at him. These guys had gotten way too used to the extra action we had seen over the past few years and they were chomping at the bit for some more. I had a feeling they would be seeing plenty.

"You seem to have snapped out of your earlier haze," he commented as we drove down the country road.

I was still scared as hell, but he had been right earlier. Maggie was counting on me to get her out and I couldn't do that if I was letting the fear take over. "Come on. It's Freckles. She's probably giving them so much hell that they'll hand her back just so they don't have to put up with her." *Or kill her.*

"Well, let's just hope her mouth doesn't get the better of her."

I was looking out in the distance off to the left, but my left eye just wasn't as sharp. I was practically blind in one eye. "Am I imagining things or do we have company headed our way."

Sinner pulled out some binoculars and checked it out. "Looks like someone saw what direction we were headed. I count two pickup trucks and a few motorcycles."

"That's what they're going to try and take us out with?"

He scanned the horizon in the other direction. "Make that another four trucks and a few more motorcycles." He dropped his binoculars and grinned at me. "Come on, Cap. You know you want to let me."

"No, I really don't."

"Aww, don't be like that. You know you want it as bad as I do."

"Actually, I'd prefer a nice, quiet drive out to the safe house."

"What are you guys talking about up there?" Cara asked from the third row.

"We've got company," Sinner said excitedly.

"Are we in danger?" Lillian asked.

"Yep," Sinner said a little too cheerily.

"What should we do?" I could hear the fear in Cara's voice and so could Sinner because his face instantly softened.

"You don't have anything to worry about. All of these vehicles are bullet resistant and we have a new secret weapon."

"No, we don't," I said testily.

"Yes, we do." He was trying to reassure them and I knew that, but I didn't want him pulling that thing out now of all times. It would be different if Knight was in the vehicle with us.

Sinner's phone rang again and he picked up on the first ring. "Yeah, we see them, also...I know. Perfect timing, right?...Well, I told Cap it was the perfect time to break it out, but he doesn't seem to think it is...Yeah, well you try telling him that."

"Put it on speaker," I demanded. Sinner did as I said.

"Cap, now is not the time to fuck around," Cazzo said. "We need to take these guys out fast so we can get to the safe house."

"Yeah, but..." I glanced over at Sinner. "It's Sinner. He's the one that'll be using it."

"It'll be fine, Cap. Let's get this shit done."

"Fine, but I don't want to hear any bitching when it goes sideways."

Cazzo hung up and I sighed. Sinner was practically bouncing in the seat next to me.

"So? Can I? Can I? Can I?" he asked excitedly.

"Yes, but try not to kill any of us. I would hate for us to die on the way to the safe house."

"Cap, you totally underestimate me."

"That's because I've seen you with your new toys. This is such a bad idea," I muttered to myself. Sinner climbed into the back and started pressing buttons. I felt the whoosh of air as the roof opened and the machine gun raised up to the top of the roof.

"This is gonna be so great." I could hear the grin in Sinner's voice and I prayed that he didn't kill anyone. Well, anyone other than our enemies.

"Hurry the fuck up. They're almost on us."

"Yeah, yeah. I'm working on it. There are so many buttons. I just have to figure out what to press."

"Do you have the controller?"

"Yeah, I'm just trying to figure out how to work it."

"Jesus Christ."

The trucks were converging on both sides of us and we only had seconds before they would be trying to kill us.

"Hurry up, Sinner!"

"I'm working on it. Don't rush me."

The first truck rammed into the front of our truck, sending us swerving off to the side of the road. Luckily, it had been more of a clip than a direct hit. I pushed the gas pedal down and tore down the road. I couldn't see what was happening behind us. My phone rang and I put it on speaker.

"I thought you guys had a fucking plan," Knight shouted through the phone.

"We're working on it," I shouted.

"Aww, fuck. You're letting Sinner do it?"

"Hey! I take offense to that," Sinner said as he pressed more buttons. The trucks were pulling up alongside all of us, trying to run us off the side of the road. The truck to my left rammed into us, sending Sinner flying in the backseat.

"Would you hurry the fuck up?" I yelled.

"Got it."

I heard the machine gun start to rat tat tat above us and then

Knight yelling through the phone. "What the fuck? Why are you shooting at us?"

"Oopsie," Sinner muttered.

"Oopsie?" Knight said furiously. "You're supposed to be shooting at the bad guys!"

"I'll get the hang of it."

"Yeah, well do that before we all end up dead." Knight ended the call and Sinner cursed behind me.

"Cap, up ahead at that intersection, pull onto the side road and park it so I can hit 'em as they drive by."

"You won't get all of them," I said.

"I'll get most of them."

I grumbled to myself as I sped past the trucks beside us and prepared to take the side road. "I really hope this fucking works. Otherwise, we're all gonna be fucking dead."

"You have no faith in me," Sinner said with a smile in his voice.

I called Knight behind us and quickly relayed the plan, hoping they would all brake in time to let the vehicles fly right by.

I yanked the wheel, turning down the side road as the tires spun on the gravel and threw the truck in park. Sinner was already firing, taking out the trucks as they flew past. I watched as all five trucks drove off the road and into the ditch. The motorcycles had pulled back at the sound of gunfire and our guys were sitting back a few feet from the intersection. The guys on the motorcycles gunned the engines to get out of there.

"Sinner, we've got a few runaways."

"On it, Cap. Let's see how the targeting system works."

I turned around and watched as he played with the screen, locating the targets he wanted and then he pressed a button. There was rapid fire for all of five seconds and the guys on the motorcycle fell to the ground.

"Fuck yeah!" Sinner shouted.

"You both okay?" I asked the girls as I turned around to look in back. They both nodded, but were quiet. I threw the truck in gear and took off, not wanting to stick around and see if more guys showed up. We had to get to the safe house and make a plan.

Chapter Eight
ALISON

Chris brought us out to a building on the back of the property. Opening the door, I could clearly see that they used this as a gun range. Chris was going to teach us to shoot and I was a little nervous. As much as I knew that Chris would teach Axel everything he needed to know, I couldn't help the anxiety that came with him learning something that would bring him that much closer to Slasher's world.

"Relax," Chris whispered as we stood in front of the arsenal of weapons. "I'm going to teach him everything about properly using a gun and when not to use one. He needs to know."

"I know," I said, swallowing hard. "I just don't like the idea of him holding a gun."

"It's better that I teach him. We're about to go to war with the Blood Devils. I need to know that you're both prepared to defend yourselves if something goes wrong."

I knew he was right and nodded my agreement.

"Alright, for starting out, I'll have you both use a Glock 19." He went through the different parts of the gun, letting us know the basics. "This is the magazine." He pointed to the bottom of the gun. "This is where you load the magazine. Then you have the front and back sights and the slide. This is your trigger, which also has the safety. Now, there is no hammer on this gun. It's built on the inside and I'll show you how that all works."

When he handed me the gun, I took it gingerly in my hands, not really wanting to use it. I let my hand adjust to the weight of it and felt the grip of it. It wasn't as bad as I thought it would be. He handed me the magazine and I loaded the gun, surprised that I was able to do it with ease.

"Rack the slide."

I did like he showed me. That part was a little more difficult. I looked over and saw that Axel was picking up on this a lot faster than I was. He looked almost natural holding a weapon.

"Now, when you stand, you want one foot to be slightly in front of the other and stand shoulder width apart." I did as he said and shuddered when his foot slid between my legs and adjusted the width of my stance. "Good. Now, raise your arms out in front of you and lock your elbows. Shoulders back and lean forward slightly."

His arms wrapped around me and he adjusted my arms and pressed down on my shoulders, trying to loosen the tension. "That's good," he whispered in my ear. My eyes slid closed as I felt his breath caress my neck. I felt my body come alive when he was near me. It was different than when we were kids. Back then, we had just been crazy in love and letting our hormones run free. Now, his strength and commanding presence washed over me and left me feeling a need deep inside. This wasn't just hormones or lust. This was my body feeling a pull to his and knowing that I was his and always would be. No matter what happened when this was over, there was only one man that would ever make me feel the way he did. I had missed the feel of him pressed against my back all these years. I had missed the deep rumble of his voice that sent shivers down my spine.

"Ali." I turned around to see Chris gazing at me in question. I cleared my throat and tried not to let him see how much he affected me. Now wasn't the time for us to figure out where we went from here, if he wanted us to go anywhere at all.

"Sorry, I was just thinking about something."

A sexy smirk curled his lips. "Yeah, I remember that look," he whispered in my ear. "Not in front of the kid, though."

I flushed bright red and cleared my throat, glancing over at Axel, who was concentrating on his stance and how to hold his weapon. He walked over to Axel and adjusted his stance and how he was holding his weapon and then took a step back, nodding as he looked at both of us.

"Alright, next is sighting your target. You always look at your target first and then follow the line of sight through the front sight on the gun and then the back sight. It's more natural and faster, so don't try and do it in reverse. Now, you see that smaller trigger in front of the main one?"

I glanced at the gun and saw what he was talking about. "Yeah."

"That's your safety. Then, you pull it back about three quarters of the way and the hammer will engage. You'll hear a small click. If you pull it back all the way, you'll fire a shot. Never put your finger on the trigger unless you intend to shoot someone. A loud noise or just someone stepping into your line of sight can scare you into pulling the trigger unintentionally."

He positioned my finger on the side of the gun and then did the same to Axel. "This is where you keep your finger until you're sure you're going to fire your weapon."

I nodded and looked back at the target. "So, I just pull?"

"Line up the sight and make sure your body is steady. The gun will kick back, so you need to be prepared for it to jolt your body. Here, bend your knee slightly. It'll help you keep your balance."

I looked down, not sure which knee he was talking about until he bent down and ran his hand along my jeans and bent my knee ever so slightly. He did the same with Axel and adjusted our stance once more before nodding.

"Next is breathing. You can't fire a gun properly if you're breathing chaotically. Since neither of you have been trained to fire a gun, it won't be natural for you to hold a gun on someone. You'll be nervous and your chest is going to be heaving from fear and adrenaline. It'll completely mess up your sight. The key is, you have to control your breathing as best you can before you shoot. Some people exhale and then pause while they fire. Others, inhale and then fire. You can also let out one long, controlled breath and then fire."

"What do you do?" Axel asked.

"If I'm in a controlled environment, I can slow my breathing and keep it even while firing. But if I'm in an intense situation, I like to exhale completely before firing. It's all in what you get comfortable with and what makes shooting most accurate for you. It takes practice."

I fired my first shot, completely missing the target and Chris came over to adjust my grip and my stance. It took several tries, but I finally hit the target, well, a part of the target. Axel was doing much better than I was. He hit the target on his first try and continued to get closer to the center with every shot. He seemed to be a natural.

"Here, let me see if I can help you," Chris said as he walked up behind me. His chest brushed against my back and his arms wrapped around mine. His hands lightly held mine around the gun. "Do you feel that?"

I was breathing raggedly. I could definitely feel that. There was an electric current that flowed from him through me. It was the same as it had been when we were younger. There was always a pull between us. Years of not being together hadn't changed a thing. "What?" I asked breathily, sure that he wasn't talking about that.

"You're tense. Your muscles are so tight that it's affecting your shot. You want to hold steady, but your body needs to be more relaxed. Close your eyes." I let my eyes slide closed and let the feel of him wash over me. His hand moved slowly up my arm and across my shoulder. "Let your body relax. Think of something that calms you." I immediately thought of his arms around me and stumbled back a step into him, feeling his erection pressing into me. "That thought won't calm either of us," he whispered.

I blew out a breath and tried to think of something that relaxed me. There was one memory in particular that I had. It was of Chris and I before our lives had gone to hell. We were sitting out under the stars, dreaming of what life would be like when we moved out into the real world and escaped the life we were living. I had been lying between Chris's legs and my head was resting against his chest. His slow breaths and the steady beat of his heart had lulled me into a sleepy state. It was a memory that stuck with me all these years.

I opened my eyes and lined up my target, still hearing the steady beat of Chris's heart against my ear, and fired. The bullet tore through the target, almost dead center. My mouth dropped open in shock and I stared at it in awe, barely hearing Axel next to me, cheering me on. I had done it.

Chris bent down and placed a soft kiss to the corner of my lips. "That's my girl," he whispered and I melted right there. He stepped away and went to help Axel for a little longer while I continued to practice. I felt stronger each time I hit the target. Chris couldn't change what had happened the last seventeen years, but he was certainly trying to make up for it now, giving me strength the only way he knew how.

Knowing now that Adam had taught me self-defense and Chris was teaching me to use a gun, I was more confident in my abilities to protect us. I hadn't felt this strength in so long. It was coming from within me, but also through Chris's eternal love for me.

When I was tired of shooting, I unloaded the gun and set it down where Chris had gotten it from and sat back watching him teach Axel. I wished that I had been able to get away sooner. It had been so hard when Axel was younger. He wasn't able to do a lot for himself and it made for a more difficult escape. After my first two attempts to escape, I decided to wait until Axel was older. Slasher had started threatening Axel's life and I just couldn't risk it. But as Axel grew older and Slasher started taking his rage out on both of us, I knew I didn't have long before our only choice was to escape or die.

"Hey," Chris said, walking over to me and taking a seat. "What's on your mind?"

Axel was still practicing and he looked good. "He's gonna be good."

"Yeah, the kid's a natural. That's not what you were thinking though. You had a far off look, like you had some bad memories floating around in there," he said, tapping my head.

"I was just thinking about how long it took us to get away. I wish it could have been sooner. I wish that Axel didn't miss out on so much time with you." I looked into Chris's eyes and smiled. "You would have been a great father to him."

"I'm sorry I wasn't there."

"It wasn't your fault, Chris. Life happens. I hate that my life went the way it did and I really hate that Axel grew up in that environment, but I don't blame you. I'm glad that you never joined the Blood Devils. I never wanted that life for you. And Axel and I survived. We got out just in time."

"Ali, I have you back now and I'm never letting either of you go. I never should have walked away all those years ago and I'm certainly not going to now. I still love you. I never stopped."

My heart leapt in my chest at his words. Was it really possible that he still wanted me? Even after he knew everything that I had been through? I wouldn't blame if he walked away from me. I was dirty, damaged. He was this great guy that had achieved so much. In my own right, I had overcome a lot, but the way I had been living...I just couldn't imagine him still wanting me.

"I want all those things we dreamed about when we were kids. I want you beside me every night and I want to put that ring on your finger that I promised you all those years ago."

Tears filled my eyes at his words and I had to look down so he wouldn't see how heartbroken I was. There was so much he didn't know yet. "Chris, Slasher is my husband." His face turned lethal and his nostrils flared. I could barely see his dark eyes under his cowboy hat, but I knew they held the promise of murder. "I didn't want to, but it was the only way to keep Axel safe."

"Well, you won't have to worry about that much longer," he said angrily.

"Chris, there's no way that Slasher will give me a divorce. He would rather see me dead first."

"You're not getting a divorce. I'm gonna kill him and every other Blood Devil so you never have to worry again."

"That's a nice sentiment, but-"

"It's not a fucking sentiment," he barked. "I'm highly trained and so are the men I work with. There's no fucking way that any of them will ever see the light of day by the time I'm through with them. That asshole took what was mine, took years from us and I won't let him get away with that."

I bit my lip, not sure if I wanted to say the rest. Seeing how he reacted to the marriage, I was sure this would make him explode. "If you really feel that way, then there's something else that I have to do. I need to go to a clinic and get tested."

He dropped his head in his hands. Taking his cowboy hat off, he ran his fingers through his hair, tightening them around the silky strands. I could see how his forearms clenched every so often as he tried to control his anger, but he wouldn't let me see his face. When he finally looked up at me, his face was controlled and calm. "We'll take care of it as soon as this is all over."

"Thank you."

He wrapped his hand around the back of my head and pulled me in closer to him. "I'd do anything for you," he whispered before he crushed his lips against mine. His tongue slipped inside, caressing mine and possessing me completely. His other hand slid to my cheek, his fingers running along my neck and eventually wrapping around my back, pulling me even tighter to him.

"Um, not that I'm not happy for you two, but it's kind of weird to see my parents making out."

I smiled against Chris's lips as he let out a small chuckle.

Chapter Nine

MAGGIE

I woke up to the feeling of my arms being wrenched and nausea rolling through me. It took me a few deep breaths before I was finally able to pry my eyes open. Darkness surrounded me, but I was able to make out two other figures in the room with me. Squinting, I still couldn't see, so I blinked rapidly, trying to clear the haze from my eyes.

"Hello?" I said hesitantly.

"Maggie? It's Kate."

"Are you okay?" I asked around the croak in my throat.

"I'm okay. My wrists are a little sore, but I think I'm fine other than that."

"Who else is in the room with us?"

"Vanessa. She hasn't woken up yet."

I leaned my head back against the wall and tried to take stock of my body. I was still in a fog and I was having trouble concentrating on anything. My arms were behind my back, handcuffed, but the rest of me was able to move around. My head was pounding and I vaguely remembered being struck in the head as I was shoved in the car. Caitlin. Panic ripped through me. I didn't know if she was safe. Had Sebastian gotten to her? I glanced around the room quickly, hoping I didn't see her small frame tucked in a corner, but there were too many dark spots wherever we were.

"Are we the only ones here?" I asked nervously.

"Yeah. It's just us."

"Caitlin isn't here?"

"No. I was awake when they brought us in. It's just the three of us."

I let out a terrified breath and took several deep breaths to try and calm my nerves. "Oh, thank God. It worked."

"What worked?"

"When they came for us, I distracted them, hoping they would forget about Caitlin."

"I haven't seen her, so I'm guessing she's safe. But I'm worried about Vanessa. She's been groaning a lot and I think she's bleeding."

"Can you tell where the blood's coming from?"

"No. I'm chained to the wall."

I yanked on my wrists, realizing that my handcuffs were also chained to the wall. "Did you see who they were?"

"They looked like gangsters. That's all I could make out. I didn't really get a chance to ask them for their names."

"Next time you'll have to be a more friendly hostage."

"Sure. I'll work on that."

We sat in silence for a while, which was fine with me because it felt like I had a jackhammer going off in my head. I must have dozed at some point because the next thing I heard was yelling in the room. I opened my eyes and saw Kate struggling with two men. They were trying to take her somewhere and she was fighting back. My heart pounded wildly. I couldn't let anything happen to her. Knight would kill me. Hell, I was Sebastian's wife. If they wanted anyone, it should be me.

"What are you doing?" I shouted.

"Getting information," one of them snarled.

"She doesn't know anything. Please. Don't do this," I pleaded.

Kate kicked out at them, but they continued to drag her to the door. I shook my head wildly, pulling at my restraints as hard as I could.

"Take me!" I shouted without thinking. "I'm Sebastian's wife. She doesn't know anything. She can't tell you jack shit!"

"And we're supposed to believe that the owner's wife will just give us whatever we need?"

"Not a chance in hell, but she really doesn't know anything. She doesn't have anything to do with the company, if that's what you're after."

One of the men threw her to the ground and stalked over to me. "So, you want us to take you instead?"

I shook in fear. My eyes flicked to Kate and I could see the terror reflecting in hers. I couldn't let anything happen to her, but that didn't mean that I wanted to take it myself. Rough hands jerked me forward and I felt the pressure release from my wrists. I was still cuffed, but no longer latched to the wall. The second man walked over to me with an evil smile and yanked me up by the elbow, shoving me toward the door. I glanced back one last time to see Kate's wide eyes staring back at me. Vanessa was still passed out in the corner.

I did my absolute best to hold my head high as I was led down a dark hallway. It smelled like piss and rot throughout the building and the room they led me into was no better. I was pretty sure the dark stains on the floor were blood and there was an overwhelming smell of vomit that had me gagging as I was shoved into a metal chair. A man with tattoos all over his face stepped forward and grinned at me. He had gold caps around his teeth and his gums looked like they were rotting.

"You want a turn, puta?"

I looked at the others and then back at the man in front of me. They all had matching grins that sent chills down my spine. I swallowed hard and tried not to show my fear, but the way they started laughing at me let me know that they knew exactly what they were doing to me. One of them circled behind me, looking at me like I was something he would devour. He yanked my arms over the chair behind my back and tied a rope around my waist, holding me to the chair.

"I see why El Jefe chose you. Are you this demanding in the bedroom too?"

He squeezed my breast hard, but the slamming of the door had them all jerking around.

"We're not here to get our dicks wet. We need information," a dark figure said from the doorway. He didn't have a Spanish accent like the others. He had a rough, but commanding voice and I didn't miss how the others stood tall when he was around. "So, you're the boss's woman." His eyes roamed over me in an assessing way that didn't make me fear being raped, but what kind of torture he had in mind for me. "You'll do just fine," he said with a grin.

He nodded to one of the men and my left hand was jerked from the restraints and pulled forward. The man held my hand out firmly, making it impossible for me to move.

"I think maybe we should send him your wedding ring. Let him know exactly what we're thinking." A glint touched his eyes and I swallowed hard. "We'll leave your finger attached."

He nodded to another man and he pulled a pair of cutters out of his pocket. I started to squirm, too scared to even make a sound. I wanted to scream. I wanted to beg for mercy, but my throat wouldn't make any noise. I was paralyzed with fear.

"Where's the safe house?" the man asked.

I couldn't answer. All I could do was stare at the cutters as they came closer and closer to my finger.

"Maybe we can convince you to answer."

The man with the cutters grabbed my pinky finger and yanked it out straight. I started to scream as the blades surrounded my finger and sliced into my skin. I kicked out, trying to hit anything to get them to leave me alone, but it was no use. The blade cut deeper and deeper until the pain was overwhelming and my voice was hoarse from screaming. The thud of my finger falling to the floor echoed in my ears.

I glanced down through the tears and saw that my pinky finger was gone. Blood was streaming from the end of my hand sending me into a blinding panic. I swallowed over and over, trying my best not to vomit from the pain.

"Where's the safe house?" he asked again. I vaguely heard the question over the pounding in my head. I looked up at the man, wishing I could wake up from this horrible nightmare. I couldn't give up the location of the safe house. I had to hold out as long as I could. Once they knew where the safe house was, it could never be used again. I couldn't betray my husband and the rest of his employees in that way. They would be attacked and killed. I had to give them as much time as possible to find me.

He nodded again to the man and this time my ring finger was held out. I looked at my wedding ring, wondering if I would ever see it again or my husband. I turned my head as the cutters closed once again around my finger. I ground my teeth together, trying my best not to scream, but when the cutters started cutting through my bone, I couldn't hold back anymore. Sobs wracked my body as I screamed with the pain. Black spots danced in front of my eyes as he sliced all the way through my skin and then my bone cracked and I felt my finger drop to the floor with a thud. How much longer could I hold out? Would I be missing all my fingers by the time he was done?

He bent down and picked up my finger, examining my wedding band. "Maybe he could put your ring on a different finger. If you last that long. Would you like to see?"

He turned my finger so I could see the exposed bone and flesh that had blood dripping from it. I jerked my head to the side just in time to vomit all over the floor. By the time I was done, I was shaking violently. I didn't know if I could make it through losing another finger. My body was begging me to give in, but my mind was telling me I couldn't betray my family like that.

"Perhaps you're not that concerned about losing a finger. Do we need to be more creative?" He looked at the man behind me. "Take off her shirt and spread her out on her stomach."

I felt the rope loosen from around my stomach and then I was thrown on the ground as my shirt was ripped from my body. I was sure my pants were next. He was going to rape me right here on the dirty floor, just feet from my own vomit. My fingers were laying on the floor in my periphery and I focused on them instead of what was going on behind me. When I felt the first slice into my skin, I screamed until my throat felt raw.

The pain started at my left shoulder blade and jagged cuts were made over to my spine and down my left side. Hands held my arms and legs down on all sides as the blade continued to dig into my skin over and over again. Through the blur of tears, I focused on my fingers, giving me something to anchor myself for as long as possible.

When the pain stopped, I took a deep breath, choking on the snot and tears that clogged my nose and throat. It started again on my right side, but I started to fade in and out. The pain was too much and all that was leaving my throat at this point were pathetic whimpers. I could see the spots dancing in front of me. I was about to pass out.

The man leaned down next to my ear, his hot breath skimming over my flesh. "Would you like us to continue or are you ready to talk?"

I knew I was done. I had held out for as long as I could, but I couldn't take any more. I hoped that Sebastian wouldn't hate me. I hoped that his teammates would forgive me. I whispered the address to the man, but when he went to leave, I grasped his hand with my three fingers I had left.

"You need the code," I choked out. "2-6-6-6."

The man grinned at me and motioned for his men to leave the room. They didn't take me with them. They just left me lying on the floor, bleeding everywhere. I could feel the blood trickling out of my back and down my sides. Everything hurt too much to move, so I let the pain wash over me and I fell into the darkness.

Chapter Ten

CHRIS

"What's going on?" I asked Alec as he stepped into the gun range.

"The Night Kings hit everyone back home. It's a fucking disaster. Kate, Vanessa, and Maggie were all taken."

"Fuck. You've gotta be kidding me." I ran a hand down my face, hating that this all started with me.

"I wish I were. Everyone's on their way here. Cazzo's place is no longer an option as a safe house. We're on lock down from now on. You need to bring them back into the house where we can be sure they're completely protected."

I nodded. "Do me a favor, don't let anyone talk about this in front of them. It'll just make them feel worse."

I turned back to Axel and Ali, trying my best to hide my rage from them. I couldn't let them see how angry I was at what the Blood Devils were doing. They didn't need to feel worse for the situation we were all in.

"We need to head back to the house. Everyone's on their way here. We need to formulate a plan."

Axel looked a little disappointed to be leaving, but Ali walked over to my side and slipped her hand in mine. We made our way back into the house and I pulled Ali aside.

"I want you and Axel to go upstairs while I talk to everyone."

"Why? Shouldn't we be here in case we can help?"

"This is going to be us strategizing for a long time. There are so many things we need to figure out first. I promise, when we discuss going after the Blood Devils, I won't leave you out of it."

Ali nodded and pressed a soft kiss to my lips before motioning for Axel to follow her upstairs. It didn't take too much longer for everyone to pull into the safe house. One by one, they all filed into the house, looking completely wiped out. Sebastian, Knight, and Cazzo looked particularly pissed and it made the guilt weigh down on me even harder. This was all coming back on them because of me. This was my mess that I hadn't cleaned up all those years ago and now their women were paying the price. And Vanessa, she had become like a sister to me. I didn't want to even think about what was going through Cazzo's head right now. I just hoped that he wasn't going down that dark path he had been down just a little over two years ago.

"Cap," I said urgently. "I'm so fucking sorry. This should have never happened."

He shook his head and placed a hand on my shoulder. "Don't fucking say you're sorry. This isn't your fault. You were protecting your woman and you did the right thing bringing this to us."

"But Maggie and-"

"We'll get them back," he said fiercely. "Sean's working with his contacts now. We should be hearing from him any moment now."

"I think we need more help than that. Cap, there's not enough of us to take on so many of them."

"I know," he nodded. "I'm gonna give Cash a call. If he can help us out, we should be able to wipe them all out."

"What's the plan?" Knight asked.

Cap turned to everyone in the room. All the men and women were staring at him, waiting for an answer, a direction. "Sean's working his contacts now. As soon as we hear from him, we head out and get our women back. Let's load up and bring all the fire power we need. Girls, you'll be staying here with Ali and Axel. This is the safest place for you at the moment. Chance, you'll stay here on their protective detail.

We'll leave two vehicles with you just in case. You know the drill if anything happens."

"Cap, I'd like to stay," I said insistently.

"No. I know why you want to, but we need all hands on deck right now. They'll be protected, but I need you to do your fucking job and right now, that's getting us loaded up and heading out with us when it's go time."

He was right. I owed him that much, especially since this was all because of me. I nodded and got to work with everyone else. When we were just about finished, I went up to see Ali before we left. I only had a minute to talk to her. I knocked on her door and slowly pushed it open, seeing that Axel was asleep, but Ali was staring out the window.

"Hey," I whispered.

She turned to me, arms crossed protectively over her chest. "You're leaving," she said, taking in my appearance.

"I have to. I'm not allowed on your protection detail and they need all the help they can get."

"Where are you going?"

"We're going to pay a visit to the Night Kings."

"But why? You can't already have a plan in place for taking them all out. You said it would take planning."

"Ali," I sighed, not wanting to tell her and make her feel bad, but I had no idea what we were walking into or what would happen when we returned. She didn't need to hear about it from someone else. "The Night Kings attacked all our homes. It was a setup to have those two guys come after us. They took three of our women. We're going to get them back."

Her hands flew to her mouth as the tears started to flow down her face. "Don't beat yourself up about this."

"But this wouldn't have happened if I hadn't come here."

"And I would have never met my son or seen you again. You'd probably be dead by now. Is that what you want?" I asked fiercely. "I will never regret you coming here and my brothers don't blame you either. This is what we do."

"Just promise me that you'll come back," she choked out.

"Always."

I wrapped her up in my arms and kissed her forehead. I pulled back and looked at her again, wanting her to see the promise in my eyes. "I swear to you. I'll always come back to you. I'll never leave you again. You and Axel have become my whole life in such a short time and I'll never let you go."

Her eyes dropped to my lips and I took the cue and crushed my lips to hers, pouring in all the lost years and minutes that I had missed her. It was all worth it to have her back in my arms again.

"Stay safe," she whispered as I headed for the door. I glanced back at Axel and then headed downstairs. The guys were all gathered in the living room because it was the biggest space. Cap was talking with someone on the phone. It must have been important because everyone was focused on that call.

"Right. Thanks, Sean." He hung up and looked at all of us, determination set in his features. "Sean coordinated with the police department and we're clear to move in. It's a little bit of a gray area, but we're good to go."

"When do we leave?" Knight asked anxiously.

"Five minutes. Chance, are you sure you've got enough people? You've got Ali, Axel, Claire, Lucy, Lillian, Cara, Alex, and three kids."

"We'll make it work. You guys need everyone you can to get Vanessa, Kate, and Maggie."

"It'll be a tight fit if you have to bug out, but we need all the other vehicles. I'll have coms on, but I won't have my phone on. I haven't heard back from Cash yet. If he calls, Becky, you take the call and explain the situation. Tell him that we could use backup if he can give it."

"Will do."

Cap looked back at everyone and he didn't have to say anything more. We all knew what was at stake here. There was no way we could fail. "Alright, the most likely location is an old factory outside of Pittsburgh. Pittsburgh PD says that there's a lot of activity over there with the Night Kings and that's most likely where they'd take our girls. We're alone on this one. We have the okay from the department to move forward, but legally, they can't do anything right now. As soon as we see something inside, we call the department and they'll be on standby to come down and make arrests. As much as we want to take out a few gang members tonight, let's play this as straight as possible."

"Not fucking likely," Knight muttered.

Cap ignored his comment, most likely because we were all thinking the same thing. If they even so much as looked at us wrong, not one of us would have a problem putting a bullet in their heads.

"Pittsburgh PD has been driving by over the past hour and said there aren't a lot of vehicles there. That should make this easier for us. We'll surround the building and enter at the same time. Knives only until absolutely necessary. We don't want any of them getting jumpy and killing someone. The plan is to get in and out before any of them have the chance to alert any other Night Kings. If they all descend on us, we're fucked. Do whatever you have to to make sure that doesn't happen."

"One more thing," Cazzo said, stepping forward. "Vanessa's pregnant."

A heavy silence filled the room as we all took in that bit of information. Cazzo looked at the floor, obviously having a hard time dealing with the fact that his pregnant fiancé was in danger.

"We'll get her back," Cap said firmly.

We nodded and headed for the doors. We all drove in silence to the location Sean had given Cap. We parked all around the building, each of us taking a different location to enter from. Cap checked in with all of us as we converged on the building. There wasn't a lot of light, which benefited us greatly. There was a single guard posted outside the various doors. When they were all removed, Cap gave the signal to move in.

Ice swung the door open and I entered first, moving silently through the large building. Ice and Jules were at my back as we descended the steps toward the basement. That was most likely where the girls were being held. We heard a creak behind us and spun around, but it was already too late. There was a man at the top of the stairs with a gun trained on us. If he fired, our location would be given away and we'd be fucked. I slipped my hand down my leg to the strap where my knife was housed. I almost had it out when a figure jumped out and broke the man's neck in one swift movement.

He gently laid the man down so he didn't make any noise and then walked toward us. Knight. Of course. The man was as lethal as they came and you never knew where he would be. He moved as swiftly and silently as you'd expect from any assassin. He paused on the stairs next to me with a quirked eyebrow.

"You didn't seriously think I would let you have all the fun?"

I shook my head and started back down the stairs with Knight beside me. There was a hallway with a series of doors. I could hear someone speaking in Spanish, but it was muffled. I nodded for the first door. We needed to clear all the rooms no matter where the voices were coming from. We couldn't afford to miss anything.

I swung the first door open and scanned the room, but there was nothing there. We moved down the hall to the next room and did the same. Movement from the corner had Knight and I aiming our weapons over there. Knight was running over the next second, huddled down next to Kate. I could see Vanessa on the floor, unconscious and pale. Her hands were behind her back, chained to the wall. Ice and Jules were keeping watch outside the room.

"Cap, come in."

"What do you have?"

"We've got Kate and Vanessa. Kate appears okay, but Vanessa is out. We need Hunter down here now. Basement level, second door. No sign of Maggie yet. There are voices down the hall. We'll need a few more teams down here."

"10-4."

I glanced over at Knight and saw that he had cutters on him that he was using to remove Kate's cuffs. Kate wasn't saying anything, just trembling and staring at Knight. When her cuffs were removed, she flung herself into Knights arms as he handed me the cutters. I quickly cut through Vanessa cuffs and pulled her arms out from behind her back. I could see now that she had blood all down her legs. There were no open wounds to see, which meant that she was most likely miscarrying. I didn't want to say anything over coms. If Cazzo heard that, it could put everyone in danger.

A few minutes later, Hunter and Cole ran into the room. Cole went over to Kate, yanking her from Knight's arms and wrapping her in a tight hug. Hunter was by my side looking over Vanessa with a grim look on his face. "She needs a hospital. We need to get her out of here now."

"Anyone found Maggie yet?"

He shook his head.

"We still have more rooms to clear down here, but we need to get her out of here."

Hunter nodded. "Cap, we're taking Cole and Knight to get Kate and Vanessa out of here. We need to get to the hospital. Cazzo, you need to come too, man."

"I'll meet you at the south exit," he said gruffly. I could hear in his voice that he was trying to hold it together.

"We're clear up here. I'm heading down to you. Alec, your team takes watch around the building," Cap said.

"Copy that," Alec's voice came through the line.

The rest of us took up posts in the hallway of the basement as Knight, Cole, and Hunter silently made their way out with Kate and Vanessa. Cap was downstairs moments later with Sinner and Burg, ready to finish clearing the building. We cleared the remaining rooms on the sides of the hallway, which left one at the very end. I could see the look of terror on Cap's face, knowing that what was beyond this door would tell us almost everything we needed to know.

We listened outside the door for a moment, hearing two voices. Cap nodded and I slowly turned the knob on the door, flinging it open as Cap stormed the room, followed by Sinner, Burg and myself. The men were surprised and didn't react right away. Neither did Cap. He was staring down at his wife, lying lifelessly on the floor, too stunned to move.

There was a black tarp on the floor and Maggie was lying next to it on her stomach. Blood smeared her back and her left hand was missing two fingers that were laying just inches from her body. Cap's eyes slowly lifted until he was looking directly at the men in front of him. He moved so fast that I didn't have time to try and stop him, not that I would have. His knife sliced across one man's throat before lodging in the other man's eye. He pulled it out and started stabbing them repeatedly until blood was pouring from their bodies and covering his. Sinner had to pull him off them.

"Cap, enough. Maggie needs you."

That seemed to get through to him and he slowly stood, wiping the blood from his face with his shirt. He turned around and swallowed hard as he knelt down beside Maggie. I placed my fingers on her neck and felt a pulse. It was faint, but it was there.

"Cap, she's alive. We need to get her to the hospital."

He just stared at her, tears in his eyes and heartbreak on his face. He was on the verge of losing it and that couldn't happen if we were going to save Maggie.

"Burg, I need your med kit."

Burg grabbed the kit out of one of his pockets. It wasn't much, but we all carried a little something just in case of an emergency. I pulled out my own and so did the others. I quickly wrapped Maggie's hand tightly with gauze to try and slow the bleeding. Her back was a different story. She had deep gouges that looked like letters, but there was so much blood that I couldn't make out what it said. I wasn't a medic. I didn't know what to do, but I knew that putting something dirty on her could cause infection. The alternative was to carry her out with open wounds and I didn't think that was too much better.

"Here," Sinner said, whipping off his shirt and handing it to me. "I have a few gauze pads we can put over the worst of it and then we'll put this shirt on her to protect the rest."

I nodded in agreement and took the pads from him, gently placing them over the worst of the cuts. Although, all the cuts were bad. I was at a total loss what to do, as was everyone else in the room. Cap was still standing there staring down at her.

Hunter rushed into the room and I breathed a sigh of relief. "I sent Vanessa and Kate to the hospital and came back. We need another team there ASAP."

"We're on it," Sinner said as he and Burg left the room.

Hunter knelt down on the other side of Maggie and assessed her injuries. His eyes flicked to her fingers on the floor and he quickly pulled out a baggie and gauze.

"Chris, put her fingers in the gauze and then in the baggie."

I did as he asked, picking up the two digits with the gauze and placing them in the bag. When I picked up her ring finger, her wedding band fell to the floor and made a dinging noise that echoed throughout the room. Cap finally snapped out of his haze and looked at the ring on the floor. He bent over and picked it up, slipping it on his pinky finger. Taking a deep breath, he knelt down next to Maggie and pushed her strawberry blonde hair from her face.

"Alright, I'm going to clean up these cuts the best I can and then we'll get out of here. Chris, I need you to call ahead to the hospital and let them know we're on our way and the extent of her injuries. We're out of here in five," Hunter demanded.

I placed the baggies in his medical bag as he finished pouring something over her cuts. As the blood washed away, I heard Cap suck in a deep breath. I looked over to see *Night Kings* carved into her back. Hunter quickly threw on some patches and covered her body. I ran up the stairs to get reception and called the hospital, relaying all the information Hunter had asked me to. When he emerged from the building carrying Maggie, we rushed to our vehicles and raced off to the hospital. I wanted to get back to Ali, but I needed to be sure first that Maggie, Vanessa, and Kate would be alright.

We made it to the hospital in no time and the girls were brought back to be checked out. Knight had to be physically held back from going with Kate. The staff was on the verge of having him thrown out. I chuckled to myself, wishing I could see them try.

I looked around the waiting room, thinking we should have some sort of plan for what we were going to do next, but Cap was too out of it to make any decisions. I looked to Cazzo and he looked equally devastated. I walked over to Derek and motioned for him to follow me. I waited for a nurse to pass in the hallway and then leaned in close to Derek.

"We need a plan and you're all we've got right now. Cap and Cazzo are out of their fucking minds and we have to be prepared."

He nodded his agreement. "I know. Something wasn't right back there. Where was everyone? There should have been more people in that building."

"Unless they got what they wanted. Maggie was pretty torn up."

"We need to figure out what they were after," Derek nodded. "They could have been after Reed Security codes, but Maggie wouldn't know the most recent ones."

"No, they aren't after intelligence. If they're working for the Blood Devils, they want to know where Ali and Axel are."

"Maggie knows that location," Derek said grimly.

"But she doesn't know the codes to get in."

"She knows one," Derek said cryptically.

Chapter Eleven

ALISON

I walked out of the bedroom, unable to sleep. Axel could sleep through practically anything, but I was too worried about Chris to even close my eyes. Every time I tried, I saw him lying on the ground, bleeding out. I went downstairs to the living room where the girls were all sitting. I felt awkward, not knowing any of them, but they were all related to someone at Reed Security, so they were Chris's friends.

"Hi, I'm Claire," a woman said as she walked over to me.

"Alison. I'm...uh, well, my son is Chris's son."

"Chris has a son?" she asked incredulously.

"Well, he didn't know. It's a long story," I said anxiously. Would she want me to go into all the details now? I didn't know if I was ready for that.

"I bet it would make a good book," she grinned. At my confused expression, her smile widened. "Sorry. I'm a librarian and I love a good story. Not that I expect you to tell me your whole life story right now, or at all if you don't want to. I was just saying that I like to read and by the sounds of it, your story would be quite interesting."

"Um...."

"Don't mind her. She rambles. Hi, I'm Lucy, her sister. I'm engaged to Hunter and she's engaged to Derek." I shook her hand and gave a tentative smile. "Come on. I'll introduce you to everyone else."

We walked into the living room and all eyes turned on me. None of them were judging me from what I could tell, which I didn't understand.

"This is Cara. She's Sinner's wife. That's Lillian, Sean's wife, but Sean isn't here. He's a detective with the police department. Cara is Lillian's sister-in-law." I nodded along, trying to catalogue that information for later.

"I have two kids, but they're upstairs sleeping right now," Lillian said with a smile.

"I didn't see them come in."

"They were pretty out of it," she said sweetly. "Rebecca is four and Caleb is three."

"Uh, well, I'm Alison and I have a son, Axel. He's almost sixteen and he's Chris's son." A few eyebrows went up and I didn't want them thinking badly of Chris. "It's a really long story, but basically, Chris and I were high school sweethearts and circumstances tore us apart. He went off to the military and I was...I was taken by a gang. It was safer for my son if everyone believed he belonged to this guy, Slasher. But Slasher wanted to initiate Axel into the gang, so we ran. I'm afraid that all this chaos is because of me."

I expected some outrage or at least some critical looks, but everyone just looked at me with sympathy, which was almost worse.

"How did you get away?" Cara asked. I could see in her eyes a kind of familiarity. Like she had lived this life before. I didn't want to push, especially since I didn't want to talk about my own life.

"I made Slasher angry enough to beat the crap out of me. I knew he was having a party and he would forget about me if I was out of commission. When they started partying, Axel and I slipped out."

"You purposely had a gangster beat the crap out of you?" Claire spluttered.

"I had to get away. It was my only chance."

"Wow," she whispered in awe. "You're like, way better than Lois Lane."

I tilted my head in confusion, not sure how to respond to that.

"I mean, she was always being rescued by Superman. You saved yourself. That's the best kind of heroine."

"Well, I had a son to take care of. I was determined," I said with a shrug.

"So, what was it like being part of a gang?" Claire asked excitedly. My eyes flicked to Lucy, who just rolled her eyes. "Yeah, yeah. We all know I have no filter. Sorry about that," she said, not so apologetically. "It's just, I've read all these romance books about women being rescued from the grips of an evil drug dealer who is determined to keep her shackled to his side for the rest of her life or until she succumbs to her tragic fate. How realistic is that?"

"Well, I haven't actually read any of those kinds of books. In fact, the only books I tend to read are medical journals."

"Wait, are you a doctor?" Lillian asked.

"No, I'm a nurse. I was able to go back to school and get my nursing license."

"He let you do that? Oh my gosh. Is he like one of those evil men that you hate to love?" Claire was a little too giddy about this whole conversation, but I found her light attitude about the whole thing kind of endearing.

"He's definitely not someone you hate to love. Or love to hate for that matter. He was just pure evil. I convinced him that I could be helpful to him."

"So, what happened when you ran? Was it an easy escape or was there danger lurking in every corner?"

I smiled at Claire's enthusiasm. "Well, considering that he had just beaten me up, I was in a lot of pain and I guess I wasn't as stealthy as I thought I was. They caught up to us in Pittsburgh."

Claire put a hand to her chest as she let out an audible gasp. "No, way."

"Be careful, Alison. Claire's about to have a book-gasm over here," Lucy shook her head.

I chuckled, not able to keep in the hilarity of the situation I found myself in. "Yes, way. It was pretty intense. Chris found us just in time, but so had the Blood Devils. Chris was carrying me back to his vehicle when they started shooting at us."

"Holy Cannoli," Lillian whispered. "Then what happened?"

"I'm not sure. I remember being jostled around a lot and I remember intense pain, but that's about it. I woke up in his bed later with a chest tube in. I guess I had a collapsed lung and he had to put one in not long after we got on the road. Axel told me a little bit about it. He said it was pretty intense."

Claire nudged Lucy and whisper hissed, "See? I told you there was something strange about the men of Reed Security. They all have like these awesome super powers."

"Just ignore her," Lucy said. "She has this weird obsession with superheroes and at one time thought that all the men from Reed Security had super powers."

"Hey, don't make fun of me," Claire pouted. "It could have happened."

"Claire lives in a fantasy world that is part book and part reality. You never really know what you're going to get with her."

I nodded to Lucy, but deep down, I thought Claire was pretty awesome. Living in your own little reality sounded really appealing at the moment. Now that I got to know Claire a little better, I was really interested in knowing the rest of them.

"So, Lillian. You're married to a detective?"

"Yes. He works with the police department back home."

"Did he not want to join Reed Security?"

She glanced at Cara. "Well, Cara went missing for a while and when the guy who took her wasn't caught, he decided to join the police force. He was determined to find the guy."

I looked over at Cara in disbelief, which was a little strange considering my own story. "Did they catch him?"

She nodded and grinned. "Yes, but I was a basket case. Technically, I still am. Sinner is kind of like my therapist."

"Wait, Sinner's a therapist? I thought he was a member of Reed Security."

"He is. I met him when I passed out in a restaurant. He helped me overcome my fears."

"How did he do that?"

She blushed furiously as she ducked her head. "Let's call it sexual healing."

I bit my lip, not sure if this was some kind of new kink that I hadn't heard of yet. And did I want to know about it? Yes. Yes, I did. I cleared my throat and tried to find the best way to ask her more, but Claire beat me to it.

"Did he throw you down on a restaurant table and ravage your body?"

"Uh, there was a restaurant one time," Cara grinned.

"Okay, so is it just me or are the men of Reed Security all pretty... large?" Lucy asked.

I thought about it and all the men I had seen were rather large. But then they were all former military and probably had to keep up their bodies.

"Definitely large," Claire said with a grin. "I would say super sized."

"Overwhelmingly so," Cara smiled.

"Oh, dear. I'm not sure this is appropriate to talk about," Lillian said primly.

"It's just us girls," Claire giggled. "It's not like they're standing right in front of us."

"But," Lillian stuttered for a moment. "Doesn't it feel like we're objectifying them?"

"Because of the size of their bodies?" I asked. All the women turned to me and I suddenly understood what they were talking about. "Oh, sorry. It's...uh, been a while since I was with Chris."

"But from what you remember?" Lucy asked. I blushed bright red and remembered our first time together. It had hurt a lot, but so had every time after that, only in a good way. He was definitely larger than Slasher and part of me always wondered if Slasher was just trying to compensate for his lack of size.

"Oh, man. Do you see how she's blushing? He's definitely hung like a horse," Lucy said. The women continued to banter around me about the men and I found for the first time ever that I was actually enjoying myself with other people. I had friends at work, but I was never allowed to hang out with them outside of work. I always went straight home when my shift was done. The closest I came was when Adam gave me self defense lessons on my lunch break.

Claire leaned forward and whispered conspiratorially. "I have this fantasy-" Lucy groaned and sank back into the couch. "Shut up," Claire elbowed Lucy. "I have this fantasy that I'm surrounded by several of them while Derek is...you know?"

"Fucking you?" Lucy added.

Claire nodded vigorously. "Ever since you told me about Gabe walking in on you and Hunter, I can't help but wonder what it would be like to have someone watching us. I think it could be exciting."

"I don't think Derek would like that too much," Cara pondered. "None of these guys seem like that type that want to share."

"Yeah, I'm with Cara on this one," Lucy agreed. "When Gabe stood there watching, Hunter got pissed that he was staring."

"That's because he thinks Gabe is gay," Claire laughed. "Derek told me all about how he planted that little seed of doubt in his head."

"Why would he do that?" I asked.

"Because Gabe was just standing there staring, and I was mostly covered, but Hunter's ass was hanging out."

"So, is he? Gay, I mean," Lillian asked. "Oh dear. You know, it's none of my business. I shouldn't have asked."

Lucy shrugged. "I have no idea, but now Hunter doesn't want to be too close to Gabe because he always thinks he's trying to hit on him. You should see the looks of confusion Gabe gives him."

A loud explosion sounded outside and all of us stood quickly, rushing to the window to see flames dancing in the sky in the direction of the front gate. A loud alarm sounded in the house and we all looked around nervously at one another. Chance came running into the room, gun up, scanning for any threats.

"Grab the kids. We need to leave now!"

We didn't hesitate in running up the stairs. I ran to my room and flung the door open, seeing Axel still asleep. I shook him violently and shouted at him to wake up. When he finally looked up at me and heard the alarm, he flung off the covers and threw on his jeans.

"Let's go," I yelled, running to the door. Lillian and Cara were each carrying a child and Claire had Caitlin in her arms. We ran down the stairs where Chance was barking orders at Becky and Rob, who were the tech specialists.

"Back door!" he shouted at us. We headed for the back and were met by Jackson and Gabe.

"We need to run!" Jackson said urgently. We followed him out the back door and ran to the back of the property to the tree line. We ran for a few minutes deeper into the woods before he started flinging back branches and leaves that covered the ground. There was what appeared to be an underground cellar. He lifted the doors and ushered us all down there with Gabe in the lead. Gabe flicked on a flashlight and quickly started leading us through the cellar, which was connected to a long underground tunnel. It was much bigger than it appeared from the outside.

The tunnel let out into a large space that echoed as we entered. Gabe flipped on a light and the space was illuminated in an instant. We were in a garage. There were two large SUVs that Gabe ushered us over to.

"We don't have car seats, but we should be able to get away easily. As soon as we're a safe distance away, we'll stop and pick up a few. For now, strap them in as best you can."

We quickly started piling into the SUVs and were joined by Chance, Jackson, Becky, and Rob a few minutes later. When we were all in, Gabe took off down another long underground drive that led us a few miles further away from where we had been. He pressed a button on the visor and a large door opened ahead of us. My eyes widened in shock.

"What the hell is this place? It's like Batman's cave," I said in amazement.

"That's exactly what I was thinking," Claire said.

"Shit," Gabe swore from up front. "I can't get ahold of Cap."

"Call Derek," Becky said from the front seat. He dialed another number and started talking quickly about alarms and getaways and whole bunch of other things that I didn't understand.

"What?...Shit. Alright. Where do you want us to go?...That's not much of a plan...Yeah, get back to us soon."

"What's going on?" Becky asked.

"They're trying to find a safe house for us. They're going to get back to us."

"Where is everyone else?" I asked. Where was Chris? I needed to know.

"At the hospital. Kate's okay, but Vanessa and Maggie aren't doing so good." Gabe said harshly. I didn't know if that was directed at me or if he was just angry at the whole situation. I couldn't think about that now. We drove in tense silence for the better part of an hour. We seemed to be going back and forth through the area and I was really confused what our destination was. Finally, Gabe turned down a road and we headed away from Pittsburgh.

"Where are we headed?" I finally asked. I couldn't hold back any longer. I needed to know what the plan was.

"You don't need to know that," Gabe sneered.

"Will we be seeing everyone again? Will they be meeting us?"

"Listen, I get that you're Chris's woman, but I don't trust you, so there's not a damn thing I'm going to tell you until I'm sure that you can be trusted."

I felt my cheeks flame, but when Claire reached over and gripped my hand, it eased some of my embarrassment.

"Why would you assume that she can't be trusted?" Claire asked.

"How about you tell me how someone found out the location of our safe house?" he asked. "That location has never been compromised and she comes into our lives and suddenly we're all at war and our safe house is given up within a day. Tell me why I should trust her?"

Claire started to say something, but I stopped her. "It's okay. I understand why everyone's so suspicious. I don't blame them."

Gabe's phone rang and he hit the speaker button. "Yeah?"

"We're in the clear. There's a twenty-four hour Walmart ahead. We should stop for supplies. We need to get the kids car seats. If anything happens to Caitlin, Sebastian will have us both gutted," Chance said.

"Who's going in? I don't know jack shit about car seats," Gabe questioned.

"Lillian?" There was muffled talk on the other end and then Chance came back on. "Uh, we have a bit of an issue here. Cara's

having an anxiety attack and we don't have her meds. Lillian doesn't
want to leave her."

"That leaves Lucy and Claire," Gabe surmised.

"I don't know anything about car seats," Claire said. "If you give me
exact information, I'll do my best."

"No good," Chance said. "We need to be in and out in five
minutes."

"I'll go," I said quickly. "It's been a while, but I know what we
need."

Gabe looked at me suspiciously in the rearview mirror, but
conceded. "Fine. I'll take Alison inside. Have Jackson come over and
watch over everyone in here."

We drove for another fifteen minutes before pulling into the
parking lot. Gabe stepped out and grabbed my arm. I looked back at
Axel in concern. I didn't like the idea of leaving Axel, especially
considering that Gabe didn't trust me. I didn't really know anything
about these people and with Chris not being here, it made me even
more paranoid. What if Gabe decided to get rid of me and say it was
an accident?

I swallowed hard and gave Axel a tentative smile. We needed those
car seats and they were all relying on me to get them. I wouldn't let
them down. Gabe and I walked through the darkened parking lot, his
body too close for comfort. I kept glancing around in the shadows,
sure that at any moment someone would jump out at me.

"Looking for your friends?"

"What?" I asked, startled.

"I don't know what the fuck your game is, but Chris is like a
brother to me and there's no way I'm going to let you do anything to
hurt him or anyone else at Reed Security."

"I'm not going to hurt him."

He snorted in derision. "Sure. Before you came into our lives, we
were just a regular security company with mostly normal lives. Now, we
have two gangs after us and Maggie and Vanessa are in the hospital
fighting for their lives." The anger in his voice scared me and I never
wished more than now that I had just run anywhere else with Axel. If
these people didn't trust me, what was stopping them from killing me

or handing me back to Slasher? "Give me one good reason I should trust you."

We walked through the doors of Walmart and grabbed a cart, then headed for the baby department. I walked by him silently, sure that he didn't really want an answer to the question, especially when there were other people around that could hear our conversation. I quickly found three car seats that would fit the kids and put them in the shopping cart.

"Is there anything else we need?" I asked.

"That's it for now. When we have a better idea where we're headed, we'll stop for anything else we need."

I nodded and followed him to the registers, noting that several people were watching us. I was starting to panic. They looked like regular people, but what did I know?

"Relax. You're going to make us look suspicious."

"It doesn't look suspicious that we're getting three car seats in the middle of the night?" I asked.

"We were just in a car accident. The car seats were totaled and we needed new ones."

That made sense. We quickly paid and headed for the exit. Just as we stepped through the doors, a large man rushed us, grabbing me from behind. I swung my fist down and low, feeling my fist connect with his balls. He bent toward me, grunting in pain and I whipped my head back, connecting with his nose. I stumbled away as he released me and Gabe instantly had him down on the ground with his arm wrenched behind his back.

"Who the fuck do you work for?" he sneered.

"No one. I just wanted some fucking money."

"So, you thought you'd rob us? Wrong choice." Gabe punched the guy several times and then tossed his body to the darkened side of the building. I was shaking by the time Gabe got back and he looked over me quickly before pushing the cart toward the SUVs.

"You want to tell me where you learned that? You just took that guy down before I had a chance to intervene."

I didn't say anything and Gabe stopped me with a tight fist wrapped around my arm. "You aren't what you seem. Chris thinks

you're some damsel in distress, but if you could do that, you would
have left the Blood Devils a long time ago."

"I have a son. I might be able to get away, but what about him? Was
I supposed to leave him behind with those monsters?" He shook his
head in disgust. "Besides, being able to take down one man doesn't
mean I could have taken on a whole group of them. I would have been
dead in five seconds. They wouldn't have hesitated to shoot me."

"Yet you still managed to get away," he sneered.

"Look, I get that you don't trust me, but I'm not some traitor. I
never wanted the life I was dealt and I tried to escape sooner. Until
you have a child to look after and make sure that he doesn't get hurt,
you don't get to judge me."

Gabe glared at me and started pushing the cart away again. There
was nothing I could say to make him believe me. I quickly followed
and tried not to stumble over my feet as I practically ran behind him.
My nerves were shot and I didn't know how much longer I could take
this. I needed Chris. I needed someone that didn't treat me like a
criminal.

When we got to the vehicles, Gabe and Jackson immediately got to
work getting the car seats out. I did my part to help and get them
strapped into the car, and then climbed back in. Gabe, Jackson, and
Chance stood outside discussing something for a minute and then
Gabe climbed back in, slamming the door and starting the vehicle.

"Everything okay?" Claire whispered.

I couldn't speak, so I nodded and closed my eyes. Taking deep
breaths, I looked in the back seat to see Axel already sleeping. Lucy
was sitting on the other side of Caitlin's car seat looking off into the
night and Claire was doing something on her phone. I finally calmed
down enough to drift off to sleep. When I woke again, we were
stopped at a gas station and I had to use the bathroom.

Chapter Twelve

REED SECURITY

Cazzo

I paced the waiting room for what felt like hours. This was just like the last time. The last time I had almost lost Vanessa, it nearly tore my world apart. I couldn't let the darkness creep in. I had to hold it together for her and for our child. I promised her I would never go down that road again and I planned to hold true to my word.

I glanced over at Kate and Knight. Kate had been released after being looked over. She was basically fine, just some minor bruising around her wrists. The way she gripped onto Knight made it obvious that she was just barely holding it together. Was Vanessa feeling the same thing right now? I needed to see her. I needed to touch her and know that she was okay.

The doors swung open and a doctor stepped through. I rushed over, hoping to God that he would give me some insight into how Vanessa was.

"Vanessa Adams?"

"That's me. I'm her fiancé."

The rest of my teammates crowded around me and the doctor quirked an eyebrow at me, but I just motioned for him to continue. I didn't have time to waste. His next words hit me like a sledgehammer.

"Vanessa suffered a miscarriage. She's doing fine other than that-"

"Was it because of trauma?" I asked before he could finish. If she miscarried because of those assholes, there wasn't a damn thing that could keep me from going and destroying their world. Hell, they were gonna pay no matter what.

"We can't be sure. She has marks on her that are consistent with a taser, but we have no way of knowing if that was the cause. There's not a lot of research on the effects of a stun gun being used on a pregnant woman. However, about one in every four pregnancies end in miscarriage. Usually it's because of a chromosomal abnormality and there's nothing that can be done to prevent that."

"So, what you're saying is that you really don't have any answers for me."

"Unfortunately, no. There's just no way to know this early in a pregnancy. She's resting comfortably and you can go see her now."

"So, other than the miscarriage, she's fine?"

"Yes. She can be released in another few hours after she's rested for a little bit. I'll send in a nurse to go over care instructions with you."

I nodded and headed for the door. I didn't bother to look back at everyone else. I had one goal and that was to see Vanessa. When I opened her door, it took everything in me to hold back the tears. This was all my fault. I hadn't protected her. Again. That was my responsibility and I failed again.

"Don't," she said sharply.

I wiped at my eyes, not even realizing that she had been staring at me too. "I'm so sorry, sweetheart."

"Me too, but this isn't your fault. Don't start blaming yourself for what someone else did."

"I was supposed to protect you," I said as I sat down next to her, taking her hand in mine.

"Listen, the doctor said that there was no way to know why I miscarried." She shook her head as tears rolled down her cheeks. "I wanted that baby, too, but playing the blame game and trying to figure out why the baby was taken won't do us any good right now. We need to focus on us. I don't ever want to see that look in your eyes again. Don't even think of leaving me."

"I won't," I said, shaking my head. "I promised you that I would never consider that ever again and I meant it." I blew out a breath and ducked my head. I had to be honest with her. She deserved that much. "I could feel those thoughts creeping in when I was waiting to hear what was going on with you, but it was a different kind of darkness. It was more...like I would go kill anyone that hurt you and damned the consequences."

She squeezed my hand and shook her head slightly.

"I know. You don't want me to do anything that could get me taken away, but I'll tell you this right now, Vanessa. You're my world and they won't get away with hurting you. I can't let them and neither will anyone else at Reed Security. When they went after all of you, they declared war on us. I'll make sure you're safe, but I'm sorry. I can't walk away."

"Just promise me that you'll come home to me."

"I swear, Vanessa. When this is over, we're going to have the life that we planned. We're going to get married right away and we're going to have a whole house full of kids."

"Don't make promises you can't keep," she said quietly.

"I never do."

Cap

"Cap," Sinner said, sitting next to me in the waiting room. "It's going to be okay. Maggie's a fighter."

I didn't say anything. I could see her lying on that floor with blood dripping off her back. Her fingers laying next to her on the ground. I really thought she was dead as soon as I saw her. The first thing that ran through my mind was that she had gotten into something really dangerous this time and I hadn't been there to protect her. Only, it wasn't something that she did. It was because of someone coming after me and my men. Then Caitlin flashed in my mind and I wondered how the hell I would break it to my daughter that her mother was dead.

I scrubbed my face with my hand, trying to wipe the images from my mind. They were so raw that every time I closed my eyes, I saw every little detail glaring at me. This had to be because of me. They knew she was my wife and they wanted to hit me where it hurt the most. And they did. They took her from me and mangled her beautiful body.

My chest started tightening painfully and I could scarcely take a breath. I gripped at my chest, rubbing and trying to ease the pain that was shooting through me. I felt Sinner's hand on my shoulder as he tried to steady me, but I was already falling apart. I wasn't sure if I had it in me to lead these guys like they needed. I had people depending on me, but right now, I just couldn't do it.

"Cap, we have an issue," Derek said as he stood in front of me. I could hear him speaking, but I couldn't respond. There was nothing I could do for any of them right now. I needed to see Maggie. "Cap."

"Just deal with it," I snapped. I stood and shoved through the group of men that had gathered around me. I thought about going outside to cool down, but I didn't want to leave in case the doctor came out. I paced around the waiting room, feeling the eyes of everyone on me. They were waiting for me to lose it.

"Maggie Reed?"

I whipped my head around and charged toward the doctor, as did the rest of my team. His face was grim as we approached and I felt Sinner grip tightly onto my shoulder.

"How is she?" I croaked out.

"She's stable. She lost a lot of blood, but we've been giving her transfusions and she's doing much better now. We cleaned up the cuts on her back and stitched her up. It took quite a lot and I would suggest looking into reconstructive surgery. It's not necessary for her to live a healthy life, but having those scars would be a permanent reminder of the trauma she suffered."

I nodded and swallowed hard. "What about her hand?"

"I'm afraid we weren't able to reattach her fingers. When a finger is dismembered that close to the hand, it's not only more difficult to recover from, but it could be harder for the entire hand to function. On top of that, the severed fingers were mangled and dirty. There was too great a risk of infection to the rest of her hand. We closed up the wounds and wrapped it, but I'm afraid that's all we could do for her."

"Will she still be able to use her hand?" I asked.

"Yes, she'll have to learn to use it differently, but because she still has her thumb and two other fingers, she'll still be able to use it quite well with time."

"Can I see her?"

"Of course."

I started to walk away, but then turned back to Sinner. "I don't..." I cleared my throat as my eyes filled with tears. How did I ask for him to come back with me? I didn't know if I could handle seeing her by myself and Sinner was like a brother to her.

"Do you want me to go back with you?"

I nodded and followed the doctor back to the room, along with Sinner. When I pushed the door open, I saw Maggie lying in the bed with her eyes closed. There was a nurse in the corner on the computer, but I didn't pay any attention to her. All I could focus on was the love of my life lying in the bed. My eyes drifted to her hand, which was very clearly missing two fingers. It was wrapped tightly with gauze. That was the only visible sign that she had been injured. The rest of her injuries were on her back.

"She just had some pain medication, so she'll be a little out of it," the nurse said as she left the room.

I took the seat next to her and placed my hand over her arm. I wanted to hold her hand in mine, but I didn't want to hurt her. I saw her wedding band on my pinky finger and tried to just be relieved that her fingers were the only thing she lost. I had no idea what her state of mind would be when she woke up. I couldn't believe this had happened. When Maggie opened her eyes, I felt like my heart was about to split in two. I could feel my face crumpling even though I tried to hold the tears back. I was supposed to be strong for her.

"Hey, I'm fine." She didn't have the strength in her voice that she normally did and she sounded like she had gone a few rounds with Muhammed Ali.

"This should have never happened," I bit out.

"It's nothing I can't come back from," Maggie said quietly. "Who needs five fingers anyway? The extra ones just get in the way."

"Freckles," I whispered. "I'm so fucking sorry."

"Sebastian, I need to tell you-"

"It can wait," I said, cutting her off. There was nothing she needed to tell me right now. Nothing else was more important than her in this moment.

"No. I'm sorry. I gave up the location of the safe house."

I shook my head. "Don't worry about that right now."

"I gave them the code," she grinned. I huffed out a laugh. Of course, leave it to Maggie to be happy that she blew something up. I had given her that code so that she could use it to her advantage if she ever needed it. Not so that she could suffer unnecessarily.

"Why didn't you just tell them right away? None of this had to happen."

"I didn't want to give up the location. You won't ever be able to use it again."

"I don't give a shit. I would give up every safe house if it meant that you didn't have to lose your fingers and have them-"

I cut myself off before I could say more. She didn't need to know how bad it was.

"Sebastian." I couldn't look at her. I was so ashamed that she had suffered so much all because she wanted to be loyal to me. "This isn't just about me. I had to give all of you enough time to find us. They were going to kill us all. If I had given up so easily, we'd all be dead right now. Just be happy all they took were my fingers."

"But your back..."

"Yeah, I'm definitely going to want that fixed," she said sleepily. The drugs were kicking in and she was starting to drift off. She turned to Sinner and gripped his hand. "Is Cara alright?"

"Yeah, Freckles. Cara's fine. We're gonna get these bastards," he said vehemently.

"As long as I get to get in on the action. I have a bone to pick with them."

Sinner grinned and leaned forward to place a kiss on her forehead, then he nodded to me and left the room. Maggie was asleep and I finally let it all wash over me. The fear, the anger, and the sadness for what she lost. My shoulders shook as I allowed myself just a few minutes to really feel everything that was running through my mind right now.

I blinked back the tears and wiped the moisture from my face. Sinner was right about something. Those bastards were going to pay and as soon as Maggie was released, I was going to hit them hard and make sure not a single one of those mother fuckers ever saw another day.

Derek

Shit was falling apart fast. Cap was barely holding on. Cazzo had just lost a baby and I was the one everyone was turning to for answers. There was one thing that was very clear. We needed to get someplace safe. If we stuck around the hospital too long, the Night Kings would come at us full force. The problem was, we didn't have anywhere for everyone to go. We needed one large location where we could all gather and make a plan to fight back. I gathered everyone in the waiting area.

"We need a new plan. The safe house was attacked, but everyone got out. Maggie gave the code that triggered the explosion. It allowed everyone enough time to get out. We don't know if any of the Night Kings survived, but I just talked to Chance and everyone is safe."

"What about our other safe houses?" Burg asked.

I shook my head. "There's not enough space. We need to stick together right now. I don't want to risk splitting up and not having enough manpower. Right now, we need a new safe house to get everyone else to. They're out there driving around and the longer they do that, the more dangerous it is for them."

"I have a place," Knight said. "We can all head there. It's a place I've had for a while now, just in case. It's on one hundred fifty acres and all the security we could ever want."

I nodded in agreement. That was exactly what we needed at the moment. "Alright. Get on the phone and give Chance all the information he'll need. We need to find out how long Vanessa and Maggie need to stay in the hospital, but it would be best if we could get out of here ASAP. We don't need the Night Kings descending on us here. We need to regroup and get a plan in place."

"What about Cap and Cazzo? They're not really thinking clearly right now," Chris said.

"I'll handle things until Cap is ready to take over. For now, everything goes through me first. Understood?"

They all agreed and I walked away, pulling out my phone. There was one more thing we needed to make sure that everyone stayed safe, and dammit, he would answer his fucking phone if I had to call him until he answered.

The phone rang and rang until finally Cash growled out a nasty hello.

"It's Derek. Any chance you're up for a fight?"

"What the fuck did you guys do?"

"Oh, you know. Took a woman and her kid that belonged to a gang. Took out some gang members. Now we've got a shit ton of trouble headed our way."

There was a moment of silence before a deep sigh. I smiled, knowing I had him. Cash craved a good fight just as much as the rest of us.

"Which gang?"

"Gangs. The Night Kings and the Blood Devils."

"Shit. You really are in a clusterfuck. I'm assuming you need as many men as possible?"

"That would be ideal."

"You got weapons?"

"Could always use more."

"What the fuck *do* you have?"

"A whole team of pissed off men who want to take these fuckers out," I growled into the phone.

"That'll do. Text me a location."

He hung up and I grinned to myself. It was about time something went our way.

Chapter Thirteen

CHRIS

It was fucking impossible to stay in the waiting room when all I wanted was to see Ali and Axel again. I had been holding off on calling them because of everything that was going on around here. There would be a lot of questions that I didn't have the answers to, but now that we knew that Maggie and Vanessa would be alright, I couldn't wait any longer. I walked over to a deserted corner of the waiting room and dialed Gabe. I knew from Knight that she was driving with him.

"Hey, Chris. Whatcha got?"

"I need to talk with Ali."

"Hang on." I heard a door shut and then some shuffling. "Why?"

"Why what?"

"Why do you want to talk to her?" he asked harshly.

"Because she's my fucking woman and I need to hear her voice," I growled. This wasn't like Gabe. He wasn't usually such an asshole. "What's going on?"

"Man, are you sure you can trust her?"

"What the fuck are you talking about?"

"I'm talking about the fact that she came to stay with us at the safe house and not even twenty-four hours later, our location was given up."

I was pissed. I felt the rage that I had been holding back the last seventeen years breaking free. "You listen to me, you motherfucker. I've always trusted you and I'm putting that same trust in you right now to keep Ali and Axel safe. They didn't have anything to do with the attack and my word should be enough for you. I swear to God, if you don't do everything you can to protect them, I'll put a fucking bullet in you myself. That's my family and I expect you to protect them the way you would protect anyone else's family. Do you understand me?"

I could practically hear him gritting his teeth together on the other end of the line. He didn't like that I wasn't backing him on this. Well, I didn't like it that he was accusing them of being traitors.

"I got ya."

"If you want to know why you were hit, you could have just asked. Maggie was fucking tortured until she gave up the location, but she also gave them the code to blow up the gate to warn you. She held out for as long as she could. So, why don't you rein in your attitude and do the job you're supposed to. Now, put my woman on the phone."

He didn't say anything else and when Ali's voice came over the line, I finally felt the first spark of relief.

"Chris?"

"Hey, Ali. Are you doing okay?"

"Yeah. We're good. What happened?"

"I'll explain when I see you. We'll be leaving soon and we'll catch up with you at the next safe house. Just do what the guys tell you and you'll be fine."

She got quiet and then she lowered her voice, almost as if she was trying not to be heard. "Chris, they don't trust me. They think I'm trying to get everyone killed."

I could hear the rattle in her voice. She was scared, probably because I wasn't there to protect her. She didn't know any of the people at Reed Security and she was relying on them to keep her safe. "Baby, I know this is hard for you right now, but I need you to trust me. They will protect you with their lives."

"Gabe won't. He already told me that he doesn't trust me. Chris, I'm really scared," she said hesitantly. It fucking killed me that she

didn't feel safe with my brothers. Although, at the moment, I was hesitant to call Gabe a brother.

"I swear to you. Nothing will happen to you as long as you're with
them. I already set shit straight with Gabe. Trust me, he won't be a
problem anymore."

She sighed and I wished that I could be there to wrap my arms
around her and tell her that she was safe with me. "I miss you."

"I miss you, too. I'll see you in a day or two."

"Okay."

"Ali...I love you."

"I love you, too, Chris."

I could practically see the smile on her face because the same
stupid grin was on mine. It was true. I hadn't ever fallen out of love
with Ali. She was the girl I knew I would marry someday, and even
when I walked away, I still wished every fucking day that she was with
me. I had been a dumb fucker to stay away so long. But that wouldn't
be happening anymore. She was mine and I would make sure that she
never questioned whether or not we would be together again.

When I got off the phone with Ali, I called Chance. As much as I
felt I had set Gabe straight, I wanted to be certain that someone else
was watching out for her and Axel.

"Chance, I need a favor, man."

"Shoot."

"I need you to keep an eye on my family."

"We are. Gabe's with them," he said in confusion.

"He's also shooting his mouth off to her. She's scared. He's accusing
her of being a traitor."

He growled into the phone and I heard him taking a deep breath.
"Don't worry about it. I'll make sure he fucking knows his place."

"Thanks, man."

"We'll see you at the safe house. Watch your six."

"You too, man. Stay safe."

I hung up and walked back over to the group of Reed Security
members that were currently taking up the entire waiting room. Derek
was looking over a map with Knight, who still had an arm wrapped
tightly around Kate. Burg and Sinner were gone, probably in Vanessa's

room with Cazzo. Hunter and Lola were sitting and arguing about something. They seemed to do a lot of that lately. Lola had been absent for months, off on a vacation. I wasn't privy to what was going on. Cap kept that information between him and Derek's team.

Ice and Jules were lounging in some chairs like they didn't have a care in the world, but I knew them all too well. They were watching everything, wanting to keep an eye on everything while Derek worked shit out. Alec, Craig, and Florrie were keeping watch near the door. Ideally, we should be spread all over the hospital to keep watch, but when we talked to security about positioning people around the building, they basically told us they would have us removed if we didn't stay in the waiting area.

Cap walked out into the waiting area looking a lot more put together than the last time I'd seen him. "Derek, what's the plan?"

"We need to get on the road. Is Maggie able to be moved?"

"If we need to. Where are we headed?" Cap asked.

"Knight's giving us a place to go. I already sent Chance out there," Derek said.

"Sebastian," Kate said quietly. "I'm so sorry about Maggie. She wouldn't let them take me."

"What?" Knight asked.

She looked at Sebastian with tears in her eyes. "They were trying to take me out of the room. She begged them to take her. She told them I didn't know anything and that she was your wife. I'm so sorry."

Sebastian pulled her in for a hug and held her tight despite Knight's growling in protest. "Don't worry about it," he whispered. "Maggie did what she thought she had to do and she wouldn't want you feeling guilty about it."

"But she shouldn't have done it. She has a daughter. I'm nobody."

Sebastian pulled back and quirked an eyebrow at her. "I think Knight would say differently. Besides, I wouldn't want to deal with his cranky ass if anything had happened to you."

Knight nodded to Cap, obviously approving of him trying to ease Kate's mind. He wrapped an arm around her again, pulling her in close to him and I found myself wishing I could do the same to Ali at this very moment.

"When will Maggie be released?" Derek asked.

"They haven't said."

"We need to get on the road," Derek said urgently. "The sooner the better. I know this is hard, but if we stick around here, we're gonna get ambushed."

"Alright, I'll get the doctors to release Vanessa and Maggie."

"Good. I got ahold of Cash. He's going to meet up with us."

"Thank fuck," Sebastian said as he ran a hand over his face. "We need something to go right for us."

I could see that Cap was exhausted and though he was trying to appear in control, he was still on edge. And it was my fault. It was hard to stand here while Maggie was in the other room suffering and not feel guilty. I had brought this on them and even though I knew they wouldn't blame me, I couldn't help but feel I needed to set some things straight with Cap. When he and Derek finished discussing plans, I nodded for him to follow me. We walked over to the coffee station and I opened my mouth to speak.

"Don't even think about it," he cut in. I just stared at him for a minute. "I know what you're thinking right now. It's the same fucking thing I think when I look at Maggie in that hospital bed. But this isn't on us. We're not going to blame each other for what those fuckers did. We're going to regroup and we're going to take out every single one of them. If I even hear you utter the words *I'm sorry*, I'm gonna make sure that you get installation duty for the next year. You feel me?"

I nodded.

"Good talk." He walked away and headed back to Maggie's room.

"Derek," Alec, from team five, came over the mic as we pulled out of the hospital parking lot. "We've got a tail."

"I see it," Derek responded. "Let's keep going and see if we can lose them on the way out of town."

I was driving the vehicle with Cap and Maggie. Usually, I would drive with my team and Knight would drive with Cap, but seeing as how they were both too preoccupied with Kate and Maggie, there was no way they could drive together. Ice and Jules drove with Knight and Kate, while Cazzo and Vanessa drove with Sinner and Burg. Derek, Hunter, and Lola had the lead vehicle and Alec, Craig, and Florrie were in the last vehicle.

Cap was in the backseat with Maggie trying to keep her comfortable. She had to keep her hand raised to keep the swelling down and she had been pumped with morphine before we left the hospital because of all the stitches on her back. I knew she wouldn't be able to make the entire twelve hour trip in one sitting. It would just be too uncomfortable for her.

We all had our earpieces in so that we didn't disturb Vanessa, Kate, and Maggie. They had been through enough and didn't need to hear every detail of what was going on.

We wound through Pittsburgh, trying to lose our tail, but there were just too many of us and it was too risky to split up at this point. We needed to stick together.

"Alright," Derek said in frustration. "We can't risk trying to take them out on the road. Not with the girls in the condition they're in. Let's just keep driving and, as long as they don't make a move, we'll wait them out. We already know that Maggie won't make the whole trip, so we'll find someplace to stop that's not too busy and we'll take them out there."

"I can't be sure, but I think there are about six of them in two vehicles," Craig said over the mic.

"Keep me informed on their movements. As long as they don't try anything, we'll stick to the plan so no one gets hurt," Derek said.

"Which route are we taking?" I asked. "Chicago or Indianapolis?"

"Fuck, neither is a great option, but I think Indy is the lesser of two evils. I don't want to risk the traffic in Chicago. I think we can bypass Indy easily enough," Pappy said. He had been studying the map before we left and since Derek was driving, we were all relying on Pappy to get us where we were going."

"I agree," Derek said. "Let's go south. Indy is the better option. Alec? Are they trying anything yet?"

"Just tailing us, Irish. Looks like they just want to see where we go."

"Let's not make this first leg of the trip too long. I don't think

Maggie will hold out long. She looks uncomfortable as fuck," I said as I kept looking in the rearview mirror.

I could see Maggie starting to squirm in the back. The morphine was only doing so much for her and no matter how Cap repositioned her, she couldn't get comfortable. We drove for a few hours, but we were still in Ohio and I could tell Maggie had had enough.

"Pappy, you need to find someplace for us to stop. Maggie's hurting."

"No," Maggie whispered. "I'll be fine."

"Bullshit," Cap said fiercely. "Derek, we need to find someplace soon."

Cap was whispering in Maggie's ear and trying to soothe her. I could tell that he needed to get her out of the SUV and into a bed.

"I'm on it," Derek said. About ten minutes later, Derek came back over the mic. "There's a place up ahead. About twenty more miles. Small town B & B about a mile outside the town. That's our best bet. I don't know how long we'll be staying, but hopefully, we can give the girls a reprieve before we get back on the road."

"Good. Let's get there fast," I said.

By the time we pulled into the B & B, Maggie was in tears from the pain and I had my hands wrapped tightly around the steering wheel in rage. I hated that Maggie was in such pain and I was just glad that I didn't have Vanessa in the same vehicle. She had just lost a baby. I didn't think I could handle seeing both of them suffer.

Derek ran up to the window and I quickly lowered it. "I'm going to check in. Why don't you guys go ahead and get everyone out. We'll get the girls settled and Alec's team can keep watch. Then we'll set up a rotation."

"Sounds like a plan."

I turned around and nodded to Cap. "How do you want to do this?"

"Fuck, I don't have a clue. I'm not sure she can walk, but carrying her is going to hurt her even more."

"Why don't you piggyback her? I'll help her onto your back and then we'll get her to the room."

"I'm going to need to change her bandages. I think she's got a popped stitch."

"I'll tell Hunter to meet you in your room. He can look her over before she passes out for the night."

We got Maggie out of the SUV and onto Cap's back. Her tears were ripping my heart to shreds as I tried not to hurt her as I helped her onto Cap's back. The woman at the front desk stared at us with wide eyes as we helped Maggie upstairs. I knew we were going to have to explain some shit to her. Vanessa wasn't in too much better condition. She was cramping as she walked up to her room. Kate was practically catatonic as Knight led her upstairs.

"Ice, maybe you want to work your charm on the lady?" I nodded toward the counter.

"Aw, come on, man. Why do I always have to do this shit?"

"It's those gorgeous baby blues. Women practically drop their panties when they see them."

"You know, I really don't like being objectified like that," he grumbled.

"Ice, I've seen the way you let women objectify you. Don't give me that bullshit."

We walked over to the counter and I turned my back, looking around the lobby of the B & B. I didn't give a shit about the interior. I was really keeping watch on the outside. Even though Alec's team was watching also from inside, it didn't hurt to have another pair of eyes keeping watch.

"Hi. My name is John, but my friends call me Ice," he grinned.

"Lindsey. Do they call you that because you look like Val Kilmer?"

He grinned his cocky grin. "Something like that."

I turned and watched her roll her eyes at him. "Very original. I'm sure all the ladies go crazy for it."

Ice's smile faltered for a second, but I nudged him on. We needed this chick to leave or she might end up hurt.

"Maybe you could take me out tonight, show me the town?"

"The town has about two thousand people. What exactly did you want to see? The four bars on Main Street? Or the grocery store that went out of business three years ago?"

Ice glanced over at me and I could see little beads of sweat forming on his forehead. He'd never had a woman act like this toward him. He was fucking lost. Best to just go with the truth at this point.

"Look," I said turning around. "We've got some bad shit following us and it would be best if you weren't here tonight."

She narrowed her eyes at me. "You really expect me to fall for that? I've poured my heart and soul into this place and there's no way I'm leaving so that you can rob me."

"Lady," Ice cut in. "Did you see those women walk in? That'll be you if you don't get the fuck out of here."

She scowled at him and her temper flared. "I'm not going anywhere and if you do anything to my property to damage it, I'll make sure you pay for every repair."

"Let's go," Ice said as he pushed away from the counter. Sinner walked up to us, giving a chin nod.

"What's going on? What's with the long face?" he asked Ice.

"He struck out. Tried to woo the lady and she wasn't taking his crap.

Sinner sucked in a breath and grimaced, then patted Ice on the shoulder. "You know, maybe it's time you found yourself someone to settle down with. Looks like you're losing your touch."

"Shut the fuck up," Ice said, shrugging off Sinner's hand. "I'm not losing anything."

"Right," I nodded. "Just couldn't snag the one eligible woman in this town."

"You don't know that she's the only eligible woman. I'm sure there are plenty of other women who don't have her bitch attitude."

"Yeah," I agreed. "In a town of two thousand, I'm sure they'll be lining up to get you. Young, old, women...men?"

He punched me in the arm and walked away leaving Sinner and I chuckling.

We waited for most of the day for something to happen. We could clearly see the two cars parked down the street. They must have thought they were being slick. We had all taken up position around the house, watching from the inside.

"I hope to God they aren't waiting for reinforcements," Ice said as he walked over to me.

"If they do, we'll deal with it when the time comes. We don't exactly have a lot of options right now. We can't risk any of the girls getting hurt."

Ice glanced over at the front desk and I saw Lindsey scowl at him.

"I don't think you're getting anywhere with that one."

"Didn't plan to."

"What the hell are we going to do when they make their move? She can't be involved in this," I said.

"Give her a gun and wish her the best," he snapped. "If she's stupid enough to stick around, she gets what's coming to her."

I rolled my eyes. This wasn't at all like Ice, which could mean only one thing: he liked her. I chuckled as I shook my head at the thought of Ice finding a woman that could wrap him around her finger. The man was fucking hard as steel on the best of days. He was a great guy, but not exactly the type of guy that women saw in the long term, which I guessed was exactly what Lindsey saw when she looked at him.

The darkness settled around us until it was nearly impossible to see anything outside. Without the lights of the town, we were working based on instinct more than anything else.

"We need to kill the lights," Ice growled.

"Yeah, why don't you go talk to your woman about that?"

He sneered at me and walked over to her. "We need you to shut off all the lights."

"I don't think so. I don't shut down the B & B until eleven and even then, I leave a light on," Lindsey snapped.

"Listen, do you want to get a fucking bullet in your head? With the lights on, we can't see jack shit outside."

"Oh, sure," she said unbelievably. "I'll just shut off all the lights and then you guys can go do whatever you want and rob me blind. Do you really think I'm that stupid?"

"Incoming," Alec said over the mic.

"Listen, we don't have time to argue. They're on their way," Ice snapped. "Do you have a fucking death wish?"

"I wish you would go away," she replied.

"Ten seconds," Alec said.

"At least go back in the office where we don't have to watch out for you," he urged.

"Two at the front door, two at the rear. I can't see the other two," Craig said.

"Lady-"

Bullets tore through the windows, shattering glass and hitting the walls, leaving holes everywhere. Ice dove over the counter and tackled Lindsey to the ground. I crept over to the front door and stood just inside out of sight. There was only one thing I hated more than being fired at, and that was idiots that didn't even have any aim. I waited for the firing to die down. They weren't shooting at anyone in particular, so it was a matter of waiting for them to run out of bullets.

I heard the crunch of glass as one of them approached the front door. Stealthy they were not. When his shoulder slid through the doorway, I yanked him inside and twisted his neck in one swift movement. It was better if I didn't give away my position just yet. I slowly lowered him to the ground out of the way and leaned back against the wall.

"Hey, mira a todos los cabrones?" one of them asked from outside.

"Todos muertos," I said in my best Spanish accent. The guy stepped through the doorway without any hesitation and I wrapped my hand around his face, cutting off any noise he might make.

"Did you call it in? Tell the rest of your gang where we're at?"

He shook his head violently and he mumbled against my hand.

"You so much as raise your voice above a whisper, I'll slit your throat. Got it, hombre?"

He nodded and I slowly released my hand from his mouth. "We were just supposed to follow you to your location."

"Then why did you come after us?"

He didn't say anything and I saw him looking down at the floor. He jerked his head toward the dead guy. "He thought we could take you all out."

"He thought wrong," I said as I swiftly slid my knife across the man's throat. "Two down by the front door," I said through the mic.

"Two down at the back door," Craig confirmed.

I heard some chuckling and frowned. What the fuck was that?

"You should see these two fuckers out here," Sinner laughed. "The one guy is trying to show the other guy how to use a gun."

I stepped silently onto the front porch and made my way over to the side of the yard where Sinner was positioned. One of the gang members was showing the other how to hold the gun. When he handed the gun over to the second guy, the second guy held up the gun like he was a fucking badass, holding the gun sideways. The problem was, holding the gun like that gave you shit for aim.

I saw Sinner walking in the trees behind them and carefully pick up a branch. He watched as the second guy pretended like he was going to shoot someone and then he snapped the branch in half. As expected the guy spun around, firing the gun before fully turning and shooting the other gang member. I heard Sinner chuckling over the mic as the gangster's eyes widened and then he spun around wildly looking for where the sound came from.

"No te tengo miedo!" he shouted. "Salir y luchar, tu coño!"

I stepped from the shadows, no longer wanting to wait out this asshole. "Pussy? You want to fight?"

He spun around, his gun pointed at me with a shaky hand. "I'll fucking shoot you," he said with a thick Spanish accent.

"Not like that, you won't." I walked slowly toward him. Sure, it was a risk considering he was nervous and had a gun pointed at me, but he also didn't have any aim. I decided to take my chances. "Here, let me show you how to use that thing before you kill another one of your friends." He looked at me funny and I continued. "Do you know why you don't hold a gun that way?" I asked as I stepped right in front of him.

He shook his head, obviously confused. I grabbed the gun quickly from his grip and shot him dead center in the head. "That's why, you stupid fuck."

Sinner stepped out of the trees, shaking his head and grinning. "That wasn't nearly fun enough. I was expecting something more."

"They were only supposed to follow us. One of them decided they could take us on their own."

"Stupid fuckers," Sinner said, kicking one of them.

"Cap, time to move out," Derek said over the mic. "We need to hit the road before anyone else shows up."

"On our way down," Cap replied.

We walked back to the house where I heard arguing and walked in on Lindsey yelling at Ice for destroying her property.

"I told you to fucking leave," Ice shouted.

"I didn't think you were serious! Who actually has a gun fight anymore? This isn't the OK Corral."

"Look, now you're fucking stuck with us. We could have handled this more discretely if you would have listened, but you didn't. Now we're going to have every single fucking gang member coming here for answers and they're going to be looking for you."

"Why me?"

"Because this is your fucking business," Ice shouted.

"I'm not going anywhere with you. I don't even know you," Lindsey shot back.

Ice pulled her out from behind the counter and pointed at the two men on the floor that were dead. "Is that how you want to end up? Because if we leave you here, you'll be joining them in the ground very shortly."

I saw Lindsey pale and then she swayed. "Is that...blood?"

She looked up at us and then her eyes rolled back in her head as she passed out. Ice caught her and slung her up over his shoulder, shaking his head and grumbling about stubborn women.

"And you wanted to give her a fucking gun," I muttered.

He took her out to his SUV and then came back in with a scowl on his face.

"Should we leave you two alone?" I asked.

"That woman drives me fucking crazy and I don't even know her."

"She'll do," Sinner grinned.

"What the fuck are you talking about?" Ice snapped.

"That, my friend, was some of the hottest foreplay I've seen in a while. Well, aside from Derek and Claire, but not many can keep up with them."

"You're off your fucking rocker," Ice said as he stormed away. I sighed and started dragging the bodies off to the back yard. I saw a lake in the back. It was a good place to drop them for now. By the time Sinner and I were done, everyone else was loaded and ready to hit the road. If we were lucky, we could hit Iowa by early morning.

Chapter Fourteen

ALISON

My back was aching from sitting in the damn SUV for so long, and my ribs were still sore from when Slasher beat the crap out of me. We'd been driving since we stopped at the last gas station and I really had to pee, but I didn't dare say anything. Gabe still looked at me like he wanted to kill me. Best not to give him a reason. Besides, nobody else was complaining, so I needed to suck it up and let them do their jobs.

I shifted in my seat again, trying to get comfortable and caught Gabe's glare in the rearview mirror. I quickly averted my eyes and looked out into the darkness. There was nothing to see, but I couldn't stand to look at anyone in the vehicle. Claire was out like a light next to me. I wished I could be that lucky. I glanced back and saw that Caitlin was also asleep. She looked so sweet in her carseat and I prayed that her mother was alright. The guys weren't telling us anything, so I had no clue what was going on. Axel, of course, was asleep against the window without a care in the world. I shook my head as I smiled. That kid could sleep anywhere through anything.

Becky was in the front seat on her computer. I had no clue what she was doing and frankly, if she tried to explain it to me, I doubt I would understand. I had big dreams after high school to go away to college. I wasn't completely sure what I wanted to do yet, but I was leaning toward becoming a doctor. Becoming a nurse was as close as I would get to that and I hadn't studied anything to do with computers. I was past the point of wanting to go back to school. Now I just wanted to live my life in peace.

I stretched for what felt like the tenth time in the past five minutes and groaned slightly when I pulled at my sore ribs.

"Relax, Princess. We're almost there and then you can get your beauty rest," Gabe snarled from the front seat.

"Why do you call me Princess? Do you really think I've been living the good life all these years?"

"Even gangs have women they hold in the highest regard."

I snorted and rolled my eyes. "Yeah, I'd like you to show me one of those. There's not a single gang member I know that wouldn't shoot his own mother if it meant that he could move up in the gang. Believe me, women are only good for one thing to a man in a gang."

"I hope you get yourself tested before you plan on seducing Chris. He doesn't deserve all the diseases you would give him," Gabe sniped.

I felt my face flush red and then saw Becky smack Gabe in the arm, reprimanding him for being such an ass. But the truth was, Gabe wasn't wrong. While I hadn't been passed around to all the other members, Slasher had definitely taken his fair share of the women that hung around. Who knew what diseases I could be carrying at this very moment.

I stared out the window for another half hour until we finally pulled down a dirt road and drove for another mile or so. When we finally stopped, I was ready to jump out of the SUV, but when I reached for the door, Gabe stopped me.

"Just hold on. We have to secure the perimeter."

He stepped out of the vehicle and Becky turned around to face me. "You know, Gabe's not normally a bad guy. He's just being very suspicious because we're all under attack. He'll come around."

"I get it. I would probably be suspicious of me too."

"Well, give it time. Chris's word means a lot around here. Gabe's just being a hard head."

"That's not what I would call it," I grumbled. I heard Becky chuckle, but sat in silence for the next ten minutes as the guys did whatever it was they needed to do. When Gabe came back, he glared at me and I immediately started to tremble. What had I done now?

"Let's unload," Gabe said sharply.

Claire yawned and stretched her arms out over her head. "Where are we?"

"New safe house," Gabe said with a softer voice. Apparently his angry voice was reserved for me. I spun around in the seat and woke up Axel. He looked like he was perfectly rested and ready for the day, even though it was about 2 a.m. I unbuckled Caitlin, careful to not wake her and held her tightly to my body. She was so sweet. Her little thumb was in her mouth and she held a little unicorn tightly in her fist. I ran my hand over her soft red curls and wished that I had gotten the opportunity to have a little girl of my own.

I stepped out of the vehicle and followed everyone inside. The place was huge. I couldn't really see anything from outside, but once the lights were turned on, it was clear that this was some kind of mansion.

"Knight bought this just in case?" Jackson asked. "In case of what?"

"Maybe he was planning to host a state dinner," Chance remarked. They looked at each other and started laughing. I didn't quite get what the joke was, so I shrugged it off and walked over to Chance.

"Where should I have her sleep?"

"Take your pick of rooms. We haven't been here before, so I don't have any idea what the best rooms are for kids."

"I think I'll stay with her. I don't want her waking up alone in a strange house."

"Right, just with a stranger," Gabe muttered.

"That's enough," Chance said sharply. Then he turned to me. "I'm sure Cap would appreciate it if you could stay with her."

I nodded and headed for the stairs, feeling Axel behind me. When we reached the top of the stairs, Axel grabbed my arm and pulled me aside. "Why do I get the feeling that we're not any more welcome here than with Slasher?"

"Chris will be here soon. I talked to him and he was on his way. We just have to hold out a little longer."

"These people don't trust us," he said angrily. "I don't like the idea of being here without Chris."

"Axel, we'll be fine. None of them would do anything to us."

"I'm staying in your room tonight."

It was like I was looking at my little seven year old boy again. I smiled sadly at him and rested a hand on his arm. "You don't have to be scared. I'll protect you."

He gave me a funny look and shook his head. "I'm not scared, Mom. I'm staying in your room so I can protect you. I want you to get some sleep and I'll keep watch. I still have that gun Chris had me practice with and I intend to use it if any of them even looks at you wrong."

I shook my head, completely amazed by my kid. Just a few days around Chris and he was already becoming the man that he would have been had he been raised by Chris. We walked down the hall to a medium sized room with a double bed. I laid Caitlin down on the bed and then slipped under the covers with her. I saw Axel opening doors and then walked through one, coming back a few minutes later.

"This has an adjoining room," he said.

"Why don't you take that one?"

Axel moved a chair to face the door and sat down, resting his gun on the table beside him. I was a little nervous about him having a gun out, considering he had only just learned to use it, but he instantly quelled my fears.

"Relax, Mom. I took the magazine out. Chris taught me how to quickly assemble the weapon. I'll be ready if I need to be, but you don't have to worry about me accidentally shooting someone."

I nodded and it wasn't long before I was drifting off to sleep.

"Get the fuck out of here." That was Axel's voice. I couldn't register what was going on. My brain was in a fog and I couldn't pull myself out of it.

"Kid, I think you're mistaken on who gives the orders around here."

"I'm not mistaken at all. You've had it out for my mom and I since we arrived. I wouldn't put it past you to put a bullet in our heads and then say that we were trying to kill you."

I finally shook my head awake and sat up, checking on Caitlin before I assessed the situation. Caitlin was still fast asleep, so I slipped out of the bed and slowly moved over to the door where I saw my son holding a gun on Gabe. My eyes widened as Gabe took a step forward, but Axel took a step back, not allowing him in his space.

"Just stay the fuck away from us," Axel growled.

"I'm just here to check on Caitlin."

"And you can see that she's over there sleeping in the bed. She's fine, so you can get the fuck out."

"Kid, you're on my protective detail. It's my job to make sure that you're safe and that includes everyone in this room. You shouldn't even have a fucking gun."

"He only has it because Chris gave it to him," I interjected.

Gabe huffed in irritation. "I can't believe he just handed over a gun to a kid that he's known all of five minutes. He may think that he can trust you, but I'm not quite that stupid. How do we even know that this kid is really his? This whole thing stinks like shit to me."

"What the fuck is going on in here?" Chance stepped in behind Gabe.

"This kid is holding a gun on me."

"After you made it perfectly clear that you think Mom and I are here to infiltrate Reed Security or some shit like that."

"Gabe, we talked about this," Chance chastised.

"They've got Cap's kid in the room with them," he said incredulously.

"Yeah and Cap was the one that said we trust them like we would any other family member of Reed Security. Get the fuck out of here and cool off. Chris is gonna hand you your ass if you don't knock it off."

Gabe's jaw tensed, but he walked out of the room and stormed down the stairs. Chance sighed and ran a hand over his tired face. "I'm really sorry. Gabe's not always the most trusting person. He won't be coming near you again. I'll make sure of it. I'll put Jackson on your personal security until Chris gets back and I fill him in as to what's going on."

"Thank you," I said quietly.

"Sorry, kid, but I can't let you walk around with a gun. That's not the way this shit works."

"I'm not handing it over. If I do, what the hell am I supposed to protect my mom with?"

Chance smirked at him. "You know, you'd do good in the military. You might want to think about that when this shit is over. Just do me a favor and keep the safety on."

Axel grinned at him. "The magazine is empty. I didn't think Gabe was actually going to try anything, but I don't trust him either. I just wanted to show him that we were protected."

Chance threw back his head and laughed. "I won't tell him that. He'll be pissed that you slipped that past him."

"When will the rest of them be here?"

"They should be here in a few more hours. They had some hang ups along the way, but it shouldn't be too much longer. I would suggest getting some more sleep before they get here."

I nodded and turned to Axel as Chance closed the door. "You're just like your father," I said with a smile. "You haven't even known him that long, but I can already see the same bravery and determination that he's always had."

"Thank God I didn't take after Slasher. I would have been such a disappointment."

"Let's not think about Slasher anymore. Soon, he won't even be a part of our lives."

———

A few hours later, I was awoken for the second time by hushed voices coming from outside the door. I looked over to see Axel fast asleep in his chair. I crept over to the door and slowly nudged it open, relieved to see Chris standing out in the hall. I ran and threw my arms around him, not even caring that everyone was watching. Tears pricked my eyes as the last twenty-four hours finally caught up with me. It was bad enough with everything going on, but then to be driving with people that I didn't know and didn't trust me, it was just a little too much to take.

"Hey, it's alright, Ali. I'm here now," Chris whispered as he stroked my back.

"Is everyone okay?" I asked as I pulled back. Darkness crept over Chris's face and I swallowed hard, not wanting to hear what had happened because of me.

"Maggie's not doing so well right now," Sebastian cut in. "She'll be fine with some rest. Chance said that you've been watching over Caitlin. Do you think you could continue to do that during the day until Maggie's doing better?"

"Of course. She's a very sweet girl."

"Sweet," he smirked. "She's got a little of the devil in her, just like her momma." Sebastian's face turned down slightly before he shook his head and gave me a soft smile. "Thank you for taking care of her. I'll take her for the rest of the night and come find you when I need help again."

"No problem. I'm glad I can help."

Sebastian walked over to the bed and lifted Caitlin into his arms, kissing her lightly on the forehead, then walked back to the door.

"Why don't you all get some sleep and we'll meet at noon to start planning?" Sebastian said to Chris. Chris nodded and I opened the door further for him to enter. I wasn't sure what his plans were for sleeping arrangements, but I needed him close to me right now.

"Where's Axel?" he asked as he stepped inside. I nodded over to the chair that Axel had passed out in. "He's a good kid, watching out for you like that."

"He is. He even went up against Gabe."

"Gabe?"

"Yeah, he doesn't trust us." At Chris's dark look, I quickly made sure he understood what happened. "Chance stepped in and set him straight. He has Jackson watching us now."

"I'm gonna have to have a talk with Gabe."

"Chris, I really don't want to cause any problems for you. We've already-"

"Please, no more. Let's just put a plug in it for tonight. I'm tired as hell and I need some sleep before we start planning."

"Okay, I can go sleep in the other room," I said, turning from him. He grabbed me around the wrist and yanked me back against him.

"Not a chance in hell. You'll be sleeping in my bed from now on."

"But, what about what I told you? You know, about needing to be tested?"

"That doesn't mean I can't hold you in the meantime. We've wasted too much time, Ali. I just want you in my arms right now. I don't care if we don't have sex. Well, for the time being, but believe me, I will be making love to you and it's going to be a helluva a lot better than when we were sixteen," he growled.

I felt shivers race down my body at his promise and wished that there was a doctor that could check me over now so that I didn't have to wait. I wanted Chris more than I did when we were kids. The only experience I had other than Chris was at the hands of a man who never tried to take care of me. I was just a body to be used. I desperately wanted to know what it would be like to have Chris take care of me now that we were both adults.

I watched as Chris shook Axel's shoulder. Axel immediately reached for the gun and then relaxed when he saw Chris. "Chris, I'm glad you're back."

"Me too, kid. I see that you're taking care of your mother," he said, gesturing to the gun.

"I didn't keep it loaded since I'm not that experienced. I kept the clip in my pocket in case I needed it."

"That was smart. We don't need anyone accidentally shot. I've got it from here, though. Why don't you go in the next room and get some sleep?"

"Thanks. I'll do that." Axel looked over at me and gave a chin lift, already so much like his dad. "You sure you're okay, Mom?"

"I'll be fine. Thank you for watching out for us."

Axel went into the other room and shut the door behind him. I waited at the foot of the bed, a little unsure of how we would be sleeping. I knew that he wanted to stay in bed with me, but I didn't know the dress code. I was so out of my element right now.

He walked over to me and slid his hand under my hair and behind my neck. "What's going on in that head of yours, baby?"

"I'm nervous."

"It's just me," he whispered. "You could always tell me anything. There was never any hesitation between us."

"I know, but this is different. We're adults now. We haven't see each other in so long. I don't look the same and..." I didn't want to say that my body had been used as a fuck hole for the past sixteen years. That would just make him mad, so I just stopped talking.

"Don't worry about all that shit, baby. When this is over, we'll do whatever we have to to make sure that you're one hundred percent comfortable being with me. For now? Just get in whatever you wear to sleep so I can hold you in my arms."

I smiled at the reassuring tone he took with me and slid out of my pants, tossing them on a chair. I also took off my bra. Having that on all day and night was so uncomfortable. I just wanted to relax and for once not worry about anything. I felt like I could finally do that here with Chris. I slid under the covers in just my t-shirt and watched as Chris stripped out of his clothes, but he didn't stop with just his pants and shirt. When he grabbed onto the waistband of his boxers and started pulling them down, I almost choked. He was larger than I remembered and I couldn't force my eyes away from him.

His body was so different now. When I last knew him, he was tall and scrawny because he never had enough food. I could see now that he not only ate well, but he did everything he could to stay in shape. His body was a work of art, with thick, muscular arms and legs and a chest that flexed and jumped with each move. God, I wanted him so much. He lifted the covers and I couldn't help but notice that he was semi-hard. I closed my eyes, sad that we couldn't do anything yet.

"Take off your shirt," he grumbled.

"What?"

"I want to feel your skin against mine. Take off your shirt."

I slowly slid my shirt up and pulled it over my head. My nipples pebbled as he stared at my breasts. They were softer than before and they weren't as perky. It made me feel very self-conscious, but I willed myself not to cover up. If he wanted me after all these years, he had to see me for the way I was now. His eyes slowly traveled over my body, darkening with every inch he took in. I felt like I was under a magnifying glass, sure that he would see every flaw about me, but he only looked at me like he wanted to devour me.

"You're still as fucking beautiful as you were when we were kids," he said softly. He slid toward me and pulled me against him. I could feel his rather impressive erection pushing against me and I closed my eyes to enjoy the feel of his hard length. His hands skimmed over my shoulders and down my back, slowly trailing the curves of my body. Tears filled my eyes and I couldn't hold back the sob that broke free.

He cupped my cheeks and forced me to look at him. "Why are you crying?"

"All this time, I've wanted you so much. I never stopped wanting you. I really didn't think I would ever see you again. And now you're holding me and I just know that everything's going to be okay."

He leaned into me and placed a soft kiss on my lips. I had thought Chris would be a demanding lover and maybe he was, but right now, he was nothing but sweet and gentle, and that was exactly what I needed from him.

He pushed me down on the bed and gently ran his large, rough hands over my body. Every touch made me shiver. I wanted to stop him, to remind him this couldn't go anywhere yet, but he didn't try for more. He just kissed me in the most random places, leaving wet trails all over my skin. I wanted to do the same to him, but every time I tried to move, he pushed me back down.

"I've missed the taste of your skin. When I was overseas, I was always trying to remember what you tasted like. It was the one thing that drove me crazy all these years, not remembering that."

"I missed your breath against my neck. It was always so comforting to me."

He moved himself behind me and wrapped his arm around my waist, pulling my ass against his erection. I groaned, not needing a reminder of what we couldn't have. His breath tickled my ear as he kissed and licked the sensitive lobe and then down my neck.

"Is that what you needed?"

"Yes," I said breathily.

"This is all I need right now. You in my arms, knowing that you're safe and mine again."

"I've always been yours," I whispered.

"You always will be."

Chapter Fifteen

CHRIS

When my alarm went off, I groaned in frustration. I just wanted to stay in bed wrapped around Ali. She was still sleeping peacefully next to me and it made me want to kick myself for every fucking morning that I woke up and she wasn't there. All because I had left without so much as a second thought about her.

For the first time in seventeen years, I really looked at her and saw she wasn't the same girl I once knew. She was an older version of the girl I once knew, but that was as far as it went. I could see the stress had worked its way into the lines on her face and silvery scars from what Slasher had done to her over the years were more obvious in the morning light. My battle scars were nothing compared to what she had lived through without me and I would make sure she never had to suffer like that again.

I gave her a kiss before pulling the covers up over her shoulders and climbing out of bed. If I was going to make things right for her, I needed to start by eliminating the threat that constantly hung over her head. I took a quick shower and dressed for the day. I had another hour before our meeting would start, but I was ready to get going now.

Cap was already downstairs looking at maps and talking over things with Becky and Rob. Looking at the security monitors, I saw that

Hunter, Derek, and Lola were on watch outside. Ice and Jules were MIA, which meant they were probably still sleeping. I was curious where Lindsey was and wondered if she was in Ice's room. It wouldn't surprise me. As much as there was tension between the two of them, it was obvious he wanted to fuck her as much as strangle her. Though, hopefully he didn't do both at the same time.

"Cap," I said, walking into the room. "How's Maggie this morning?"

"She's asleep," he said wearily. "Kate cleaned her up when we got here and she's been keeping an eye on her."

"Kate's doing okay?"

"I think as long as she's busy taking care of everyone else, she won't be thinking about what happened. What about Alison?"

"I know she's feeling guilty, but she's doing fine. Axel..." I let out a little chuckle as I shook my head. "That kid is something else. He was sitting guard in her room last night. He wouldn't even let Gabe in the room."

"Definitely your kid."

I nodded as I stared off in the distance. It was so weird that just a few weeks ago, I didn't have anyone but the Sergeant and his wife for family and now I had my very own. I had missed out on so much time with them.

"Hey, stop that." I shot Cap a questioning look. "You can't change how things happened. Just be happy that you have them now."

"I am. I just want this shit over so I can actually have a life with them."

"On that note, I've been thinking about how to deal with this. We have Cash coming in with everyone he's got."

"It's not enough to just take them out, Cap. I want this over, but I want those fuckers to suffer. I want them to know what it's like to be hunted."

He grinned and slapped me on the back. "Then we're on the same page, but we have to be smart about this. Nothing leads back to us. I can get Sean to look the other way on a lot of stuff, but he's not going to be a part of this. He can use his contacts in the department, but that won't mean jack shit if we aren't careful."

"What do you have in mind?"

"Guerrilla warfare. We're going to have to attack at the same time. I'm thinking we send OPS to the Night Kings while we go after the Blood Devils. If we do this right, we'll make them each think they're being attacked by the other gang. We set it up for them to take each other out and we take out any stragglers."

"No," I said angrily. "After all they did to Axel and Ali, I want them to pay. I want them to know that they're being hunted and they have no way out. I want them so fucking scared that they're pissing their pants when they see us coming."

"There's a greater risk of us getting caught that way."

"Cap, we know how to do this right. We know how to stay concealed. Besides, Tennessee will be thanking us by the time we're through with them."

Cap sighed and thought for a minute. I could tell that he didn't want to do things my way, but I could tell that he wanted blood just as much as I did. "I'm with you on that, but I won't ask anyone else to risk their lives. This isn't just a job. This would mean jail time if we're caught. I can't ask everyone to take that risk."

"I get it, but this is the way it has to be for me."

He held out his hand and I took it, shaking it firmly. "Then let's get this shit done."

"I get Slasher. That's non negotiable," I said fiercely.

"Just keep your head in the game. Slasher's not a total dumb fuck. He has a power over you that could tilt things in his favor."

"What the hell are you talking about?"

"Your woman and your kid."

I shook my head. "He still thinks the kid is his."

"And it's best it stays that way. If he finds out that Axel isn't his, you know he'll take him out just to fuck with you. We'll keep them safe, but you know how shit happens in war."

"I want in." I turned to see Axel standing just a few feet behind us. "I want to be the one to take out Slasher. I deserve to after all he's done to my mom and me."

"Axel, I know you have a bone to pick with him, but I've been dealing with this asshole since I was seventeen. He killed my brother-"

"You dealt with him for a few years. I've lived with him my whole fucking life," Axel shouted. "I've been his punching bag and I've watched him beat my mom within an inch of her life and that's after I heard her screaming while he was raping her. There was nothing I could do about it then, but I can kill him now. I can make him pay for everything he ever did to us."

I hated that he had seen and heard all that over the years. No kid should have to grow up that way. But I wasn't about to let him become anything like Slasher. "That's not going to be the way this ends. I won't have you starting your new life by taking his. That's not what I want for you."

"Chris, no offense, you may be my dad, but this has been my life for the past sixteen years and you're not going to step in now and tell me how to live it. Knowing you for just a few days has given me an idea of the kind of man I want to be and that starts with me taking out the man that has tortured me my whole life. You don't get to take that away from me."

I could see I was getting nowhere with him, so I conceded. "If, *if*, the opportunity presents itself, I won't stop you. But I'm not bringing you along on this. You're not trained and I'm not risking your life so you can get revenge."

"But you'll risk yours when we just got you back?"

I looked to Cap for help, but he just shrugged. "I've been trained to kill fuckers like this. I have a whole team to back me up. I'm not going anywhere."

He snorted and crossed his arms over his chest. "Is that what you told Mom before you got her pregnant?"

He turned and walked out of the room before I could say anything else. I tried not to let his words get to me, but he was partially right. I had promised Ali the world and then walked away. He had every right to be pissed at me for the way he grew up.

"Let it go, Chris. He's pissed. Just give him a chance to cool off."

"I'm so fucking lost. I don't know how the hell to start being a parent when my kid is almost an adult. I missed out on so much."

"Just do your best, man. Look on the bright side. At least he's not a girl."

My eyes widened as I thought of the possibility of having a teenage daughter. He was right. That was even more terrifying.

"Cash, thanks for coming." Cap shook Cash's hand like they had been life long friends instead of men that met through Sinner.

"We couldn't let you have all the fun. The boys were getting bored out in Cali. Too many heiresses needing a hot bodyguard. It gets old fast."

Cap smiled and led him into the room. I had yet to meet all the men of OPS and I was impressed with what I saw. I could see why Sinner had chosen to go there a few years back.

"Alright, let's make introductions and then get to the planning. I want to take out these shitbags and get back to my life."

Pretty much all of Reed Security was in agreement on that one. Not that we really had homes to go home to. All of our homes would need extensive repairs after we'd been attacked. Cap introduced all of us and then nodded to Cash.

"I'm Cash Owens, owner of Owens Protection and Security. We're not quite as big as you right now. We only have three teams. Team one is Jerrod Lockhart, Ed Markinson, Brock Patton, and Scottie Thacker." He pointed them all out and they nodded in acknowledgement. Then he pointed to another group of men.

"Team two is Marcus Slater, Mick Jeffries, and Tate Parsons. Team three is Bradford Kavanaugh, Eli Brant, and Red Warren."

"Here's the deal. The Blood Devils and the Night Kings have declared war on us. They attacked our homes and they tortured our women. Now, this all started with Chris's woman and we've talked about how we want to deal with them." Cap looked around the room at the men and women that were standing with us. "No mercy. By the time we're through with them, there won't be a single one of them still standing. What we're going to do isn't legal and it could land us in jail if we're caught. If you don't want any part of this, you can walk away. Some of you have families to think about and you won't be thought less of for wanting to protect them. OPS can go back home and the gangs will never know that you were tied to this if something goes wrong. If you're with Reed Security, you can stay here and be on protection detail while we're gone. The choice is yours."

I looked around the room and saw that no one was backing down. No one even looked hesitant.

"After what they did to Vanessa, you can bet your ass I want in," Cazzo growled.

"They didn't get Claire or Lucy, but they fucked up my house," Derek said. "No one gets away with that."

One by one, everyone from Reed Security put in their two cents on the matter.

"They shot my dog," Jackson glowered. "I'm in."

"My pillows are destroyed," Chance sneered. "You can bet I want to fuck them up."

The room went silent as everyone stared at Chance.

"What?" He looked around the room at the raised eyebrows and confused faces. "That bed cost me $3000. It was the most comfortable room in the house, and the pillows were $200 a piece. They were hypoallergenic."

Still, everyone just stared at him. He rolled his eyes. "Hey, I don't have a family or a fucking dog, but I do have creature comforts and it pisses me off that someone destroyed that."

There was no arguing with that. The man had a point.

"I need a team to stay behind to guard the women and children." Cap looked around the room for volunteers, but everyone wanted in on the action. "I was thinking Lola could-"

"No." Lola had always been outspoken and fierce, but there was a command in her voice right now that even Cap didn't question. I had no fucking clue what was going on between the two of them or her and her team for that matter, but whatever it was, Cap wasn't challenging her.

"How many people are we talking?" Cash asked.

"We have eight women and three children," I spoke up.

Cash shook his head. "That's too many for one team. I'd say we should leave behind two teams to be on the safe side."

"Cap, we'll take over Alison's security detail," Alec stepped forward. "We don't have as much in this as everyone else. Not that I don't want a piece of them," he muttered.

"I appreciate it," Cap nodded.

Cash turned to his group of men and jerked his chin at one of them, who nodded in return. "Team two will stay behind. Do you have a preference which teams go to which states?"

"I'm going after the Blood Devils," I said firmly.

"Your team will go to Tennessee with Cash, but the rest of us are going after the Night Kings," Cap confirmed. "They fucked up Maggie."

"Alright. When do we leave?" Cash asked.

Chapter Sixteen

ALISON

"What can you tell me about the Blood Devils?" Chris asked. All his friends were hanging around in the living room and I felt a little bit on display. It was very uncomfortable.

"Um, what do you want to know?"

"We need anything you can give us. Different gang members and where they live. Where they meet up. What they deal in. Anything that will give us a leg up."

I saw Gabe looking at me and I could tell that he was assessing me, still trying to decide if I was a traitor or not.

"Okay," I said, shifting my eyes from his gaze. "I can write out a list of gang members and where they live. I don't know all of it and I don't have addresses, but I can give you directions to the best of my knowledge."

"What about meet up locations?"

"I wasn't really privy to that information."

I heard a scoff, but so did Chris. His head whipped around and he glared at Gabe. "You got a problem, man?"

"I can't believe you trust her," Gabe leered at me. "She's been with them for over sixteen years."

"Gabe, that enough," Chance interjected.

"No. I've kept my mouth shut about all this, but someone has to be the voice of reason. She needs to give us something big that will prove that she's on our side. Otherwise, how can we be sure that she's not playing us?"

"What exactly do you think I did? Run away from the gang and draw them to Chris? For what purpose? Chris hasn't been a part of my life in years. What could they possibly want with him?"

"I don't know, but we've been fucked over before. I don't think it's wrong to want proof first," Gabe said.

"I agree." I looked over to see a woman step forward. "I don't think that you're a traitor, but I've been on the wrong side of someone betraying us. I think it would make us all feel better if you could give us something."

"Lola," Chris said angrily.

"No, Chris. This affects all of us. We all want to be certain that no one here is going to screw us over."

"I don't understand. You already know that I didn't give up the safe house and someone is always around me. When could I have even contacted anyone?"

Chris moved in front of me protectively and crossed his arms over his chest. "This is absolute bullshit. I've stood by all of you when you needed help and I never fucking questioned a thing. Since when is my word not good enough?"

"It's not that I don't trust your judgement," Gabe said, "but you haven't seen her in seventeen years. Do you really think that nothing else is going on here?"

"What could she be up to?" Chris questioned. "I haven't had contact with the Blood Devils since I was a fucking kid. The only reason they came after us was because she ran to us to get away from them. They only want her and my kid. Whatever you're imagining is going on, it's all in your fucking head. Now, if you don't want to help me take these fuckers out, then walk away right now. If you don't trust her, that's the same as saying you don't trust me. So decide. Who's fucking side are you on?" he growled.

Gabe shook his head and walked out of the room. Chris glared at him the whole way and I just stared at Chris's back. I felt awful that

Chris was having to deal with all this unrest because of me. I hated that his teammates didn't trust me. I didn't realize that I was crying until Chris turned around and cupped my cheeks in his large hands.

"Hey, don't do that. I trust you and that's all I fucking care about right now."

Sebastian's voice boomed over the group of men. "I trust Chris completely on this and Alison has given us no reason not to trust her. If you don't want to be a part of this, walk away right now. But you won't be staying under the safety of Reed Security. This is a safe house and everyone in it needs to feel safe and that includes Alison and her son. You have a problem with that? Get the fuck out."

Nobody said anything, but everyone looked at each other, wondering if anyone was going to follow Gabe out the door. Nobody followed and I felt some of the tension leech out of Chris's body.

"Alright, let's stop this bullshit bickering and get on the road."

Sebastian walked out of the room and the rest of the men filed out to follow him. Chris stayed with me until everyone was gone and then kissed me hard. "I don't want you to even think about this bullshit. You know I trust you with my life."

"I know. I'm just sorry that people doubt me. I don't want things to be harder for you."

"I can handle it. I just want this to be over so we can move on with our lives."

"Chris."

We both looked over to see Gabe standing in the doorway. Chris stepped in front of me again and I felt his muscles flex under his shirt.

"I'm sorry, man. I do trust you and if you trust her, then I'm with you all the way." Chris nodded and Gabe walked in closer, looking at me. "And I'm sorry that I've been so hard on you. I've always questioned everything and I'm probably the most skeptical person on the face of the earth. It won't happen again."

"Thank you." Chris looked at me with a raised eyebrow, like he couldn't believe that I would brush all that aside so easily, but the truth was, I didn't want everyone leaving here angry. They were basically going to war and needed to have each others backs. "I'll get to work on that list right away."

I walked away, leaving Chris with Gabe. If they had some guy shit to work out, I didn't need to be around to hear it.

Chris had left with the other guys early this morning and the rest of us were left to roam the house. I was starting to feel out of sorts. I liked to stay busy and I didn't really feel like I could do that if I was stuck in this house for too much longer. It was weird because even though this wasn't the cage that my last home was, it was still a cage. I wasn't allowed to leave and someone was always watching me. Even if it was for my own good, I still didn't like the feeling.

When I walked into the living room, I was surprised to see Maggie there. She hadn't been out of her room since we'd arrived and I assumed that she wouldn't be up to the company after what happened to her. All the girls were gathered and even though I had spent some time with Lucy, Claire, and Cara, I felt like an intruder on the group. Then I saw Lindsey sitting there looking just as awkward as I felt. Only she looked pissed. I would be too if my place of business had been shot up and I had been taken away from my home against my will.

Maggie smiled at me brightly and I briefly wondered if she had been drinking. She seemed way too cheerful. "I was wondering when you would come down."

"I, uh, wasn't really sure what to do here. Are we allowed to wander around the house?"

"Of course," Kate smiled. "This is partly my house, even if Hudson insists that he runs it."

"Who's Hudson?"

"Sorry, I forget that everyone calls him Knight," Kate said with a wave of her hand.

"Why do they all have nicknames? It's so confusing."

"I think it all started when they were in the military and just kind of went from there," Maggie said. "Like my husband, Sebastian, is called Cap. He was a captain in the military and it just kind of carried over."

"And they call Chris *Jack* because he likes his whiskey?" I asked.

Vanessa nodded. "Yeah, but he's lucky. Sam, my fiancé, his nickname is Cazzo. It means *dick* in Italian."

"He lets them call him that?" I asked incredulously.

"He doesn't know what it means," she snickered. "He's too hard headed to look up the meaning."

"So, all this time he hasn't known what his name means?" Lindsey asked. When all eyes turned to her, she almost looked like she was cowering in embarrassment for having intruded on our conversation. Vanessa smiled at her reassuringly and nodded.

"Yep. He's just too stubborn to look it up."

"I'm sure he'll break someday," Kate said.

"So, what are the other guys' names?" I asked.

"Well, Mark is Sinner. That's Cara's husband. He had a bit of a reputation with the ladies before he met Cara," Maggie smiled.

Cara rolled her eyes. "His last name is Sinn. It just kind of worked out that way."

"Right, it had nothing to do with how many women he used to bed," Maggie smirked.

"Okay, how about we not bring up my husband's former bedmates?"

"You mean like Vira? We still don't know exactly what happened there," Maggie raised an eyebrow.

"Uh, do we have to talk about that woman?" Lillian rolled her eyes.

"Fine," Cara huffed. "If you really want to know, when he moved out to California, as you know, we were broken up. He thought he could screw me out of his mind and he tried with Vira, but," She bit her lip and grinned. "He couldn't get it up all the way for her. Vira said it was the worst fuck of her life."

Gasps sounded around the room and I didn't really understand why everyone seemed so shocked by that. Were these men so fantastic in bed that it was a sin for one of them to be less than worthy?

"No way!" Lucy said in shock. "He's just...sorry, Cara, but your man is big time eye candy. I don't really see how he could be bad in bed."

"He's not," Cara said smugly. "He's amazing in bed. But he didn't want to be with Vira. He told me that the whole time he was trying to get off, he kept thinking about how much he wanted to be with me."

"Aww, that's so sweet." Claire held her hand to her chest with a desperate look on her face.

"Great Caesar's ghost," Lillian sighed. "I hope I never see or hear from that woman again. She just ruffles my feathers so much."

"How do you know Vira?" Lucy asked.

Lillian looked down at her pants and rubbed a small pattern for a few seconds before speaking. "Sean was involved with her before me, and sort of at the same time. He was over the moon for her, or at least, he thought he was for awhile. But she kept dragging him along and he got tired of it. She kept coming back into his life and we almost didn't get together. I wasn't very experienced with men and she's...well, she's a professional at public relations."

Cara snorted. "That's a nice way to put it."

"She's really not that bad," Maggie chimed in. Cara and Lillian glared at her. "What? You have to remember that I knew her before you. She was a friend of one of the girl's I met through Sebastian. She's really a lot of fun, but yeah, she's a bit of a slut and people don't like her for that. But if you just go hang out for a good time, she's hilarious."

"You'll never get me to see her as anything other than a trollop." Lillian gasped and covered her mouth as if she had just said a horrible word. I got the feeling that swearing was not something that she did, which was kind of endearing.

"The guy that dragged me out here, Ice? What's his real name?" Lindsey asked curiously.

"John," Maggie answered.

"John? He doesn't look anything like a John," Lindsey wrinkled her nose.

"I know, right?" Lucy stared off in the distance with a dreamy look in her eyes. "Can't you just see him saying, *You! You're still dangerous. You can be my wingman anytime.*"

"Bullshit, you can be mine," Claire laughed. I felt like I was missing something here.

"I don't get it." Everyone stopped laughing and looked at me, stunned.

"Val Kilmer? Iceman? Top Gun?" Lucy said urgently.

"Sorry, I never saw it."

"Shut the front door," Lillian gasped. "Even I've seen that movie."

"Well, I..." I was about to say that I hadn't really had the luxury of watching movies, but I didn't want to sour the mood. "I guess I'll have to rent it."

"And then there's Hunter," Maggie said after a beat. "He goes by Pappy because his last name is Papacosta."

"And Hunter is your husband, right?" I asked Lucy.

She nodded vigorously. "Well, he will be soon enough." She shoved the ring in my face and grinned. It was a beautiful ring, not too large and gaudy.

"Maybe you and Claire should have a double wedding," I grinned.

"I don't think Derek or Hunter would like that," Claire smirked.

"Why not?" Lucy put her hand on her hip.

"Well, I was talking with Derek about having a Superhero themed wedding. Sort of an inside joke. I don't think Hunter and Derek would agree on the decorations." Claire's eyes twinkled as she spoke and Lucy's nose wrinkled in disgust.

"You're right. Hunter and I will definitely have our own wedding."

"Does this have something to do with why they call him Irish?" I asked in confusion.

"No," Claire waved me off. "That's just because his family is Irish. Very creative, these men."

"Yeah, just like Burg," Maggie grinned. "His last name is Reasenburg. Very creative, right?"

"Which one is Burg? I'm getting them all confused."

"He's the one that looks like the size of an iceberg. He's huge, like way bigger than Hunter," Lucy said.

"And who is he with?" I looked around the room, counting all the women and not seeing anyone else, but I thought Chris had told me he was taken.

"Her name is Meghan. We've hung out with her a few times," Maggie said. "She was on vacation with her mom when this all happened, otherwise you would have met her too. They've been together for over a year now."

"Wait. Isn't *Knight* Hudson's last name?" Claire asked.

"Yes," Kate said. "It's not really a nickname. But that's what they call him." She looked down at the ring on her left hand and sighed. "We were supposed to get married soon, but I've been so busy at the clinic that I've been putting it off."

I sat down in an empty chair across from her. "What clinic do you work at?"

"I have my own clinic," Kate informed me. "I didn't want to work at a hospital, so I opened my own clinic and I help out when Sebastian needs me."

"Oh. So, you know the area pretty well then. I'm a nurse. I'm going to have to find a job when all this is over."

"What kind of nurse are you?" Kate asked.

"Well, I've always worked in the ER."

"That would be perfect for Sebastian if he needs the help, but you could always send me your credentials. I'm always looking for a good nurse. It can be a little boring compared to the ER, but it's steady hours."

"That actually sounds really nice. I'll definitely send you everything if we ever get out of here."

"Oh, we'll get out of here," Maggie insisted. "I'm not staying locked up here while they're all out having all the fun."

"Don't you need to rest?" I asked, a little concerned that she was ready to run out of here after all she had been through.

"I'll be fine," she waved me off. "So I'm missing a couple fingers. It's really not that big of a deal. It'll slow down my typing, but I can work around that. I can still fire a gun and pull the pin on a grenade."

"I'm confused. Are you a part of Reed Security?"

The girls all snickered around me. I felt like I was missing some vital piece of information.

"She's not, but her and my husband like to pretend that they're the Lone Ranger and Tonto," Cara grinned.

"And Sebastian's okay with that?"

Maggie waved her hand at me, brushing off my concern. "Ah, he doesn't like it, but Sinner and I have so much fun when we're together. I think he's actually a little jealous because he doesn't get out of the office as much as he'd like."

"And you still want to go shoot a gun and throw grenades after what happened?"

She looked at me funny. "Why wouldn't I? If anything, I want to even more. I crave the excitement and while I don't like what happened, I'm not going to sit down and take it. You know exactly what I mean."

She looked at me pointedly and I did know what she meant. Just because something happens doesn't mean you stop living your life and that was precisely what I meant to do when we left this place.

"Yeah, I definitely get it."

"So, your son is older than all our kids. Is he already looking at colleges?" Lillian asked.

"Actually, with the way our lives were, we hadn't really had the opportunity to plan much of anything. I would love for him to go to college, but I think he's actually thinking of going a different way. He's been really questioning Chris about his time in the military and his face lit up when he learned how to use a gun. I have a feeling he'll go that way."

"It'd be good for him," Vanessa said. "After what you've been through, it'll give him the feeling of control. That was something that was really important to Sam after he was injured."

"Well, if he follows in Chris's footsteps, I can't say I would be disappointed. He was about to be initiated into a gang, so anything is a step up from that."

"That would make Chris so happy," Maggie smiled.

"You think?"

"Definitely. To know that the son he didn't know about already wanted to be like him?" She nodded like it was dumb logic. "All of these guys hope that they can have little boys that want to follow in their footsteps."

Alex, who had been quiet the whole time finally spoke. "I think that really bothers Cole. We aren't able to have kids. I was pregnant once a few years ago and I miscarried. I just shrugged it off as fate, but I can tell it really bothers him. He wanted me to keep trying to get pregnant, but it never worked for us."

"Did you talk about adoption?" I asked.

"Yeah, but honestly? I think he wanted it more than me. I'm okay with not having kids. I just wanted my life with Cole, but I think after everything that he went through in the military, he just wanted that normal life."

"I guess that's all I want at this point, a normal life and I don't really care if it includes more kids or just what I have. I'm just glad to not be in that hellhole anymore."

"That's exactly how I felt." Alex threw her head back and laughed. "I'm so glad someone else gets it."

I didn't know her story, but I wasn't about to ask in a room full of women either.

"I think when we get back home, we should head to the Reed Security building and blow some shit up," Maggie said after an awkward pause. We all looked at her like she was crazy. "What? I'm telling you, it'll make you feel so much better."

Chapter Seventeen

CHRIS

Tennessee

"We've got three inside," Ice said in my ear. He was on the other side of the house, scoping out our target through the back window. "They're all headed for the living room. Looks like they're just gonna hang out. They have beer with them."

"Copy that," I said quietly. I was laying on my belly in the trees across the street from the house. Jules was closer to the house, but would have a harder time getting there unseen.

"Don't be a fucking cowboy," Ice growled. "There's one for each of us."

"No problem, man. As long as I get to spill some blood, it's all good."

"Aw, fuck. He's going without us," Jules said.

"I said I would let you have some fun too," I said with a grin. I had no intention of letting them have any fun tonight. I had been waiting to take out these fuckers since Ali came back into my world and I wasn't letting anyone take that from me.

I stood up and crept across the road, not waiting for Ice and Jules to tell me they were ready.

"Ice, he's moving," Jules said urgently.

"Fuck, Chris. Wait for us."

"I'm just getting into position."

I sidled up along the house and peeked in the window. They were all sitting around, drinking beer and bullshitting. It was fucking perfect.

"You're just getting into position to fuck us over." I could hear Jules breathing heavily as he ran. I only had seconds to do this before they would be coming in behind me. I ran up the steps to the house and banged on the door.

"Son of a bitch," Ice swore over coms. I heard a bang on the back door. Fuck, he was trying to break the door down. The front door swung open and I lashed out immediately, slicing my knife across the fucker's neck. Blood squirted everywhere as his hands went to his throat as he tried to staunch the bleeding. The back door flew in as Ice kicked it open. I flung my knife across the room into the second guy who was standing there staring at his friend. The knife plunged into his heart and he dropped to the ground. Ice ran toward the room as Jules's footsteps pounded up the stairs. I jumped over the bodies to the third guy and kicked him in the nuts before snapping his neck. When he dropped to the ground, I turned around to see Jules and Ice glaring at me.

"What? You guys weren't here yet. Did you expect me to wait around for you all night?"

"We weren't here because you went in without us, you asshole," Ice growled.

"I wouldn't have had to go in without you if you weren't so fucking slow. I swear, old age isn't working well for you."

Ice stepped over to me, shaking his head before he punched me in the fucking face. I honestly wasn't expecting it, but I couldn't say that I didn't deserve it.

"Fine, I'll let you two get the next one."

"Gee, thanks for being so accommodating," Jules muttered.

I pulled my knife out of the asshole on the floor and made my way out of the house, making sure that I hadn't left any evidence behind. Jules and Ice followed me out of the house and we made our way back to our truck that was parked a block away.

"The next fuckers are ours," Jules said as he slammed his door, getting in the truck.

"Fine. They're yours. I won't touch them."

We drove to our next location in an old apartment building in a shitty part of town. I remembered it from growing up here. Back then, it had always been a drug haven and it didn't look like that had changed over the years.

"I doubt anyone here will call the police over gunfire, but better to keep things quiet," Ice said as we parked a block away. We walked to the building and easily slipped inside. There wasn't any security or cameras in sight. Still, I lowered my head as I made my way inside. I followed Ice and Jules up to the third floor and down the hall to the last apartment that happened to be by the window with the fire escape.

Ice pounded on the door and it swung open, reeking of pot. Ice grabbed the man by the collar and threw him across the room. He crashed into a glass table that was covered with lines of heroin. I pulled a rag out of my pocket and quickly tied it around my face so that I didn't inhale the drugs. Jules and Ice did the same.

"Dude," one guy said as he looked at the man on the table. "You totally just fucked up my line."

I started to stalk toward the table, but Jules put out his hand, stopping me from moving forward. I turned a glare on him, but he just raised a brow.

"This one's ours, remember?"

I huffed in irritation and crossed my arms over my chest as they went toward the other room. There were four guys sitting around, fucked out of their minds. It was an easy kill for Jules and Ice. It wouldn't be any fun anyway. The guys didn't even try to defend themselves at first. They just watched in awe as Ice pulled out a knife and rammed it into one man's gut.

Another man started laughing and slapping his knee. "That was totally fucking awesome."

Jules turned to him and chuckled. "You think that was awesome?" The guy nodded. Jules motioned for the guy to come closer and he did. I shook my head at the idiocy of these assholes. They were so fucked up that they didn't even realize they were being taken out. When the man was close enough, Jules snapped his neck in one swift move, dropping him to the floor and stepping over him to the next guy. As he approached, I saw the fourth guy looking a little nervous. He started making a move for the window. Ice saw him too and started after him. I whipped out my knife and threw it across the room, stabbing the man directly in the neck, nicking his carotid artery. He started bleeding out immediately. I crossed my arms over my chest and leaned back against the wall as if nothing had happened. Ice turned to me and growled. I shrugged like I didn't know what had happened.

"I fucking told you they were ours."

I raised my hands in surrender. "I didn't touch them."

Ice walked over to the man and yanked the knife from his neck, wiping off the blood on the man's shirt before tossing the knife back to me.

"Asshole," he muttered as he shoved past me. I smirked and walked out behind him.

"Let's see how Cash and his boys are doing," Ice said as we got into the truck. He pulled out his phone and dialed, leaving it on speakerphone. I immediately heard screaming in the background and felt a little bit of anger that my kills hadn't been quite so gratifying.

"Cash here."

"How's it going on your end?" Ice asked.

"Not bad. I gotta say, I'm a little disappointed that they're not putting up more of a fight."

"They aren't scared yet. They're still too fucking high to realize we're coming for them," I surmised.

"Let's leave it for tonight. We'll see how they react tomorrow. I have something special in mind to fuck with them."

"Alright. We'll meet you back at the safe house." Ice ended the call and sat back in his seat. "I feel like I should be happier about tonight, but it was kind of a let down."

"That's because Chris took all the fun out of it," Jules glared at me.

"It's because they were too fucking high to care that we were there to kill them. We need them sober so that we have a worthy adversary," I shot back.

"Still wouldn't be worthy, but maybe at least they could put up more of a fight. I guess we call it a night and see what Cash has in mind for tomorrow."

He put the truck in drive and we headed for the safe house, all of us hoping that tomorrow would relieve a little more tension. Hopefully things were going better for Cap.

Eli from OPS pointed to a building on the city map, pointing out our next location. "I scoped out this location yesterday. This is where they meet up every day. It's sort of like their clubhouse or something. As far as I can tell, they just kind of sit around doing drugs all the time. This is where we want to hit."

"You want to take them out all at once?" I asked. "I thought the plan was to make them suffer?"

"Did I mention this is a sniper's paradise?" Eli said with a grin. "I'm suggesting we all set up around the building and take out one person each."

"Just one?" Jules asked.

A grin split Eli's face. "On any given day, there's thirty guys there at once. There's eleven of us. That's a lot of guys that see their friends murdered and wondering when we're coming for them."

I nodded, liking his idea. It really was a great plan. We could take out a bunch of them and scare the shit out of the rest of them all at once.

"I'm guessing they'll be meeting tomorrow to discuss why their men are being taken out. Let's slip in there tonight and set up coms so we can hear what they're saying. We need to know if they suspect us and what they're planning," Cash said.

We got to work, gathering up the supplies we needed and headed for the building. Eli was right. This was a sniper's paradise. Tomorrow would be too easy.

"I'm fucking telling you, man. That was a professional hit. Someone's after us and they're letting us know they're coming."

I watched through my scope as the man tweaking in my line of vision ranted about us taking out other members of the club.

"Would you calm the fuck down?" Slasher yelled. "If you guys weren't so fucking high all the time, this wouldn't have happened. That house last night was packed with smack. We're fucking lucky that we cleaned it up before the police could get there. We would have been fucked. They would have looked at anyone wearing our colors and then most of you would be in fucking jail right now. We don't have the kind of dough to fight that shit."

"That's because you gave all our money to the Night Kings. You should have just cut that bitch loose," T-Bone yelled at Slasher.

"She took my fucking kid. I couldn't let her just walk away."

"That's the fucking problem, man. Ever since you took over for Bullet, you've been taking everything and we get nothing. We're fucked if anything happens."

"Ice, you catching all this?"

"Loud and clear," Ice responded.

"T-Bone is gonna start a mutiny and take everyone out before we get the chance," I said irritatedly.

"Everyone got eyes on their target?" Cash asked. We all answered in the affirmative. "Remember, no one takes out the higher ups yet."

I looked through my scope again at my target. I took in a few deep breaths to slow down my breathing. I wasn't a sniper by any means, but I had been trained enough to know how to shoot long distance.

"On my mark. Three, two, one, mark."

We all fired simultaneously, shattering the glass from the windows and hitting our targets. They dropped instantly to the ground, every one of them a kill shot. The rest of them dove for cover, thinking they would be hit next. We waited as chaos ensued inside the building. Men ran, trying to find a way out of the building, thinking that at any moment they would be hit. It was really quite funny to watch.

I watched as Slasher started yelling at people and I looked back through my scope, finger on the trigger and ready to fire. I really wanted to take out that asshole, but I wanted it to be up close and personal. Still, the thought of him being in my sights and not pulling the trigger didn't feel right.

"Stand down, Chris. You'll get your revenge. Stick to the plan," Cash ordered.

I took my finger off the trigger and sighed. After a few minutes, the remaining Blood Devils started slipping out of the building, watching their backs the whole way. We had them scared and that was the whole point. Now I just had to be patient and wait for my opportunity to take the rest of them out.

"He's coming out the back of his house," Ice said over coms.

"I'm on it," I said as I slipped through the bushes around the house. This fucker was a low level peon, not even worth the trouble of torturing. He didn't know anything and he probably had nothing to do with Ali, but he was a part of the Blood Devils and I was here to send a message.

I walked up behind him, careful not to alert him of my presence, and instantly locked him in a choke hold. I didn't want to kill him, yet. I just wanted him to pass out so I could easily get him into position. When his head dropped, I released my hold and dragged him behind the garage to the tree where Jules was waiting with a rope. I tied the rope around his feet and hauled him in the air. Ice tied another rope around his wrists behind his back.

Working with rope, there were too many possibilities of leaving skin cells behind or blood if we were cut. All three of us were wearing black from head to toe and when we finished, we would burn everything we were wearing, including our gloves and masks. Even our shoes had a protective cover so that we didn't leave prints behind.

I leaned back against a tree, pulled out my knife, and started sharpening it as I waited for the guy to wake up. It took longer than I would have liked and I started to get bored. So did Jules and Ice because they kept sighing as they sat on the ground with me.

"Did you ever see Robin Hood?" Jules asked.

"The one with Russell Crowe?" Ice said as he leaned back against a tree.

"No, the one with Kevin Costner."

I stopped sharpening my knife as I looked up at him. What the hell was he getting at? "You want to rob them first and give the money to the poor?"

"No, I want to cut out his heart with a spoon," Jules smiled maniacally.

"Why a spoon, cousin?" Ice asked in a British accent. "Why not an axe or a knife?"

"Because it's dull, you twit. It'll hurt more," Jules laughed.

Ice leaned forward with one arm resting across his bent knee. "Serious question. Our best fighter versus Kevin Costner's Robin Hood. Who wins?"

"Me," I said, almost insulted that they had to ask.

Jules huffed out a laugh. "Yeah, I don't think so. Definitely Knight."

"Why Knight? You don't think I could take on Kevin Costner?"

"Since when do you know how to use a bow and arrow?" Ice laughed.

"Since when does Knight?"

"He has a point and Robin Hood didn't use guns, so that leaves knives." Jules shrugged. "Sorry, Chris. Knight wins out against you."

I stood and flipped the knife blade so it was resting in my hand. "You don't think I could take Knight?"

They both started laughing and I smirked. "Belly button."

"What?" Ice asked. I spun around and threw the blade directly into the man's belly button, hitting it dead center. That woke him up. He screamed in pain and tried to curl into himself, but the pain was too intense. I looked back at Jules and Ice who were staring in surprise.

"Didn't know I had those skills, did ya?"

Ice shook his head slowly and Jules started nodding. "Okay, fine. You could take Knight in a knife throwing contest, but I still don't know about Robin Hood. That man was a badass."

"Robin Hood wasn't a real person, asshole." I walked over to the man hanging in the tree and yanked out my knife, causing him to scream. "It was a name given to petty criminals during the 13th century. Get it? Robin?"

"Oh, shit," Jules said in awe. "That makes so much sense."

I nodded and turned back to the man hanging from the tree. "You know something else they used to do in the 13th Century?"

The man hanging upside down from the tree shook his head violently as blood spilled from his stomach. "They used to hang, draw, and quarter people convicted of high treason. Now, since we're not in the 13th Century, that seems a little drastic, don't you think?"

The man nodded vigorously as he moaned. I nodded and flipped my knife a few times in my hands as if I was thinking things through. "The thing is, I don't really give a shit which century we're in. Technically, I was supposed to hang you from your neck until you almost died and then cut you down, but I thought it would be more fun to gut you as you hung upside down. Which do you prefer?"

The man breathed heavily and looked to Jules and Ice for help. When they just stared at him, he started crying. "Please, I just joined. I don't know who the fuck you guys are."

"And I'm truly sorry that you felt it was necessary to join such a vicious gang, but when you run with these assholes, you die with these assholes."

I slapped some tape over his mouth and plunged the knife into his groin, dragging it down to his ribcage. Tearing through that muscle is a lot harder than it looks, especially when the victim is trying to get away. I sliced across his belly to make an equally deep cut. Gravity did the work for me and started spilling his innards all over the ground. He was on the verge of passing out. Either that or dying. I had no idea how long it would take.

Ice walked toward me and crossed his arms over his chest as we stared at the man that was dying in front of us. "You know, I think you got just a little too much pleasure out of that."

"Probably. Can't say I'm sorry about that. They fucked with the wrong man."

The guy jerked a few more times as his innards spilled all over the ground. I did get a sick kind of pleasure out of watching it, and this was only the beginning. I would be making sure that every single fucker I came across suffered a similar fate.

We walked into the barn where Red, Eli, and Bradford were currently holding one of the other gang members. They had called us an hour ago and gave us a location to meet up if we wanted in on some fun. I was all for it. One kill tonight just wasn't enough to satisfy the need running through me.

"Glad you guys could make it," Eli grinned. "We're just about to get this party started."

There was a large whiskey barrel standing up with the lid removed and a man strapped to a chair next to it.

"What do you have planned here?" I asked.

"Hydrofluoric acid," Red nodded to the barrel. The man in the chair squirmed, trying to yank his hands free of his binds. The gag in his mouth was so tight that he was practically gagging.

"Who is this guy?" I asked. It seemed like a waste to use acid on some nobody in the gang, but when Red smiled, I knew he had someone good.

"This here is T-Bone, second to Slasher. We caught him staggering outside Slasher's house to take a piss. Yep, sobered him right up when he saw the acid over here."

"Tell me something, T-Bone. Why did you join the Blood Devils?"

He mumbled around his gag as snot dripped from his nose. I yanked the gag out so he could speak. "Same reason as you." I narrowed my eyes at him, wondering what the fuck he was saying. "I didn't want to join. I had no choice."

"I didn't join. I walked away."

"Only because Slasher killed your brother in front of you. I didn't get the chance to walk away."

"That was almost twenty years ago. You stood by and watched as Ali and Axel were used as punching bags. You didn't do anything to stop him when he sent the Night Kings after us."

"I didn't want him to do it." His voice shook and I could see the fear in his eyes. He was telling the truth. This guy never wanted to be a part of the life, but he made his decision and now he would pay. "I tried to change his mind, but he was determined to get them back. He wanted his kid alive, but he didn't give a shit about Alison. He blew all the money we had to pay off the Night Kings. There's nothing fucking left."

"So, he blew all your money to get his kid back and now you're fucked," I grinned. "What's wrong? Drug trade isn't as lucrative as you hoped?"

"Slasher keeps most of the profits."

"Why do you stick around?" Red asked.

"There's no walking away," he said solemnly. "If I tried, he'd just kill me and all my family. You were lucky," he jerked his head at me. "Bullet wouldn't let Slasher kill you all those years ago. He was different. He was softer than Slasher. That's why Slasher took him out," he rambled. "Slasher's always wanted all the power and he'll do whatever it takes to get it."

"Where's he staying?" I asked.

"Man, come on. You know I can't tell you that."

Bradford grabbed him by the front of the shirt and stood just inches from his face. "You see that barrel over there?" T-Bone nodded. "It's gonna be a painful death. Now, I can make it quicker for you or I can make it excruciatingly painful. Which do you want?"

"I can't," T-Bone whimpered.

Red sneered at him. "You're being loyal to a man that would hand you over faster than his worst enemy if it meant sparing his life. You fuckers have no idea what brotherhood is all about."

When T-Bone didn't say anything, Eli pulled out a length of chain and wrapped it around the man's arms and waist as he yanked him out of the chair. Red attached a metal hook to the chain and hit the power button on the winch. T-Bone was slowly raised in the air and Red swung him over to just above the barrel. He stripped the man's socks and shoes and dropped them in the acid as T-Bone watched the acid eat through the material.

"Please," T-Bone begged quietly.

Red hit the button on the winch and began lowering T-Bone into the acid. When his toes touched the acid, he yanked his legs up, screaming in pain.

"You know, I'm not sure his whole body's going to fit in this barrel," I said as I examined the size of it.

Eli pulled out an apple and took a bite out of it. "Don't worry. When the acid eats away at his flesh and organs, he'll squeeze right in there."

"I hope that barrel didn't have any Jack Daniels in it," I said pointedly. "Sure would be a waste to empty out such a fine whiskey."

Bradford snorted. "You and your whiskey. Don't worry. This was an empty barrel."

T-Bone's feet were approaching the barrel again and he couldn't lift his feet any higher. I watched as Eli slowly chewed his apple as if he didn't have a care in the world. Something told me he was getting more enjoyment out of this than I was. We all took a step back as his feet slowly entered the barrel. We didn't need him splashing acid all over us.

"Ahhh!" His screams echoed around us, but no one made a move to help him. He thrashed his legs as he tried not to sink any further in, but the acid was starting to make his body shake uncontrollably as it ate away at his skin. His nerve endings had to be on fire at this point, but his body wouldn't give out until it reached his vital organs. When his calves became submerged, Red stopped the winch and let him hang in the barrel.

"You know, I was thinking..." He glanced over at T-Bone, who was panting hard and trying his best not to scream. "We should probably get a drink after this," he said turning back to us.

"I could go for some Jack," I agreed.

"You could always go for some Jack," Red said with a shake of his head.

"Hey, you don't mess with perfection."

"Stop," T-Bone screamed. "Just fucking stop! I'll tell you anything."

"What's the magic word?" Red asked in a sing-song voice.

"Fuck, man. Please stop," T-Bone whimpered.

"No. That's not it," Red shook his head in thought.

I watched T-Bone's legs as he tried to kick them around the barrel and get them out of the acid. The skin from his legs was starting to slip off into the liquid below and his whole body was shaking. We didn't have too much longer before he would be useless to us. Still, he could take a little more.

"I don't know the fucking magic word or secret handshake. Please, just fucking stop this and I'll tell you anything!" His words were stilted and rife with pain, but that just made me happier. All these fuckers deserved it. By the time I made it to Slasher, he would know that he had fucked with the wrong group of men.

Red raised the winch and T-Bone was lifted from the barrel. All that was left of his legs was bone and even that was becoming porous.

"Where would Slasher run off to?" I asked.

He shook from pain and looked at me pleadingly. "There's a new place on the lake he goes for drug deals. It's about a half mile down river from the bridge. There's an abandoned cabin. That's the only place I can think of."

I nodded to Red and he released the winch, letting T-Bone's whole body splash down into the barrel of acid. His screams only lasted a minute before his body gave out and he sank all the way into the barrel.

Chapter Eighteen

REED SECURITY

Chance- Pittsburgh

I flipped my knife over and over in my hand as I watched the asshole on the bed piss himself. I had snuck in here and tied him to the bed in the middle of the night and then waited for the sun to rise so that I could draw out the torment. Whether he pissed himself from fear or because he had to piss didn't matter to me. All I cared about was getting revenge on the fuckers that came after us.

"Are we gonna do anything any time soon?" Gabe asked. "I'm fucking bored."

I stood and walked over to the bed, flipping the knife a few more times before slamming the knife down into the bed between his legs, just south of his nuts. I saw his eyes widen as he screamed around his gag. I ripped the bedding with the knife, watching feathers float out of his comforter. The fucker deserved it after everything he did to my bed.

I pulled out a larger knife out of my thigh holster and almost started cracking up as his eyes widened. I stepped closer to him and slid the knife along his thigh. He tried to pull his leg away, but the restraints around his ankles prevented him from moving.

"You know, that bed was the most comfortable bed I've ever owned. Did you know they stopped making that bed two years ago?" I asked the guy. He shook his head wildly. "Now I have to go find a new fucking bed. I'm not too happy about that." I slid the knife closer to his balls and pressed the point of the knife lightly into his thigh. "And that comforter cost me close to a thousand dollars. Now, it's just a bunch of feathers floating around my house."

The man looked from Gabe to Jackson. I saw his throat working hard to swallow down his fear.

"Did you know that those sheets were fucking bamboo? Best sheets I ever owned. I put a lot of work into making that room my sanctuary. Fucking $200 hypoallergenic pillows." I dug the knife in a little deeper and chuckled when he whimpered in pain. "You know, when I came home after a long day of work, the one thing I really looked forward to was falling down in my luxurious bed and and shutting out the world."

I sighed and sat down on the bed next to him. "Now what the fuck am I supposed to do? My house is fucked up and my bed is destroyed. It really pisses me off when people have no respect for other people's property. You know what I'm saying?"

He nodded vigorously and I smirked. "I think you know exactly what I mean. The only way I can truly show you how pissed I am is to take something that you cherish."

I dug the knife further into his leg, letting the knife slip down and nick his sac. He whimpered as snot dripped down his nose and he squeezed his eyes shut. I picked up the knife, watching him tense. I slammed the knife down, slicing into his pillows and sending the stuffing flying everywhere. He cringed when he felt the whoosh of the knife, but then slowly peeked open his eyes and looked at the knife that wasn't anywhere near his balls. He sagged in relief and I started chuckling.

"You thought I was going to cut your balls off, didn't you?" I laughed.

He nodded and a mixture of crying and laughing left his mouth. I pointed the knife at him and smiled.

"I really had you going. You thought I was gonna go all psycho on you and start tearing you to shreds over a bed."

He laughed along with me and turned with a smile to Gabe and Jackson, who were looking at me in boredom.

"I'm not really that psycho," I said, making my face wide and scary-goofy looking. "Can you imagine, killing someone over a fucking bed and pillows?"

I threw my head back in laughter as his chest shook from his own laughter. I stopped laughing as I quickly took a step forward and pressed my face just an inch from his ear.

"You haven't seen fucking psycho yet. You think I would kill you over my bed? Sure, that fucking pisses me off, but what you're about to get is for coming after all of us. For hurting our women when we didn't do a fucking thing to you," I growled. "I'm going to make sure you suffer and my friends over there are going to get just as much pleasure out of it as I do."

His eyes shifted to mine, wide with horror. I grinned maniacally at him, baring my teeth just to scare the shit out of him. "You fucked with the wrong men."

I slashed my knife across his sac, cutting off his balls in one swift cut. His muffled screams echoed around the room as blood squirt from his privates. Gabe stepped forward and pulled his own knife out, watching the light gleam across the blade.

"I'm not quite as sadistic as him. I don't like to see people suffer." Gabe pressed the knife to his scalp by his ear. "But for you, I'll make an exception."

He cut off the man's ear and Jackson hurried over. This guy wasn't too long from passing out. We had to make the rest count. Jackson pulled out the gag, ignoring the man's pleas for mercy.

"Don't worry. It'll all be over soon." He pulled the man's tongue out and sliced quickly as far back as he could, then shoved the man's tongue down his throat. He would choke to death on blood and his tongue in no time. We all stood there watching as the man took his final breaths. I wished that I could feel some remorse for what we had just done. I thought I would feel like a monster after that, but when I thought about all the people that could have been killed and how much Maggie and Vanessa suffered, all I wanted was to make them all pay just as dearly. I was sure Cap wasn't taking it easy on anyone.

Cap

"Alright, boys. Let's do this nice and smooth. Everyone in position?" I said through coms.

Check came over the line five times, letting me know that everyone was in place. The plan was for each of us to take out one of the members of the Night Kings as they came out of the building. We would leave one or two of them to really scare the shit out of them. They would run and tell everyone else that they were under attack, which was perfect for the next part of the plan. As much as I wanted to be there to personally make sure they all suffered, I also wanted to get back to Maggie. Vengeance was burning deep within me, but the need to get back to my wife and daughter was stronger. It was what kept me on the straight and narrow.

"Doors are opening," Cole said.

"You're up, Knight."

I watched as the men walked warily out the door of their little clubhouse. It was cute how they organized like they were some badass force to be reckoned with. After tonight, the Night Kings would cease to exist. After the last person walked out and the door slammed shut, I watched as Knight snuck out in the shadows, slipping in behind the last King and slit his throat. Knight dragged him off into the darkness, the others never knowing what had happened. That was the point. We wanted to be able to take as many of them out before they could alert the others what was happening. It wasn't as fun this way, but we needed to ensure success.

"Cole, you've got the next one."

Cole stepped out from behind a dumpster and broke the man's neck. Watching through my scope, I could see the rage on Cole's face when he took out the man. He enjoyed every second of the kill. Nobody fucked with Cole.

"Irish, you're up."

He snuck up behind the third in line, but just as he was about to slit the guy's throat, the guy in front of him turned around to say something to him. I moved my gun, ready to take out whoever I needed to, but Irish was faster. Irish flung his knife into the second man, hitting him right in the throat as he wrapped his arm around the other man's neck, snapping his neck as soon as the knife left his grip. Two down.

The thump of the second man hitting the ground caused the other guys to turn around. Immediately, guns were raised and pointed directly at Irish. Hunter and Lola stepped out of the shadows, each of them taking out one of the men. One of the Kings must have thought Lola was an easy target because she was a woman. I chuckled as he stepped up behind her with more confidence than he should have had. I saw Lola smirk through my scope as she felt the man behind her. She could have made it easy. She could have killed him with the flick of her wrist, but Lola chose to have some fun. And I couldn't blame her. She had been out of the game for weeks now. Lola needed this fight for her sanity.

His hand reached over her shoulder and she gripped his wrist tightly, flinging him over her shoulder and onto the ground. The heel of her stiletto boot dug into his chest as she stood over him with a maniacal grin on her face. He screamed in pain as she pushed the heel through his skin, puncturing his lung as she rammed it down into him. I winced, thinking of what it would feel like to be on the other end of that.

I watched her lean down and whisper something in his ear before sliding her knife across his throat. I could see him gasping for air seconds before his body went still. The last two Kings stood there watching in fear before turning and running away.

"You fucker," Pappy said to Irish. "You took out my guy."

"It was necessary. Besides, you still got one. What are you complaining about?"

"You took out two. Lola took out two. I only got one," Pappy pouted.

"All of you can fuck off," I said with a grin. "I didn't take anyone out."

"I offered to trade places with you," Knight said.

"And let someone else run this? You know I don't ever give up control."

"You snooze, you lose," Knight responded.

"Irish, let Cazzo know that we've sent them his way."

Knight

"Knight, where the fuck are you? You were supposed to meet us at the clubhouse an hour ago."

Cazzo was practically yelling at me over the phone. Yeah, I was supposed to follow orders and get to the clubhouse to take out the rest of The Night Kings. I had other plans though. I had followed one of the fuckers home and hit the jackpot. There were six of them hanging out at the house, completely unaware that the rest of the club had been under attack.

"I'm taking care of a few things. I'll be there in an hour or so."

"Knight, this isn't the way shit works. You were supposed to follow orders."

"Yeah, I've never been too good at that."

I hung up the phone before he could give me any more shit about how I wasn't following the plan. I watched from outside the window. All of them were hanging around the living room, drinking beer and smoking pot. I made my way to the back of the house where the utility room was. Quietly opening the door, I slid inside and opened the panel for the breakers. I flipped them all off and grinned when the lights all went out in the house. It was dead silent besides the curses coming from the other room. I waited for one of them to come back here and wasn't disappointed when one of then stumbled through the kitchen to the utility room. I had no desire to take them out quietly. I wanted a fight and I would get it however I could.

"Did you really think you could fuck with what's mine and get away with it?" I growled from the darkened corner of the room.

The man spun around wildly, trying to find my voice. I stepped from the shadows and flung my hand out until I had a firm grip around the man's neck. His eyes bulged as his hands scratched at my arm, trying to get me to release him. "You fucked with the wrong man and now there's no way any of you will survive the night. Take a good look at me. It's the last thing you'll ever see."

I tightened my fingers around his neck until his eyes rolled back in his head and his body went limp. I dropped him to the ground and stepped over his lifeless body.

"Hey, dude. Turn the fucking lights back on!"

I stepped into the living room and grabbed a floor lamp that was to my right.

"Who the fuck are you?" one of the Kings said, standing and dropping his joint on the ground.

"I'm your worst fucking nightmare." I swung the floor lamp at his head, knocking him out right away. Another guy charged me, trying to knock me to the ground. I flung him over my shoulder, tossing him into the table that was covered with drugs. Yanking the cord from the lamp, I wrapped it twice around the man's neck as my legs entwined around his, holding him in place. His fingers clawed at the cord for only a few seconds before he passed out. I jerked it one last time, ensuring that it had cut off his air supply.

Two men charged me at the same time and I grinned at their foolishness. They really thought they could take me on, but they didn't know what the hell they were up against. A throat punch to one and he was on the ground struggling to breathe. He would be dead in minutes. The second man tried to run away. He didn't want to die like his friends had. I didn't give him the chance to run though. A kick to the knee and he was down on the ground in pain. He crawled on his elbows, trying to get away from me. I heard his whimpers as I stalked behind him, letting him think he had a chance to get away. He rolled over onto his back and with the faint light streaming in from the window, I could see tears running down his face.

"Please, don't kill me. I didn't do shit."

I knelt over him and whispered in his ear. I could hear his ragged breaths from fear and it made me smile. "Unfortunately, you ran with the wrong crowd and now you're going to pay for it," I said as I slid the knife into his heart. I pulled back enough to see the pain and fear in his eyes. I wanted to be the last thing he saw before he took his last breath.

Yanking my knife from him, I stood and faced the man who was too stoned to react to anything. He looked around and started laughing. "Dude, that was fucking awesome. Do me next." His laughter cut off when I flipped my knife a few times in my gloved hand. The rage that had been building inside me was at a tipping point and I was ready to release it. The man finally realized that I was about to kill him. He swung wildly and I sidestepped him, slamming the knife into his ear. Blood trickled out and the man fell to the ground, not dead yet, just paralyzed. His jaw was clamped down tightly as he shook on the ground.

I sighed, a little disappointed that there weren't more here to kill. That had felt good and I didn't get the opportunity to kill very often. I didn't enjoy the kill, I enjoyed taking out scum. It was the one thing that separated me from a psychotic killer. At least, that's what I told myself. I wouldn't have come after them if they hadn't gone after what was mine. Even though Kate walked away fine, she almost hadn't. She was going to be the one that was taken and tortured and if it wasn't for Maggie, Kate would never be the same woman again. She was strong, but she didn't have the strength that Maggie had. In fact, I was a little surprised that Maggie hadn't insisted on coming along. If she wasn't doped up on pain pills, she probably would have. And Sinner would have helped her escape. It was just who she was. Just like this was who I was. No matter how much I tried to hide it, I still had that dark side to me that craved a good kill. I wasn't sure how Kate would feel about that when she realized that I hadn't changed as much as she thought.

Cazzo

. . .

While everyone else was strategizing on how to make the Night Kings pay painfully and slowly, I was just itching to get my hands on them and slice them from ear to fucking ear. But I wanted Vanessa more than anything right now. So, I didn't care if they died slow, painful deaths. I just wanted to wipe out as many of those fuckers as possible. I wanted them to know that you didn't fuck with Reed Security and I wanted to be sure that there wasn't another fucking person on the face of the planet that suffered because of them. As long as they were dead, I would sleep peacefully at night.

We had set them up perfectly, scared them all into gathering in one place. We had set the explosives hours earlier and now we were waiting for them all to arrive. They were running scared and they should be. They just didn't realize they were running right where we wanted them.

"Looks like that's all of them by my head count," Burg said over coms.

"You sure you don't want to press the button on this one?" Sinner asked.

"I don't give a fuck who presses the button as long as they all burn in hell," I grumbled.

"Fuck me, this is gonna be fun," Sinner's happy voice rang through the line. Sinner was always the fun one to be around. Never had I met a man who had more fun killing people than that man. Not that he liked to kill people, but he liked to play with new toys. So, if he wanted the honors, he could have it. I just wanted to watch the show.

"Alright, ladies and gentlemen," Sinner said in an announcer's voice. "Take your seats. The show will start in five, four, three, two, one, mark."

I watched through my binoculars, but nothing happened. "Sinner, what the fuck? When you say *mark*, the building is supposed to explode."

"I pressed the fucking button. I don't know what happened," he said in confusion.

"Did you press the right button?" Burg asked.

"Of course I did. What kind of moron do you think I-"

Bright flames burst into the sky as the building was ripped apart from the force of the explosives. The sound was deafening and there would most likely be cops and firemen crawling all over here within minutes.

"Our job's done. Let's hit the road." I could hear Burg's breath huffing through the mic, telling me he was already heading to the truck. I double timed it back and met up with Sinner and Burg, hopping in the van and taking off just as we heard the sirens in the distance.

"What happened?" Burg asked Sinner.

"Uh, well, you see there was this one button that was red and then the other was black."

"You pressed the wrong fucking button."

"Well, wouldn't you think the red button would stand for fire? I mean, come on, red means danger."

"Red also means stop," I informed him.

"Whatever, the job's done, the bad guys are dead, and now we can get back to our fucking lives," Sinner grumbled.

"It's a shame we didn't get to personally take them all out," Burg sighed. "I gotta say, I would have loved to have strangled every last fucking one of them."

"I just want to get home to Vanessa," I said grimly. "I don't want to be in a fucking war where I have to worry about her being hurt. I've had enough of that for one lifetime."

"Have you talked to her?" Burg asked.

I nodded, but didn't elaborate. I didn't want to go into details about how torn up I was every time I heard the sadness in her voice. I couldn't make that pain go away and I couldn't make her forget that she might still have her baby if it weren't for the assholes that took her from our home. It would take her awhile to get past all that and for us to move on with our lives.

"I'm fucking glad that Meghan wasn't around for all this. I was so pissed when she told me she was going on vacation with her mom for a couple of weeks. It was the best fucking thing she ever did."

"I'm pretty sure that if Cara had been taken with Maggie, Kate, and Vanessa, that she would be catatonic by now," Sinner said. "I don't think she would have survived being taken again. I hate that I'm not there for her now. Alec told me that she's been having panic attacks a lot since they've been at the safe house. She doesn't have her medicine with her."

"She has Kate with her. I'm sure Kate is doing everything she can to help her out," I tried to reassure him. Although, I wasn't sure how Kate was doing, so it was very possible that Kate was in just as bad shape. I hoped that wasn't true though.

Chapter Nineteen

CHRIS

"I just heard from Sebastian," Cash said as he walked in the room. We were holed up in the safe house, planning our last attack against Slasher. Once he was killed, it would all be over. "They finished off the Night Kings. They're headed back to the safe house now."

"They got away clean?" I asked.

"Not a trace left behind. We need to do the same. Let's finish this so we can all get back to our lives."

"The property is pretty isolated," Jerrod Lockhart said, pointing to the map where we would be headed. His team was going in with us on this one. Ed Markinson, Brock Patton, and Scottie Thacker made up the four man team and would give us six men in total with Cash and I. It should be a pretty simple job. "It looks like he headed out there alone. We scoped out the property and there are two issues. First is the river. If we do this right, he won't be able to get to the river. Second, the house is built into the side of a hill. We'll have to position one person on top of the hill, but we have no idea if there's an escape built into the hill. With him being a drug runner, I would bet that he chose that house specifically because of what it could offer for hiding. We scoped out the property for an escape hatch, but if there is one, it's hidden well."

"Alright, Ed, you'll take the hilltop. Shout out any movements as you see them. Brock, you'll cover the east side of the house. Scottie, you've got the west side," Cash said, pointing at the map. "Jerrod, you'll cover the river. Chris and I will take the front of the house. We'll move out at dark. Gear up."

"We've got movement inside. He's headed toward the southwest corner of the house," Brock said over coms.

"Shit. He's headed for the hill. Any chance he knows we're here?" I asked.

"Anything's possible. We came in clean. Don't know how it would have happened, but I'm sure he's prepared for a lot of shit as a drug runner," Cash said next to me.

"Then let's go take him out before he has a chance to escape," I grumbled.

I needed to get this fucker. He was mine and everyone knew it. It was the reason that I came here with Cash's team instead of heading to Pittsburgh with the rest of Reed Security.

"Moving in," Cash said beside me as we crept through the darkness. He motioned for me to approach the east window as he looked in through the west. It was difficult to see in the dark, but one thing was very clear. Slasher knew that we were coming and he was fucking prepared. There were small boxes on the support beams of the house with wires leading out of them to the next box.

"Move out!" Cash shouted as we turned and ran from the house. Within seconds, the house exploded, sending pieces of the house flying into the night. Cash and I were thrown from the force of the explosion and when I landed, covering my head, I could see Ed being thrown from the hilltop, rolling down the side.

"Anyone hurt?" I could hear Jerrod's ragged breathing as he ran toward us. He had been stationed at the river and was farthest from the blast.

"Just a bruised ego," Scottie grumbled over the mic.

"All good here," Brock answered.

"Fuckers coming out of the side of the hill," Ed said forcefully. "Damn, I think I fucked up my ankle. He's headed for the river."

I was on my feet and running before I could think twice. The plan was simple. Kill. I had to finish this. There was nothing I wanted more than to take out that fucker. I pushed myself faster and faster as I ran across the property. I could see him in the distance running for a small boat. The sound of my own breath in my ears was accompanied by the other men that were running behind me.

He was in the boat now, starting the engine. It was now or never. I pulled my weapon from my leg holster and dropped to one knee, lining up my sights. "Come on, come on," I whispered as he moved around. When he stood straight, I unloaded my clip into him. His body jerked and he fell from the boat into the water. Standing, I ran for the boat, hoping to see his body floating in the water. It was too dark to see anything, but one thing was clear, he was nowhere to be seen.

"Fuck!" I yelled as I flung my cowboy hat to the ground and ran my fingers through my hair. "He's fucking gone," I said as Cash ran up beside me.

"You got him. For all we know, he's fucking drowning as we speak."

"That's not fucking good enough. I need to know that he's dead."

"We can't stick around for long. That explosion is going to send at least a few departments out here. We can't be here when they arrive."

I swiped my cowboy hat off the ground and smashed it onto my head. "I know," I grumbled. The rest of the guys joined us as we watched the water for any sign of Slasher emerging.

Brock held up a device and wiggled it in front of me. "This is how he knew we were coming. He probably saw us scoping out the property yesterday."

"What is it?"

"Trophy Cam. Hunters use these all the time. It signals a phone whenever it takes a picture. He would have pictures from yesterday and we didn't see them because they're made to blend in with the trees."

"Fuck. That's why he was so prepared. He fucking knew we would be coming for him and he was trying to kill us off in the process."

Sirens could be heard in the distance and I sighed.

"We have to go. Sorry, Chris, but we can't wait any longer. We'll reach out to our contacts and find out if any bodies wash up."

He placed a hand on my shoulder in consolation, but it did little to make me feel better. How would Ali ever feel safe not knowing if Slasher was still out there? We all double timed it back to the trucks and tore out of there before we could be spotted. After packing up our shit and closing up the safe house, we hit the road for the long drive back to Iowa.

Seeing Ali sleeping in bed was the most beautiful sight I had seen in a long time. It was all over. In the morning, we would be heading home and starting our lives all over again. Only this time, we would be together and things would be fucking perfect. I slipped into bed beside her and pulled her in close. God, I was hard just thinking about being next to her. I wanted her so bad.

"Hey," she said sleepily, rolling over and snuggling into my chest. "Is it all done?"

"Yeah, baby. It's all done." I kissed her on the head and ignored the fact that I was lying to her. Until I knew whether or not Slasher was a threat, I wouldn't be telling her anything. I didn't want her worrying. I just wanted her to be able to move on with her life.

"Thank God. I can't tell you how glad I am to hear that. What do we do now?"

"Now, we go home and live life."

"It just doesn't seem real. I feel like I'm going to wake up in the morning and I'll be back with the Blood Devils."

"That'll never happen again. We took them all out."

She snuggled closer to me and ran her hand up and down my chest. I closed my eyes and let out a deep breath that I seemed to have been holding for the last seventeen years. I had thought my life was fantastic when I joined the military and afterwards, but that was all just fluff. Stuff that I had to go through to get back to the man I always wanted to be. The man that had Ali by my side. I realized now how foolish it was to think that I could walk away from her all those years ago. She was always meant to be mine.

"I talked to Kate. She said I could apply for a job at her clinic. Just think, I could have a job and it'll be all mine."

"I thought you had a job before?"

"I did, but it was tainted. It was never really mine. Slasher took all the money I had and I was never free to go on my own. Now I can get a car and drive myself to work. It's just going to be so different."

"Are you going to put Axel in school?"

"I don't know. He's never really gone to school, so I don't know if he would want to after all these years. I know he's really smart and he could get into a good school if he wanted."

"I hate to say this, but part of me hopes he wants to stick around here. I just want to soak up all the time with him that I can."

"I know, but he needs to have his own life now."

"I know," I said around the lump in my throat. I hated that she was right. I wasn't mad at her. When I first found out that Axel was my kid, I didn't want to believe her because that would mean that I had walked away and left her all alone. But I couldn't go back and change the past. All I could do now was spend as much time with them as possible.

"I guess that Axel and I will need to find a place to stay when we get back," she said hesitantly.

"Ali, I already told you that you were staying with me."

"I know, but I...I think maybe I want to get my own place. I was with Slasher for so long, not living on my own. I kind of want to know what that's like."

I pulled back so I could look at her. "Ali, you can always come and go as you please with me. But I don't want to miss out on any more time with the two of you. I want it to be our house and you can do anything you want to it. Make it your own, but please, don't go stay somewhere else."

"Okay," she said quietly. "We'll stay with you."

I pulled her back into me and rested my chin against her head. I was damn lucky to have this woman and there wouldn't be a day that I forgot that.

Chapter Twenty

ALISON

I was so nervous as we pulled up to Chris's house. It was strange to think that this was all over. Could we really just go home with Chris and pretend that we were one big happy family? I mean, I loved Chris more than anything, but it just seemed like this was all moving too fast.

"Hey, stop thinking so much. This is going to be good."

He shut off the engine and stepped out of his truck. Axel and I followed with our meager belongings to the front door that was barely on its hinges.

"Oh, my gosh. Is this from the Night Kings?" I asked.

"Yeah, Sebastian hired his friend to come around and fix up all our houses, but it's going to take time. I'll board up what I need to and put up a new door." He turned to Axel and did a chin lift thing. "Maybe you can help me with that, kid."

"Sure," Axel nodded, trying to hide his excitement. "I mean, I don't really know how to fix anything."

"That's okay. There was a time I didn't know either."

He pushed the bullet-ridden door open and we walked inside. It looked like a war-zone. There were holes in the walls and broken glass on the floor. As much as he told me to stop worrying about it, I couldn't help but feel terrible. Chris took my hand and squeezed it tightly in his. The last time I had been here, I was in so much pain and so out of it that I didn't really get to take in the place.

"So, our room is upstairs," he told Axel. "There is one more room, but there's also the basement if you want." The house was a split level with the living room and kitchen on the main level and a bathroom and two bedrooms upstairs. Off the kitchen, there were stairs to the lower level that had another bedroom and a family room. "We can make that into your own space. Look around and tell me where you'd like to stay."

Axel's eyes drifted to mine in confusion. "You mean, like choose a room?"

"Yeah. You're almost a man. You need your own space. We haven't talked about what you want to do when you get out of school, but if you stay here, I'm sure you'll want space of your own. Like I said, check it out and let me know."

Axel swallowed hard and looked right at Chris. "Thank you. That means a lot to me."

Chris nodded and then pulled me toward the kitchen. "So, this is where you'll be most of the time. I like breakfast by six and lunch precisely at noon. Dinner no later than five-thirty."

"Excuse me?" What the fuck was he getting at? "Chris, I didn't come here to be your own personal chef."

"I know," he laughed. "I'm just fucking with you. Glad to see you still have that temper." I narrowed my eyes at him just to be sure he was telling me the truth. He held up his hands as he walked backwards. "I swear. I was just messing around. Come on, let's get your shit put in our room."

I followed him up the stairs to the master bedroom. It was huge and there was a hallway with closet space on both sides for hanging clothes. He had exactly three things hanging up.

"As you can see, this comes with plenty of closet space. Feel free to fill it to the brim."

"Sure. When I get a job," I said morosely.

"Hey, what's mine is yours. It doesn't matter if we're married or not. I will always provide for you and Axel."

"I don't need a man to provide for me," I snapped. I immediately felt bad. It was a stupid reaction brought on by years of being told what to do. I just wanted freedom now and not to feel like I was shackled to someone.

"You want to tell me what the fuck is wrong?" He asked as his eyes darkened into a lethal glare.

"I'm sorry," I sighed. "I just want to be sure that you understand how this will be if I live here. I won't be told where to go or what to do and part of that is not relying on you for everything."

"Have I given you the impression that I want you at my beck and call? Or that I'll expect you to sit back and be the good little housewife?"

I bit my lip as I shook my head.

"Good. Because I just want to make up for lost time. I wasn't there for so long and no matter what you tell me, I need to know that I'm taking care of my family. If you want to go back to work, go ahead. I'll make sure that you have a car to get where you're going. You don't need to get anything approved by me first or come to me for consent. This is our home and if you want to redecorate the whole fucking thing, you do whatever you want so you feel comfortable."

I had to bite my tongue to keep myself from letting the tears fall. I felt like such a bitch. He had been so good to me from the moment he found me and I was treating him like shit.

"Hey, I know what that asshole did and how he treated you. I just want to make sure that for the rest of your life, you get everything you deserve and more. I can't believe I made it so fucking long without you in my life, but I can tell you this, it's been fucking lonely without you."

He wrapped his arms around me and pulled me in close. I let my eyes drift closed as I listened to the steady beat of his heart. It had always calmed me so much. Even if I didn't want to admit it, I needed Chris more than ever. I was lost here, going out on my own for the first time. Axel would adjust fine, but I wasn't so sure about myself. I was snapping at Chris like he was mistreating me.

He took my hand and showed me the bathroom, which had a huge tub for soaking. I would definitely be using that soon. Tonight, if possible.

"So, what do you think?" It was an innocent enough question, but I saw the lust in his eyes. He wanted me more than ever now that we were in his bedroom, but I still had to make an appointment to be checked out.

"I think it's great. I'm definitely going to be soaking tonight."

"Go for it."

His hands slid down my body until he was cupping my ass, pulling me against his erection. He dropped his lips to my neck and nipped at the exposed skin. I felt his tongue leaving wet trails over my skin and I groaned, wanting him more than I ever had before. "Chris," I moaned.

"God, I want you." His lips found mine and soon he was taking my breath away, kissing me with all the pent up aggression of a man that had gone without for seventeen years. I doubted he had, but he kissed me like it had been that long. His tongue stroked mine aggressively. He bit at my lip and slid his hands down my pants. I pushed against his chest, needing him to stop this.

"Chris, we can't. I need to be checked out first."

He groaned and kissed me again. "I really wish we didn't have to wait."

"I know," I breathed out as he continued to kiss my neck and then nibble on my ear. "God, I want that too, but we have to be safe."

He pulled himself back from me and stood a good two feet away breathing hard. "I'm going to take Axel to get some shit and fix up what I can. You go take a bath. And you better be fully dressed at bedtime, otherwise, I won't be able to help myself."

He walked away, leaving me shaky and needy. This was the right choice though. I couldn't risk giving him an STD if Slasher had given me something. He had been with enough whores that my odds weren't that great. I stripped down and sank into a warm bath that I ran and tried to forget about everything. There were so many new things going on in my life and it was too stressful to deal with tonight. I was just happy that I was with Chris again and was safe at last.

A week later, I was on top of the world. I had gone into Kate's office and talked with her about her job offer. I informed her that I was waiting on my STD tests. She reassured me that with all the treatments nowadays for STDs she didn't think it would be a problem. She offered me the job and said I could start next week. I was over the moon to finally be getting back to some sense of normalcy. This was the first time that I would not only be able to have a job, but keep my paycheck and come and go as I pleased. I didn't have anyone picking me up or taking me home. I could stop at the grocery store and I could go shopping for clothes if I wanted. This was my life and this was just the beginning of taking it all back.

After I left her office, I was just pulling up to Chris's house when I got the second great piece of news. My test results were back and I was clean. I was shocked to say the least. How a man like Slasher managed to stay STD free over the years was beyond me, but I was just happy that he hadn't passed anything along to me. Without going inside, I decided to make a special trip to Victoria's Secret. Chris had given me his card to go shopping for clothes until I started earning money of my own. I hadn't used it very much, but I thought he would appreciate me spending a little on something for tonight. I planned to make it worth his while.

It was a little difficult for me to figure out what to get. I was no longer a spring chicken. I mean, I wasn't old by any means, but I was no longer at the age that I could get away with wearing something that a twenty something would wear. Or at least, I didn't feel comfortable wearing it. I felt too long like I was Slasher's whore and while I wanted to feel sexy, I wanted to stay away from anything that screamed slut. I might change my mind after some more time, but for now, I just wanted to feel sexy for Chris.

When I got home, I was practically jumping up and down with excitement until I realized that I had a kid and I couldn't really have sex with him in the house. That would be weird. I didn't want to hold back my first time with Chris and I didn't want to be thinking about if my son might walk through the door at any minute.

I dialed Chris's number and waited for him to answer.

"Hey, baby. What's going on?"

"Uh, Chris?" I was so nervous about saying that I wanted to have sex with him tonight that I just breathed heavily into the phone for a moment.

"What's wrong? How fast do I need to be there?" His voice was urgent and demanding. I shook my head as I realized how ridiculous I was being. We were both adults. I could talk to him about this.

"Nothing's wrong," I finally said. "I just got the results back from the doctor and I'm clean."

There was silence on the other end.

"Chris?"

"Sorry," he said, clearing his throat. "I had to find somewhere to be alone. I've got a bit of a situation over here."

"Oh, I'm sorry. I didn't mean to interrupt."

"No, baby. I mean you just gave me a bit of a situation, if you catch my drift."

"Oh...oh!" I said as I caught on to what he was saying. "Sorry about that. I was calling because I was thinking that tonight we could...get reacquainted."

"Damn straight we are."

"But we have Axel and if he's there, I won't be able to really let go."

"So, you want me to get rid of the kid?"

"Crap. That sounds so bad, doesn't it?"

"Not at all. I've got it covered. Just be ready when I get home tonight, because you won't be coming up for air until I've had my way with you all night."

Shivers ran down my spine and I smiled. "Promises, promises."

"You bet your sweet ass it's a promise."

He hung up before I could say anything else. I bit my lip as I remembered what it had been like when we were teenagers. It had to be better now, right? I mean, he was older and had more experience. Surely, it would be a lot better. I shook those thoughts from my head as I went to the bathroom to prepare for the night.

After showering, I pulled out a new razor to use on my legs. I wanted to be as smooth as a baby's bottom tonight. I winced as I nicked myself several times and decided by the fourth cut to use some oil. I rubbed it down my legs and started again, getting a much closer shave this time. I couldn't believe how smooth my legs felt. When I was done with my legs, I decided that maybe I should do a bit more shaving for him. Maybe make my downstairs look just as pretty.

I rested my foot on the ledge in the bathtub and did my best to oil myself up. God, I really didn't want any cuts down there. That would probably be painful. I had trimmed, but never shaved before. I hadn't ever wanted Slasher to think that I was trying to entice him into my bed. I pulled the skin as taut as possible and started shaving. I was surprised at how often I had to rinse out the shaver. There was a ton of hair!

I was also finding it difficult to shave as much as I wanted. I was too nervous about cutting myself. Adjusting my footing to get a better, wider stance, I turned to face the shower curtain and faced the spray against the wall. Facing this way, I was able to spread my legs further apart and I didn't worry as much about cutting myself.

The shower curtain was yanked back and I jerked up in surprise as I held my pussy lips apart. The shock of seeing Chris standing in front of me had me trying to quickly put my legs together. I stumbled, knocking the oil over and slipped as I tried to regain my footing. I crashed down into the base of the tub, landing on my hip and just barely keeping the razor from landing on my face.

"Oh," I groaned as I rolled over in the tub and tried to sit up.

"Are you okay?" I heard him rumble with laughter. He was fucking laughing at me. I was doing all this for him and he found this funny.

"Just help me up," I grumbled.

"What were you doing?"

"What did it look like? I was shaving."

"Yeah, but why?"

"Because," I said nervously. "I thought you might like it. I didn't know how you...prefer your women. There's no way I'm getting a wax, but I thought this might be nice too."

I stared at the tub floor and wished that I could sink down the drain to keep him from staring at me any longer. Not only was I naked, but he had caught me spreading myself wide open. Just the way every girl wants the man she loves to see her after seventeen years. Not to mention that I had a kid and nothing about my body looked like it had when I was seventeen. I had stretch marks and belly flab that just didn't want to go away. It was fine in clothes, hardly noticeable. But naked? That was a different story. And not just naked, but in the harsh light of the bathroom where everything was more visible.

"Come on out." He handed me a towel and I wrapped it around myself, unable to look him in the eye. Not that I could anyway. That damn cowboy hat he always wore was blocking me from seeing his dark, stormy eyes.

He led me over to the bed and pushed me down on it, then opened my towel, which I immediately tried to pull closed.

"Wait. Not yet."

"Hold still, woman."

"No. I had a plan. It wasn't supposed to happen like this. I have lingerie and I was supposed to be sexy."

"You are sexy. Damn sexy and you don't need fucking lingerie. Not that I won't let you put it on for me, but you don't need to be filling your head with that crap. Now, I'm going to shave that pretty pussy and then I'm going to eat every inch of it until you're screaming my name. Then we'll see about the lingerie and the what happens from there. Got it?"

There wasn't really a question in there. He was just telling me how it was going to be and I was supposed to go along for the ride. He stood up and walked into the bathroom, coming back with a straight razor and the oil I had been using in the shower. He pulled me to the edge of the bed and knelt down in front of me.

Oh, God. This was so embarrassing. He was going to be looking at me up close and personal, and while I knew that happened during sex, this was different. I wouldn't be distracted by the feelings going on in my body and he would be concentrating on not my pleasure, but trimming the hairs from my lips. Was it ugly? I thought so, but then I hadn't had a satisfying sexual experience since the last time I was with him.

He spread my legs and I immediately pulled the covers over my face to hide my embarrassment.

"What are you doing?"

"The light is in my eyes," I lied.

I heard him chuckle and I sighed. I couldn't slip anything past him. I felt his rough hands start massaging the oil into my trimmed hair and then after a few moments, I felt the cool steel of the blade against my skin. To say that it was a little terrifying would be an understatement. Having a person with a sharp object that close to your delicate areas was not something that I really thought I would ever have to experience. I forced myself to take deep, long breaths to keep myself from flinching. Every time he pulled my skin, I wondered if he was almost done yet. Then his fingers slid lower and massaged around my ass hole. I flung the covers off and sat up immediately.

"What are you doing?"

"Shaving you."

He pushed me back down, but I sat back up. "I realize that, but why are you shaving there?"

"Because when I fuck you, I want to see that tight hole and hope that someday you'll let me in there." The glint in his eyes had me blushing like a schoolgirl. Not knowing what to say, I laid back down and pulled the blanket over my head again. God, this was so embarrassing. Why did I feel worse now than when we were teenagers?

"Relax, Ali. You're fucking beautiful. You don't have anything to hide from. I like staring at your pussy."

I bit back my smile as I continued to hide under the covers. When a warm rag started wiping me down, I finally started to relax. He was done. But then I felt his hot breath on me and I jerked my knees closed. Or, I tried to, but they hit the sides of his head and then his hands were pushing my thighs apart. With a flick of his tongue, my whole body tensed. It felt so good, but I wasn't prepared for it. I hardly remembered what it was like to make love to a man and Chris had never gone down on me when we were kids.

This was my first time and suddenly, I was filled with all these fears. Would I taste good? What if he didn't like it? What if I smelled? That area wasn't exactly the cleanest area of the body. This was gross. I couldn't do this. I scurried back on the bed, completely ignoring what his tongue had already started doing to me. His strong hands latched onto my ankles and pulled me back to the edge of the bed. I squirmed and tried to get away, but his grip was too strong. He flung the covers off me and looked at me intently under his cowboy hat. Damn, he was sexy.

"Baby, this is happening. There's nothing I want more than to taste you on my tongue. Stop moving away from me so I can sink my tongue into your sweet honey."

"But it's gross!" I shouted. "I'm sorry, Chris, but I can't do this. I've never...and we...what if you don't like it?"

He leaned forward on his elbows until he was just inches from my face. He ran his nose up and down mine before placing a sweet kiss on my lips. "Baby, there's no way I wouldn't like the taste of you. All these years, I've been dreaming of what it would be like to have you in my arms again. To know the taste of your skin again. I was just a fumbling kid when we were together, but now I need to know what I was missing out on. Trust me, you won't be thinking about anything but how much pleasure I'm giving you when I get started."

I let out a slow breath as he slid down my body, trailing wet kisses along my skin. I closed my eyes and concentrated on the feel of his slick tongue against my now smooth skin. His tongue circled my clit, making me pulse into his tongue. My breathing was erratic to say the least. I felt like I was on the verge of a total body breakdown as he lapped and nibbled at my pussy. When his tongue thrust inside me, I came undone, shattering in his arms as he drove me higher and higher until I couldn't feel a thing.

I heard the clank of his belt as he undid it and let my eyes slide open just enough to see him ripping his shirt off his muscled chest. The way his biceps flexed and his abs crunched had my pussy clenching in need. I couldn't wait any longer for him. I sat up and slid the zipper down on his jeans and shoved his pants down just enough for his cock to spring free. I didn't need him completely bare. I just needed his cock now.

His hand moved to his head to remove his hat, but I shook my head. "Leave it on. It's sexy."

He grinned and slid his cock inside me. His hands were under my ass, lifting me up to him as he took me hard and fast. This was nothing like when we were kids. His thrusts were controlled and hard. He maneuvered my body like he had been doing it for years. He tilted my hips further and pleasure roared through me as he hit me at a new angle. I wrapped my legs around his back and pulled him in tight to me. He bucked into me like a cowboy on a bucking bronco. Holy fuck, it was hot.

His shaggy hair slipped out of his hat and sweat slipped down his cheeks. His jaw was clenched tight and I realized that he was trying to hold back. "Let go," I panted. "Fuck me hard."

"I wanted this to be different. I wanted to make love to you."

"You are. Now take me."

His eyes grew impossibly dark as he pounded into me, holding my legs tight to him. Each thrust was pushing me higher up the bed, but he kept me from scooting too far from him.

"God, I waited forever for this, Ali. I never thought I would have you again."

I groaned as he pushed inside me one more time and jerked as he spilled himself inside me. The feel of him jerking inside me pushed me over the edge again. My nails dug into his forearms as I came hard around him. He collapsed onto me, smothering me under his humongous body, but I didn't care. I loved the feel of him on top of me. I pushed up his cowboy hat so I could look into his eyes. What I saw filled me with so many feels. There was love, need, hunger, and what looked like a question.

"What?" I asked as I ran my hand down the side of his face.

"I don't want to spend another day without you by my side, Ali. I want you to marry me. Say that you will."

"Don't you think we should take some time to get to know each other again? It's been so long."

"I don't need another fucking minute to get to know who you are. You've been a part of my life for as long as I can remember. Just because I was fucking stupid and walked away doesn't mean that you ever weren't a part of me. I know that the woman you are today is a hell of a lot stronger than when we were kids. I know that you're a great mom to our son. And I know that you still crave me the way I crave you. The rest will work itself out."

To say I had stars in my eyes would be an understatement. I looked up at him like he was my life. And he was. Besides Axel, he was the only man who ever owned my heart and he would be the only one that ever did.

"I'll marry you," I said quietly. The grin on my face said it all.

He pulled me up onto the bed with him and held me in his arms. "That's all I needed to know. So, Vegas this weekend?"

I snorted and looked back at him. "Are you crazy? You ask me to marry you and then you want a quick wedding? People are going to think I'm pregnant."

"With any luck, you are now. I want to fill you with so many babies that you'll be popping out one a year."

"One a year?" I asked incredulously. "I hate to tell you this, but I'm already thirty-five. The chances of me giving you any more than one baby are slim."

"You have plenty of child-bearing years left in you," he grinned.

"That may be, but I don't want to just start popping out kids. I want some time with just you and me."

His face fell slightly and I knew that he was thinking about all the time he missed out on with Axel. I rested my hand on his chest, feeling the steady thump underneath my hand. "Hey, I know that you missed out on so much with Axel and I'm not saying that I don't want to have kids with you, but I just want you for now. I want some time with just the two of us. I want to be able to take you to bed whenever I want and not worry about the baby waking us up."

His eyes softened and he kissed me hard. "I'll wait if that's what you want, but I want at least one more kid with you."

"I make no promises," I said hastily, "but I won't prevent you from trying every night if it means that much to you."

He kissed me hard again and slid between my legs. I could feel his erection pressing against me, prodding at my entrance. I couldn't believe he was hard already.

"We just finished like two minutes ago. How can you be ready again?"

"I've been fucking hard since you came back into my life. It's gonna take a lot of fucking to calm him down."

I leaned in to kiss him and then jerked back. "What about Axel? Where is he?"

Chris grinned at me. "I told him I was going to be fucking his mother all night and if he didn't want to be around to hear it, he had to go hang out at Ice's house for the night."

"You did not!"

"Baby, he's practically a man. If he hasn't had sex yet, he's thinking about it."

"Yeah, but I can guarantee he wasn't thinking about his mother having sex."

He shrugged. "Maybe it'll make him rethink having sex for another year. Think of all the sex talks it'll save you."

"That's disgusting."

"Don't worry, baby. I'll have a talk with him and make sure he knows everything he needs to about sex."

"You mean, how to be responsible and make sure that he's emotionally ready."

"Right," he chuckled. "That's exactly what I was going to talk to him about."

I went to protest, but he covered my mouth with his and took me again for the rest of the night.

Chapter Twenty-One

CHRIS

"Any word on Slasher's body?" I asked Cap as I walked into his office the next day.

"Nothing yet. According to Sean, they've been dragging the river, but no sign of him yet."

"Dammit." I hit the arm of the chair I just sat in and leaned my head back, blowing out a deep breath.

"Relax, man. You shot him. You saw him fall in the river. You were there for a good ten minutes. He didn't surface. What are the chances he survived?"

"Would that be good enough for you if it were Maggie?"

"No, I suppose not," he said as he ran his finger across his lips. "Look, I wish there was more I could do, but if I start asking too many questions, it'll look suspicious. We got away clean, but I don't want to make any waves. Sean's going to keep in contact with the department down there as much as possible. They promised to keep him in the loop. Right now, all we can do is sit and wait, but they may never find his body. The Tennessee River is large and who knows where his body would end up."

I nodded, knowing he was right. I just wished I had some closure. It would make me feel better about everything.

"Hey, Chris. Your kid is about to take on Knight," Ice grinned as he walked into the room. I stood from my chair so fast that it went flying backwards.

"What the fuck are you talking about?"

"He's down in the ring. Said that he wanted to start training. Did you know that kid is going to enlist?" Ice shook his head and tapped his head. "Hard headed just like his old man."

This was not happening. Knight was a ruthless killer and there was no way I was letting him in the ring with my kid. I stormed down to the training area and slammed into the room. Axel was loosening up and Knight was wrapping his hands. Fuck no. There was no way this was happening.

"Axel," I barked as I walked across the room. "What the fuck do you think you're doing?"

"Training," he said firmly, getting back to his warm up.

I glared at Jules, who was outside the ring, talking to him about different defensive moves. What the hell was going on here? When did everyone just start doing shit without talking to me first? This was my kid they were putting up against a killer.

"Jules, you want to tell me why the fuck you're giving my kid pointers?"

"Oh, sorry, man. Did you want to do it?" he smirked.

I growled low at him and walked right up to him, pushing him back a step. "You fucking know that he shouldn't be in the ring."

"Relax," Jules brushed off my concern. "Knight's not gonna kill him. I hope."

"You fucking hope? What the hell is wrong with you?"

"Look, if it was anyone else, you would say that this'll show you what the kid is made of. Here's your opportunity to find out."

My eyes widened comically. Was I really fucking hearing this right? "Let Knight take out his frustrations on some other kid. Not mine."

"Let's do this," Knight said, jumping up and down as he got in fight mode.

"Chris, chill." I looked at my son, that still called me Chris, and tried to put myself in his shoes. If he was going to do this, if he was going to train to be in the military, I wanted him to be the best of the best. I couldn't train him. I would be too easy on him. Knight really was the best option for training him. I just hated that everyone else seemed so relaxed about it.

"Knight, you fucking hurt my kid and I'll put a bullet in your head."

"Sure, Chris. I'll let you think you're that good." He rolled his eyes, which pissed me off even more. I took a step back from the ring and watched as the fight began. The first round was over before it began. Knight took one well placed punch and Axel was down on the mat. The second round was slightly better. Axel got in a few swings before Knight knocked him down. The third round had me holding my head in my hands, praying that Knight didn't fucking kill my kid. Blood was dripping from his face and he had a slight limp. I couldn't watch anymore.

"Oh shit," Ice said next to me. I didn't want to look. Whenever someone said *oh shit* and Knight was around, it was usually because Knight was about to go into kill mode. He wouldn't really take things that far would he? I looked up and my brows furrowed. It wasn't Knight that everyone was looking at. It was Axel. He had a crazy look on his face that I knew all too well. It was the same look I got in my eyes when I knew exactly how shit was going to end.

Knight stepped forward with all the confidence he normally had, but then Axel stiffened and somehow I knew it was all over. Knight was being too cocky and went at him with all the intensity that he bottled up during the fight, and Axel just watched him come. He was patient and I saw him calculating Knight's moves. Knight spun, swinging his leg to kick Axel in the chest, but Axel saw it coming and grabbed his leg, slamming his elbow down into Knight's knee. For the first time ever, I saw Knight fall to the ground, Axel taking him down with his body weight on top of Knight. He rolled back, putting himself behind Knight and wrapped his legs around Knight's neck, pushing himself off the ground to give himself leverage. Knight couldn't get his hands anywhere near Axel's head and with his leg fucked, there wasn't much he could do.

I watched as Knight struggled for control, struggled to break the hold, but he was done. His hand slammed down on the mat as he tapped out. The whole fucking room was silent as Knight gasped for breath and Axel took in deep breaths next to him.

"Holy fucking shit," Ice whispered. "Your kid just took out Knight."

I nodded, unable to say anything else.

"Where the fuck did you learn to do that, kid?" Knight asked as he stood, limping on one leg.

"What? Did you think I was just a pussy and didn't know what I was doing?" Axel asked.

"Well...yeah. Fuck, I didn't know you could fight."

"Never been trained," Axel responded. "But I've been beat on enough to know that you watch and learn the other guy's moves. You wait for your moment and you strike. I honestly didn't think it would happen here, but I guess I got lucky."

"You're one hell of a fighter, kid. You come back every day and train with me and you'll be a better fighter than me some day."

They shook hands and I still stood there completely fucking shocked. I didn't know what the hell just happened, but I was damn proud.

Knight limped over to me with a rare grin on his face. "Your kid's not bad."

"Tell me something. Did he really take you down or did you let him take you down?"

"A little of both," he shrugged. "I was planning on letting him beat me. You know, give him some confidence. The kid has moves though and I had let my guard down. I was just planning to see what he would do. Lesson learned." He slugged me in the arm and headed off for the locker room.

When Axel walked over to me with a bloody grin, I winced, wondering what Ali would say to me.

"Relax, I've had worse," he said as he rinsed water around in his mouth.

That didn't exactly ease my mind. It did just the opposite. Now I was fucking pissed that he had had a worse beating than that.

"I don't get it. If you could fight like that, why didn't you try to get away sooner?"

He shook his head slightly and looked away. "Don't kid yourself. Knight let me win. But it was different with Slasher. I would have tried harder if I thought it would have made a difference, but there were always other people hanging around. Even if I had been able to take him out, I wouldn't have gotten very far. We got lucky that night we escaped. If even one of those guys hadn't been totally fucking stoned, we wouldn't have made it out of there alive."

I placed my hand on his shoulder and squeezed tight. "You're never gonna have to deal with that fucking shit again. I swear it."

"I know. Why do you think I want to train so badly? I'll never allow myself to be put in that position again."

"So, what are you thinking? You want to join the military? Because you know I would send you to college if you wanted."

"I know," he nodded. "But I have something else in mind."

"Yeah? What's that?"

"I, uh...I want to be a SEAL."

"A SEAL."

I stared at him, gauging the seriousness of his expression. There was no wavering or uncertainty. He was fucking serious. I nodded.

"Alright, then, You have a lot of fucking training to do and we'll make sure you get there. It's gonna be fucking tough, but if you stick with it, you'll be ready for BUDs."

A gleam filled his eyes, but then he frowned. "There's just one problem."

"What's that?"

"I don't know how to swim."

My head dropped back and I swore. "Fuck, I guess I know what's first on the agenda."

"Your son wants to join the most badass branch of the military and he doesn't know how to fucking swim," I said to Ali as I walked through the door of our house.

"Which branch is the most badass?" she asked curiously as she headed into the kitchen. When she came back out, she handed me a beer, which I immediately chugged.

"SEALs."

"And why are they the most badass?"

"That's some of the most intense training he'll ever have to go through. First he has to meet the basic requirements and then he has to pass BUDs training before he even makes it into the SEAL training program."

I was almost expecting fear or something in her eyes, but she just shrugged. "I'm not surprised. As soon as he met you and you started telling him about the military, he's been talking about it nonstop."

"You're not mad?"

She walked over to me and wrapped her hands around my waist. "If he becomes even half the man you are, he'll make me the proudest momma in the world."

"He's already better than either of us, Ali. He's gonna make us fucking proud by the time he's done." I rested my chin on her head and wished that I hadn't missed out on so much of his life, which Ali must have been thinking too.

"I wish that you would have raised him."

"Me too, but things work out the way they do for a reason. Who knows what kind of man I would be today if I had been raised differently. Aside from not having you and Axel in my life the last seventeen years, I'm pretty happy with the way things turned out. I have one hell of a family at my back."

"I have a feeling that things are gonna be pretty good from here on out. I'm not worried about a thing."

That was exactly the way I felt. I pressed my lips to hers and let my tongue slide in when she opened for me. This was heaven right here. I slid my hand to her hip and gripped her tightly, grinding myself against her. I needed her right now. Her moan had me tripping over myself to get her up the stairs. After a few seconds of not being able to detach myself from her and walk at the same time, I flung her over my shoulder and skipped two stairs at a time to get to the bedroom. My zipper was about to burst open and when I slid my hand under her shorts, I felt that she was already wet for me.

I set her down just inside the doorway and pressed her up against the wall inside our room. We fumbled for each other's zippers and I was sinking inside her moments later. I groaned at the feel of her tight, warm pussy surrounding my cock. Her feet were still stuck inside those damn shorts and I was still in my pants. I lifted her and let her shorts and underwear fall onto the floor and then lifted her around my waist, holding her up by the ass.

I toed off my pants and shorts and started fucking her against the wall. I could have been more romantic. I could have taken her to bed, but part of me wanted these memories spread all over the house. Just her and me and every place I fuck her flashing through my mind. I was ramming her hard when I heard the slam of a door downstairs. Ali's eyes went wide and she started shoving at me to put her down.

I grinned and shook my head slightly. There was no way I was pulling out of her right now. I held her tight as I reached over and quietly shut the door.

"I'm not having sex with you while our son is downstairs," she whispered.

"I'm not finished with you and I'm not pulling out just because our kid is here. He can take care of himself."

I pulled out and sank into her ever so slowly, rubbing my cock against her clit every time I pulled out. Her eyes were fluttering and her moaning was getting louder and louder. I put my hand over her mouth to keep the sound in, but it must not have worked because I heard footsteps on the stairs.

I flipped the lock on the door and sank into her again. She looked over at the door, chest heaving as the footsteps stopped outside our door. I thrust into her again and again, loving the little gasps she made when I shoved in hard.

"Guys?"

"Go away!" I shouted with a smile.

"How can you still be hard?" she whisper-hissed. "Your son is on the other side of the door."

"Eww. Are you guys fucking in there? Nasty." I heard his footsteps clomp down the stairs and then the front door slam. I chuckled as I looked back at a pissed off Ali.

"What?"

"He's our son and he was looking for us."

"He'll get over it," I said as I thrust in again. I nipped at her neck and licked at the salt of her skin as I took her harder and harder. "Fuck, Ali. God, I love you."

Some incoherent mumbling fell from her lips and then she was pulling on my hair and slamming her hips against mine. "Oh, God! I'm so close."

I winced in pain as she yanked harder and harder on my hair. I didn't mind a little pain during sex, but this was fucking brutal. And a total fucking turn on when I saw the pleasure filling her face. When she let out a breathy sigh, I fucking came hard and I had a flashback to coming in my shorts to that same sigh when we were kids and she was rubbing up against me. When I set her down, I had to hold her up so she didn't slide down to her ass.

"That was so wrong," she mumbled. "I can't believe I let you do that to me when our son was outside the door."

"I'm pretty sure when he has sex for the first time, he'll completely understand why I didn't let him interrupt us."

She rolled her eyes at me. "Men. You're all pigs."

"But you love me for it."

She tried to hide the smile, but the way her eyebrow was raising told me she was failing miserably. "Fine, I love you for it, but I still think it's wrong to have sex when our son is in our house."

"Well, I'll let you tell him when we'll be having sex so that he can stay away during those times."

"And when do I get a copy of this schedule?"

"Oh, you don't need one. Just assume that any time we're home, I'm going to be balls deep inside you." I stepped back, sliding out of her and watching my cum drip down her legs. "That's fucking beautiful."

"Like I said, men are pigs."

"Oh, thank God!" Axel said as he plopped down on the couch later that night. "I wasn't sure if you two would be done when I got back and I was running out of things to do."

"That's going to change as of tomorrow." I handed him some papers and crossed my arms as I stood in front of him and watched him look them over.

"I don't understand. What is this?"

"That's your training schedule. Since you've been homeschooled, I figure there's no need to put you in school now. I hired a tutor for you. You'll be waking up at five every morning for swim practice. That goes for three hours. Then you'll have a short break to eat again, and you're gonna need it. Then you'll be tutored for four hours every day and after that you'll go to train in the gym with Knight. You'll get a dinner break and you'll train some more. Your day ends at seven o'clock and you'll come back to do your homework."

Ali and I watched him as he studied the schedule. I was worried that he was having second thoughts, but then he looked up at me in question. "Are you sure this is enough training to get me into BUDs?"

"We'll start with that, kid. We'll adjust the schedule as needed, but this should set you on the right path."

"Are you okay with this, Mom?"

"Is this what you want?" Ali asked him.

"Yeah."

"You're sure? You don't want to go to college or a technical school?"

"Not a chance. This is what I want."

"Then, I guess you'd better get to bed early tonight. You have an early start to your day tomorrow. I'll have breakfast ready at four-thirty."

A faint smile touched his lips and he nodded, heading downstairs for the night. He had chosen to make the basement his own space and now that we had a plan in place, I thought that was for the best. He was going to be pushed to the limit before he even entered the military and there would be times that he really needed some room to breathe.

"This is gonna be hard on him, Ali. I just want you to know that if he really wants this, we're gonna push him hard."

"Good," she said smugly. "I'd expect nothing less from you."

Damn, I got lucky with this woman. How the hell she never blamed me for leaving and somehow still came back to me the way she did, I'll never know. But I was fucking grateful every day that she was mine again.

Chapter Twenty-Two

ALISON

I fumbled with my jewelry for the tenth time. I was so nervous about tonight. We were all getting together at a pub in town and I was going to be meeting a bunch of new people. I already knew that I got along great with Lillian, Lucy, Claire, Maggie, and Cara, but all these other people? What if they didn't think that much of me?

Chris walked up behind me, wrapping his arms around me and pulling me close. "Would you relax? It's going to be fine. Everyone's going to love you."

"It's just been...well, I've never actually had a night out with friends before. I don't know how this works."

He spun me around to face him and smiled sweetly at me. "It works like this, we go to the bar, have a few drinks, talk with our friends. If you want me to stick by your side the whole night, I will. If you want to leave early, we will. It's not a big deal."

"I know. I'm just letting my mind get carried away."

"What are you so worried about?"

"That they're going to judge me. That they'll think I'm some kind of weirdo."

"Well, let's put it this way. We're all humans and we all have our own issues. Cara has anxiety issues and I don't even know if she'll be there tonight. Lillian is...well, let's just say she gets a little creative when she drinks. You already know that Claire is a little out there. Lucy, you have to watch out for her having sex someplace that you'll see. Maggie might decide to blow something up. I don't know if you know this, but Vanessa is kind of like a sister to me. I was on her protection detail and I became close with her. Believe me, she has her own set of issues. And that's just the women I know. There are going to be a bunch of other women there that I don't know all that well. I'm sure you'll find all sorts of women that will be even more fucked up than you are in their own way. We all have our own issues that we hide from everyone. No one is going to know about yours unless you choose to tell them."

I smiled at his attempt to make me feel better and kissed him on the lips. He was still the same sweet man that I knew from when we were kids. The only difference was that he didn't like anyone to see that side of him now. His eyes were always harder around other people, like he had to keep up a persona.

"Are you sure it's alright to leave Axel here by himself?"

"He's a good kid," Chris said with a lazy grin. "He'll be fine. Besides, I'm sure he'll enjoy the freedom for a few hours."

I took a deep breath and headed out with Chris. To say that my nerves were on edge was an understatement, but I did my best to stay calm as we walked into the bar. Claire ran up to me immediately, her face shining bright as she wrapped me up in a hug. I could smell the alcohol on her already.

"I'm so glad you're here. We're going to have so much fun tonight."

I glanced at Chris and he mouthed *Do you want me to stay?* I shook my head, confident that with Claire by my side, I could weather anything.

"So, the last time I was here, I was trying to figure out how to pick up a man and Hunter was trying to give me pointers. Let's just say that didn't work out so well for me and I ended up insulting a few people."

"You seem pretty loose tonight," I said with a smile.

"Yeah, well, put a few drinks in me and I'm not quite as socially awkward as normal. But I make no guarantees that I won't embarrass you at some point tonight."

She dragged me over to a few tables where women were scattered all around. She started the introductions and I was so confused by the end that they all started laughing. There were just too many women to keep track of.

"So, do you guys normally all get together for birthdays?" I asked Claire.

"No, but with all that's happened this year, Sebastian wanted to gather all of Maggie's friends for her birthday. It's really very sweet. Did you see the cake he got her?"

I shook my head and followed the direction of her hand. There was a huge three tier cake on a table in front of the window.

"Wow. That's amazing."

"Yeah, Sebastian and Maggie have had it bad for each other since they first met."

"I got a chance to talk with Maggie when we were hiding out. She's pretty fierce. I haven't seen them. Shouldn't they be here if this is their party?"

"Knowing Maggie, she's probably following a story and Sebastian is trying to drag her back here."

Lucy made her way over to me and pulled me off to the side. "Alison, can I ask a huge favor?" Lillian and Sarah were deep in conversation, so I didn't feel bad about walking away.

"Of course."

"Hunter's been kind of a possessive asshole since all this shit went down. I want to teach him a lesson."

She bit her lip and grinned at me. Whatever she wanted made me very nervous.

"Um, I'm not sure that's a great idea."

"Please, please. It'll be fun. I promise."

I looked into her pleading eyes and found that I couldn't say no to her. She was one of my first friends and I really wanted to have some fun with her.

"You tell me what you want first and I'll think about it."

"Okay," she said excitedly. "I want you to ask the bartender to send Hunter a new drink every time his is empty. Ask him to tell Hunter that it's from Gabe."

"From Gabe? But then he'd think-" I shook my head as I laughed. "Why don't you do it?"

"Because if he sees me talking to the bartender, he'll figure out that I'm the one doing it. Pretty please with sugar on top and a cherry in the middle?" She stuck out her bottom lip as she begged me. I had to admit, it sounded kind of fun.

"Do you have a running tab?"

"Yes!" She fist pumped and then grabbed me for a tight hug. I walked over to the bar and very discreetly put in my request to the bartender. He didn't like the idea at first, but when I explained that it was a practical joke, he was all on board. I watched as he grabbed a beer, popped the top, and headed over to Hunter at the other end of the bar. When Hunter's head whipped around and he saw Gabe, he glared at him. Gabe met his eyes and gave him a chin lift, which only seemed to piss Hunter off even more.

"Drinks on me!" Lucy said to the women at our table. Lucy placed an order for shots with the bartender and a few minutes later, we were sucking down drinks and laughing hysterically at Lillian's British accent.

"So, is he a poof?" Lillian whisper-hissed to Lucy.

"I don't know, but it's fun fucking with Hunter."

"Don't you think Hunter might be a little cheesed off when he finds out you were taking the piss?"

"Taking the what?" I asked in confusion.

"It's from my British slang dictionary. It means to mock someone."

A woman came stumbling up to the table that I had met, but I couldn't remember her name. She was a blonde with wavy hair and her clothes were rather disheveled.

"Having fun, Harper?" Sarah smirked.

"Oh my gosh. Jack just pulled me into the bathroom and fucked me against the wall. It was so hot."

My face went slack as I stared at her. Anger rose up inside me. That asshole. He had just basically promised me the world and the second he sees a hot piece of ass, he's off fucking around. "Jack?"

"Yeah. It was so hot. It's been a while since we've done anything like that."

I stumbled from my seat, my chest heaving in fury. I glanced around the bar, sneering when I saw Chris stepping from the hallway that led to the bathrooms with a grin on his face. I couldn't believe that I had fallen for all his lies.

"Listen," I said, spinning around and planting my hands on my hips. I may have been a pushover before, but I wouldn't live one more second of my life like that. "You keep your hands off him. He's my man and if you touch him again, I'll scratch your fucking eyes out."

"What? Jack. My Jack," she stuttered.

"No, my Jack."

"That man," she pointed over to where Chris was talking to a man with dirty blonde hair. "Jack."

"Yes, that man. I have a kid with him. Keep your fucking hands off."

"How old is your kid?" she asked in shock.

"Sixteen."

She shook her head, not sure what to make of what I was saying. "No, that's not…I would have known. I have kids with him."

"Well, it looks like he's been making a lot of promises all around. Just stay away from him."

Her eyes turned feral and she charged at me instantly. I sidestepped her and shoved her into another table. Beer went flying and she was instantly covered.

"Alison, what the hell is going on?" Lucy asked, looking at me like I'd lost my goddamn mind.

"She's fucking Chris."

"No," Lucy said in shock.

"I just asked her. She even pointed him out."

A hard body hit mine and we went crashing into another table. She shoved me onto the top of the table. Beer soaked my shirt and nacho cheese landed in my hair.

"You slut! He's mine, so stay away from him."

I kicked her off me, aware that most everyone in the bar was staring at us now. Chris and the blonde man were charging over to us. Harper grabbed onto my hair and spun me around, but I fisted her shirt, taking her down with me as we both crashed into the birthday cake that was on the table for Maggie.

Chris and the blonde guy stood in front of us, looking down at us with angry expressions. I looked at Harper out of the corner of my eye and scowled.

"What's going on here, Harper?"

"I don't know. Why don't you tell me?" Harper sneered at the man. "I'm not the one spilling beer all over and landing in cake."

"I'm not the one fucking other men," she shouted.

All the men looked at Jack and discretely took a step back. I was confused. What was she talking about?"

"I'm not fucking anyone else," he shouted.

"Really? Because she tells me that she has a kid with you that's sixteen years old!"

"What?" I gasped. "No. I don't even know that man."

"You said Jack," she huffed as she turned to me.

"Yeah, Jack." I pointed to Chris and laughter filled the air. Harper and I looked around in confusion.

"That's not Jack. That's Chris," she laughed.

"I know his name is Chris, but people call him Jack. For Jack Daniels."

I glared up nervously at Chris, but he was smirking down at me and "Jack" had his head thrown back in laughter.

"My husband's name is Jack," Harper laughed. "That's Jack. Jack, my husband, was the one that fucked me in the bathroom." She slapped a hand over her mouth when she realized that she said that rather loud and everyone heard. A large glob of cake fell off the table and landed on my head with a plop.

I cringed and looked at her apologetically. "Oops?"

Maggie and Sebastian walked into the bar right then and I hung my head in embarrassment. I had destroyed his wife's birthday cake and it was supposed to be so special for her.

"Don't tell me you started a food fight without me." I looked up and a huge grin was on her face and her hands were braced on her hips. She walked over with Sebastian to us, an evil look on her face and scooped up some of the cake. I was waiting for her to throw it at me, but then she winked and smeared it all over Sebastian's face. I watched with my lips pulled between my teeth, trying not to laugh as Sebastian blinked slowly, trying to get the cake out of his eyes. He swiped the beer out of Chris's hand and chugged it down. Maggie chuckled as Sebastian nodded.

"I'll give you that one, Freckles, but only because it's your birthday."

She turned to Harper and me triumphantly, a sassy look on her face. My eyes widened as Sebastian scooped up a tier of the cake. I tried to warn her, but the shock of what was about to happen was too much to get the words out. She turned back to him and the whole tier of cake was shoved into her face.

He grinned at Chris and Jack. "Now this is what I call a party." He turned and walked away, taking Chris's beer with him.

Chapter Twenty-Three

CHRIS

"What the fuck?" Hunter said as he walked over to our table. "You guys have to help me out. Fucking Gabe has been sending me drinks all fucking night."

"Why would Gabe send you drinks?" I asked.

"Man, ever since he saw me fucking Lucy, I just get this feeling around him. Like he's looking for more with me."

"I don't know. I've never gotten that feeling from him," I said disbelieving.

Hunter rolled his eyes at me and stiffened. "No offense, Chris, but it's all in the muscles. You're too lean."

"Excuse me?"

"Look, I get that you're fucking deadly and that look you get on your face could make someone drop dead in two point five seconds. But next to me, you're a fucking string bean."

I tried really fucking hard to keep the grin off my face, but it was difficult. "So, you think that Gabe is hitting on you because he wants your body?"

"Well, yeah. It's fucking obvious, isn't it?"

I kept my eyes trained on Hunter as Gabe walked up behind

Hunter and rested his hand on Hunter's shoulder. "Hey, man. Everything alright?"

Hunter flinched at Gabe's touch and jerked back from him. "Fine. Everything's totally cool." His eyes flicked to mine in panic.

"You seem tense. You should get a neck massage or something." Gabe lightly touched the back of Hunter's neck, giving a light rub. "Dude, you have so much tension back here."

Hunter stumbled back, spilling his beer down the front of his shirt.

"Sorry about that, man." Gabe grinned and held up his hands in a back off gesture. "I'll buy you a new beer. Didn't mean to freak you out."

He turned and headed for the bar as Hunter plopped down in his stool across from me. "What the fuck am I going to do? You saw the way he touched me, right? You don't seriously think he wants something from me, do you? I mean, he knows I'm with Lucy."

"Maybe he's looking for a *menage* situation," Ice shrugged.

"There's no fucking way I'd do a *menage* with another dude. That's fucking disgusting."

"Hey, babe. Did I just hear you talking about a *menage*?" Lucy asked as she ran a hand along his shoulders. "Cuz that sounds kind of sexy to me." I watched as Lucy bit Hunter's earlobe and then winked over at me. She was totally fucking with him. "Chris? You game?"

I cleared my throat and shook my head. "Not me. I'm not into that. Hey, Gabe." I gave him a nod as he approached. "Lucy might be looking for a little threesome action. How do you feel about that?"

Gabe looked a little uncomfortable as he ran his hand along the back of his neck, nervously looking over at Hunter. "Uh...No offense, Lucy, but I'm not really into that. I mean, you're beautiful and all, but not really what I'm looking for." His eyes flicked back up to Hunter and for the first time, I wondered if Gabe really was fucking gay. He almost looked desperate. Like he was longing for something. Maybe something he almost had when he walked in on Lucy and Hunter?

Hunter wrapped his arm around Lucy possessively and pulled her in tight, shooting Gabe a *back off* look. Gabe cleared his throat and jerked his thumb toward the bar.

"I'm gonna go grab a beer," he muttered as he walked away.

Ali walked over to me after cleaning up in the bathroom, still trying to wipe cake from her face. I had an extra shirt in my truck that I had given to her. "How you doing?"

"Good. Your friends are nice."

Her face was red with embarrassment and she wouldn't look me in the eye.

"See? I told you it would be fine. I mean, aside from confusing me with another man and destroying the bar."

"I swear, it was a big misunderstanding. I-"

"I know. Relax. The truth is, this is pretty normal for Harper."

"I just feel so bad that I ruined the birthday cake," she pouted.

"Well, now you're officially part of the group. You're really not one of us until you embarrass the shit out of yourself."

"Oh, thanks. That's so reassuring."

"Just telling it like it is, baby. You want to head home?" She looked exhausted and a little overwhelmed. She hadn't hung out with a group this large in a very long time. Even with how fun it all was, I knew it was too much for her.

"I don't want to make you leave your friends," she said hesitantly.

"Ali, I know this is a lot for you. If you're ready to go, we'll head out. There'll be plenty of other parties to go to. You don't have to push yourself to do too much too fast."

"Yeah," she finally agreed. "I'm ready. I'm just not quite comfortable with all this yet."

"I know. It's fine. Let's say goodnight and we'll head home."

Chapter Twenty-Four

CHRIS

We had gotten into a good routine over the last month. Axel was doing great with his training, but I was pretty sure that it was more than he thought it would be. But he never complained. He just kept on moving. I was proud of him for taking on such a hard training schedule.

Ali had been working for Kate for a few weeks now and she was really liking the slower pace of the clinic. After everything she had already seen with the Blood Devils, this was exactly what she needed. Our house had just been finished last week. Our house wasn't in as bad of shape as some of the others, and we didn't have little kids running around. I started fixing up the basement on the weekends for Axel. He wanted to help, but he didn't have enough time in his training schedule. Besides, this was something I wanted to do for my son.

Sebastian had kept our load pretty light over the past month while we were all trying to get our lives back. Between houses needing repairs and the need to be at home with our families, nobody really wanted to take on any jobs just yet. We stuck with security installations until we were all back to normal. Cazzo had taken some time off to be with Vanessa. She was pretty devastated over the loss of their baby and Cazzo was pissed as hell that his sanctuary had been destroyed and someone had been able to get to Vanessa.

Sinner and Burg spent a few weeks helping him install new security measures around his house, along with a panic room. Personally, I thought that might be taking it too far, but when I saw the room when it was completed, I asked him for the specs so I could have one installed at my house. A few of the other guys felt the same way and it wasn't long before we were all trying to find the latest and greatest to secure our homes.

We had a meeting this afternoon to discuss taking on jobs. It was time we all got back to work or we wouldn't have a business to run anymore. I walked into the conference room and waited for everyone else to arrive. The guys all bantered, making fun of each other like they always did and I grinned, thinking that we were all finally getting back to normal.

"Alright, guys. That's enough. Let's get this meeting started so I can get home to my wife."

"Still got you by the balls, Cap?" Ice laughed at Sebastian.

"Firmly, but at least she's my wife. How long is Lindsey staying with you again?"

Ice glowered at Cap and shook his head. "What the hell was I supposed to do? Kick her out after we ruined her business?"

"We could always put her up in a hotel," Cap offered.

"I think she's planning on opening a B&B around here," Ice said, almost to himself.

"Bets in everyone," Sinner said as he pulled out a pen and paper and started a pool.

"Thirty days," I said instantly.

Ice glared at me. "I'm not involved with her."

"Fucking her isn't the same as being involved," I grinned.

"Damn straight," he said.

"But it sure does lead to it," I added.

Ice's face went lethal, just like his name implied. Sinner started taking bets on how long it would take before he bit the bullet and accepted his fate. Ice was getting more pissed by the minute. For as much as he acted like he didn't want what we all had, I knew that he was needing something more in his life. Something that grounded him.

The room got quiet and I pulled myself from my thoughts as I looked around, finally seeing that Lola was standing in the doorway. Hunter stood, but Lola shot him a glare that said to sit his ass down.

"About time you came back, Lola."

"Well, where else do I get to shoot at people?"

She took a seat and propped her feet on the table like she owned it.

"My rules still stand," Cap informed her.

"Got it, Cap."

"Knight has been working with Axel on training him for the military." Cap turned his attention back to everyone at the table. "You'll continue with that," he nodded to Knight, "but we need to make sure we still get our training in for our guys-"

"And girls," Florrie cut in. "What?" she said as we all looked at her. "Just because I like to kick ass and shoot a gun doesn't mean I'm a guy. I still like stilettos and looking pretty."

I caught Alec's eyes drifting down Florrie's chest where he blatantly stared at her breasts until his eyes flicked to mine and he quickly looked away. Very interesting. I wondered if they were just fucking or if Alec was just wanting to fuck her.

"Anyway, work out your schedule with Chris," Cap spoke to Knight. "If we're lucky, that kid'll be working for us one day. Let's make sure he's trained right."

We finished up the meeting and I headed down to the training room to get Axel. He was finishing up his workout schedule that Knight had put him on. He was on the treadmill right now, so I sat down and waited for him to finish. After this, we were heading home for dinner and he had his school work to finish. Ali wasn't going to be home until late tonight because she was helping Kate with paperwork. They were trying to catch up still from when we were all out of town. Kate had a partner at the clinic, but her being gone had set them all back.

"Ready to go, Chris?"

I stood and walked over to him, slapping him on the back and instantly regretting it. "You sweat like I do."

"Well, working out most of the day will do that. I know I need a shower, but can we just go home? I'm exhausted."

"Sure, kid." Normally, he showered here in the locker room when he was done with a workout. He was done in today. I could see it in the way he was standing.

We headed out to the truck and swung by the Chinese restaurant for dinner. Fuck cooking tonight. As much as I loved Ali, I couldn't subject her to my cooking. When we got home, Axel headed straight to the bathroom for a shower while I laid out all the food. I heard the front door slam and smiled, loving the sound of Ali walking through my front door. I turned to greet her, but was met with the butt of a gun to my head. I dropped to the floor, my head spinning as I tried to get my bearings.

Shaking my head, my vision cleared just enough that I could make out Slasher's figure in front of me right before he swung the gun at my head again.

My head was killing me and I could hear faint voices in the distance, but I couldn't figure out why I couldn't open my eyes. Everything was so fucked up in my head. My throat was on fire and my mouth was dry. What the hell happened?

My neck hurt from my chin resting against my chest, but I couldn't seem to move it in any other position right now. I pried one eye open and saw concrete below my feet. I was in a chair. I tried to shake my head slightly, but everything hurt to move. I opened my eyes further and saw my cowboy hat pulled down low on my head. At least I still had that. I never went anywhere without it if I could help it.

I used the brim of the hat as a shield and glanced around the room, careful not to move my head and give away that I was awake. Waking up like this was never a good thing and based on the tingling in my hands, I had some kind of rope tied around my wrists and it was cutting off the circulation.

Out of the corner of my eye, I could make out Axel's shoes not too far away. There was another set of shoes standing with him, but I couldn't make out who was in them.

"This was always going to be your life, you ungrateful bastard. We're gonna start over and your first job is to take out this fucker."

I knew that voice. It was a voice that I thought I had snuffed out just a month ago. This couldn't be real. I had fucking prayed that he was dead, but we had never gotten confirmation that he was dead. I shouldn't have let my guard down. I should have had someone tailing Ali all the time, but I was too focused on making sure that she had a normal life. I hadn't wanted her to feel like she was still in danger. Not to mention that we were all cleaning up still from being attacked. Nobody really had the time to follow her wherever she went. It was just too much to ask of the guys right now.

I turned my head slightly. Standing not fifteen feet from me was Slasher, the man I could have sworn I had killed. Yet here he was, standing with my kid and handing him a gun. I squeezed my eyes shut and tried to get my bearings. If I was going to get us out of here, I had to figure out what the fuck was going on and how I was going to get out of this mess.

"It's simple, kid. You shoot this fucker and I'll let you live. You need to prove to me that you're worthy of my name."

Axel shook his head in disgust. "Guess what, asshole-"

"Looks like your son is just as much of a pussy as you are," I cut in before Axel could say any more. If he told Slasher that he wasn't his kid, Slasher would put a bullet in him before I had a chance to stop him. Axel looked at me in confusion and maybe a little hurt. I narrowed my eyes at him, trying to convey my thoughts.

"He's not a pussy. He's gonna put a bullet in you and I'm gonna watch." Slasher held a gun to Axel's head and nudged him toward me. "Now or never, kid."

Axel looked back at Slasher and then to me. I could see the gun trembling in his hand. He was scared as fuck, but he had to do it. There was no other way out of this right now. If he shot me, he might still have a chance to get away. If he didn't, Slasher would kill him and then me. Axel's eyes filled with tears and I gave a barely imperceptible shake of my head. I glanced down toward my stomach and then back up at him. His hand slowly raised until the gun was pointed at me.

"Come on, Axel. Prove to me that you're not the pussy he thinks you are."

I swallowed hard as I saw a single tear fall from Axel's eye. I nodded at him with my eyes, trying to tell him it was alright. He didn't have any other choice. I held my eyes firmly on his, hoping to give him strength. When the gun fired, I did my best not to blink or show any signs of weakness. I blocked the pain for as long as I could.

The kid had done good. He had remembered what I'd taught him about where to shoot a person. While a shot to the stomach was extremely painful, a person could live up to a day or so after being shot if nothing vital was hit. That's what I was praying for.

"I wanted you to shoot him in the fucking head," Slasher yelled, pushing his gun hard against Axel's head.

"This is more painful. He could live for hours, dying slowly and in pain. More enjoyable for us, don't you think?" A slow grin curved his lips and I thanked God that he was able to pull himself together. Now all I needed was for one of my brothers to figure out where the hell I was.

Knowing that Axel would be fine, I finally let my eyes slide closed as the pain tore my insides apart. I couldn't tell where exactly the bullet hit, but it was fucking excruciating. The more pain I appeared to be in, the better it would be for Axel. Luckily, I didn't have to pretend all that much.

Chapter Twenty-Five

ALISON

I watched Slasher drive off with my son and Chris. I had been driving down the road to our house when I saw him shoving Chris in a van and pointing a gun at Axel. I was too late to do anything, but I could follow them. I saw them about a half a mile ahead of me and tried to catch up, but I got stuck at a light. I slammed my hand on the steering wheel in frustration when I saw the car turn down an alley.

"Fuck!"

When the light turned green, I slammed on the gas, racing through the intersection. I thought I saw a Reed Security SUV and it vaguely crossed my mind that I should call someone and let them know what was going on, but I couldn't stop looking for the car. If I did, I might never see Chris and Axel again.

I turned down the road that I thought Slasher had taken, but I couldn't see the car anywhere. I slowed down so I could check side streets and then I started driving up and down any road I could until I found them. I was just about to give up when I spotted a car up ahead. It was pulled up to a building that looked abandoned, but no one was in the car. Not wanting to be too close in case he had seen me, I parked a few blocks down and pulled the gun out of my glove compartment that Chris had stuck in there a few weeks ago. I checked the gun quickly, trying to remember what Chris had told me about how to use the weapon. This was the same one I had practiced with when he showed Axel and I that first day.

I stuffed the gun in the back of my jeans and hoped it didn't somehow fire and shoot me in the ass. That would be just my luck. I ran along the sides of the buildings, trying to be as stealthy as possible, and then ducked down when I got to the window outside the building. Peering in from the corner, I saw Chris tied up in a chair and Axel holding a gun on him while Slasher had a gun to his head. Vomit rose in my mouth and I swallowed it down, needing to be strong if I was going to get them out of this.

I took a few deep steadying breaths and pulled my gun out, checking it with shaky hands. *You can do this.* I repeated it over and over in my head until I heard the sound of a gunshot and flinched down. When I realized that the gunshot was from inside the building, I peeked in to see Chris staring down Axel. What had happened? Slasher pushed the gun against Axel's head and a grin took over Axel's face.

This didn't make any sense. Why would Axel be grinning at Slasher? I looked back to Chris and saw him slumping in his chair. Blood was dripping on the ground beneath him. I had to go in there now or I might never get another chance. I ran for the door and flung it open before I could think better of it, but the bright light from outside had temporarily blinded me in the dark space.

"Just in time," I heard Slasher say. I held my gun up, but was still seeing spots and didn't want to accidentally shoot Axel. I heard the door open behind me and then a gun fired. I was hit hard about the same time and then another gun went off.

Chapter Twenty-Six

AXEL

This was fucking insane. I had just shot my father, the one man that I felt I would truly be able to rely on the rest of my life. The man I looked up to and wanted to be just like. I had been about to tell Slasher to go fuck himself, that I wasn't his kid, but I saw the look in Chris's eyes. He knew as well as I did that if I said anything, Slasher would kill me, and that would fucking gut Chris. He wanted me to shoot him. He wanted me to put a bullet in him. How the hell was I supposed to live with myself?

I was breathing too fast and my palms were sweating. If I didn't calm down, I was going to get us all killed. I had to pretend like it didn't kill me to shoot my own father. I had to hold it together. I had shot Chris in the stomach because he had told me that someone could survive for days with a bullet wound to the stomach. He had also told me that it was a slow, painful death. If I had shot him in the shoulder, it wouldn't have been a life threatening wound. My only choices were the head or the chest and either of those would have killed him. He might survive this though.

The door slammed open and I saw my mom enter. Panic filled me. I knew that Slasher didn't give two shits about her. He would kill her in a heartbeat, but what the hell could I do about it? Slasher still had his gun pointed at my head. I wasn't fast enough to shoot him before he could pull the trigger. My eyes flicked to Mom. She was holding a gun, but she wasn't shooting. I didn't know if she didn't want to or couldn't.

I wanted to yell at her and tell her to run. I wanted to tell her that she should save herself. She shouldn't be in the middle of all this, but then Slasher pointed his gun at her and I spun around, not even thinking as I pulled the trigger, shooting him in the head just as his gun went off.

I watched as his body slumped to the ground. I didn't feel a fucking thing but relief. I stared at the blood draining from his head and knew that this wasn't over for me. This was just the beginning of the life I would build for myself. I looked over at Mom and saw that she was covered on the ground by Gabe. I had seen him slip in just before Slasher turned his gun on her. I ran over to Chris, praying that I hadn't just killed the man that had saved me from certain death.

Chapter Twenty-Seven

ALISON

I was smashed against the ground and I could barely breathe. Someone big was on top of me and I still didn't know what was going on with Axel and Chris. I started wiggling to get away, but I couldn't move the stiff body on top of me. Then there was a groan and I froze.

"Stop fucking moving," the voice whispered. Slowly, whoever it was rolled off me and I could finally see who had been on top of me. It was Gabe. He was holding his chest and grimacing in pain. I looked up quickly to see Axel next to Chris, pressing something against his body and Slasher on the ground, unmoving. I couldn't process what was going on around me, so I scooted over to Gabe and started looking for injuries.

"I'm fine," he groaned. "I'm wearing a vest. Just give me a minute."

The shaking that was in my hands earlier was now a full on body shake. I was cold and then I was hot. I plopped down on my butt as spots appeared in my eyes.

"Deep breaths," Gabe bit out. "Put your head between your knees."

I tried, I really did, but I just couldn't make myself move. I was the nurse. I was supposed to be the one taking care of other people, but I couldn't even seem to take care of myself at the moment. Gabe's face appeared directly in front of me. His eyes were creased with pain, but still, he grabbed my hands and squeezed tight.

"Come on, Ali. Snap out of it and breathe."

My eyes flashed over to Chris again and all the blood on the floor around him. All that blood. It reminded me of being in the ER. I had seen gunshot wounds hundreds of times over the years, but it was never from someone I loved. It was never my heart and life on the line.

"Ali!"

A hard slap landed across my face and then I finally focused on Gabe shouting at me. *Breathe*, he was saying. I could do that. Simple, right? I took a strangled breath in and realized that I was really close to passing out if I didn't start really breathing. I gulped in more air over and over until the dizziness passed and the spots disappeared. Gabe held my hand the whole time until I calmed down.

"Chris. I have to get to Chris," I whispered.

"He's over there. The ambulance is on the way."

Tears spilled down my cheeks as I got up and stumbled over to him. His shirt was soaked with blood and his eyes were just barely open.

"Chris," I cried. "Hold on. Help is coming."

"Ali." It was faint and I could barely make out his words, so I leaned in closer. "Love you, Ali."

"I love you, too," I cried. "Don't talk like that, though. You're going to be fine."

I sucked back the tears and wiped at my face as Gabe untied his bonds. He slowly lowered him to the ground and I ripped open his shirt to see where his wounds were. "Okay, okay. I can do this."

I pressed my hands over his wound, pushing harder when he cringed in pain. Pain was good. It meant his body was still feeling something. I just had to slow the bleeding. Gabe handed me his jacket and I quickly placed it over his wound and pressed hard again.

"Don't leave me, Chris."

"I'm not going anywhere, Ali. I already lost you once," he whispered. I could barely see those dark eyes that were usually so full of life. Now they looked like they were barely hanging on. I could hear the ambulance in the distance and I could hear Gabe's footsteps as he ran for the door, but my eyes were focused solely on the man in front of me. I watched as his breathing slowed and prayed when his eyes slid closed that it wouldn't be the last time I ever saw him.

"Mom," Axel said from behind me.

I shook my head as the tears slid down my face. "No," I whispered. I couldn't answer his questions right now. I couldn't tell him whether his father would live or die. I couldn't fathom the thought that we had fought so hard to be together again only for him to be ripped from my life by the man that had initially torn us apart. This wasn't how our story ended. It couldn't be.

"Chris, you fight," I said forcefully. His eyes fluttered, but he didn't move. I pressed down hard with one hand over his wound and gripped his hand firmly in mine. "Chris! Do you hear me?"

His head tilted slightly toward me and his eyes slitted open. He nodded slightly, but it wasn't good enough.

"Don't give me that shit, Chris. You're a fighter. You always have been. Fight, goddamnit!"

He still didn't say anything, but he let out a harsh breath that almost sounded like a light laugh. His eyes opened just a little more and we connected once again. I wouldn't let that connection slip away.

"Keep fighting. We have too much left to do. Do you hear me?"

"How can...I not. You're...fucking yelling...at me." The words were choppy and forced, but even through all that, I could hear the humor in his voice. He was fighting with all he had and I knew he wouldn't give up on me. There just wasn't another way that this could end. Anything else wasn't something I could even consider.

"Ma'am, I need you to step aside. Ma'am."

I moved away, but my eyes never left Chris's penetrating gaze. He stared at me the whole time they worked on him, grimacing when they started poking and prodding him. As they lifted him on the stretcher, I grabbed for his hand and felt his weak grip hold onto me.

"Ma'am, you can follow–"

"Bullshit. I'm going with you."

I could tell the paramedic wanted to argue, but that was just tough shit. Right before the ambulance door closed, I shouted to Gabe.

"Gabe! Take Axel to the hospital."

He nodded and then the doors closed. I was shoved aside so they could work on him. The whole ride to the hospital, I did my best to keep my eyes on his. I was annoyed every time the paramedic moved in front of me and broke our connection, even though I knew it was necessary. Right before we arrived at the hospital, Chris's eyes slid closed and they didn't open again.

My heart thudded loudly in my ears. The paramedics spoke loudly to each other and I was pushed further toward the back of the ambulance. If it was anyone but Chris, I would have known what was going on. I was an ER nurse. But it was Chris and I couldn't look at him as just any patient. All I saw was my life slipping further and further away.

I was pulled from the ambulance and shoved to the side as they rushed him through the doors. Everything was a haze around me now that Chris was no longer connected to me. I felt so lost. I didn't know what to do. I just stood in the doorway of the hospital as the automatic doors opened and closed because I was still standing on the mat.

I looked down at the blood staining my hands and clenched my fists tight. That couldn't be the last time I spoke with Chris. There was so much that we had missed out on over the years. He didn't get to teach Axel to ride a bike or how to skate. He didn't hear his first words or see his first steps. But there were still things that he could be a part of. His first day of college, getting married, his first child.

"Mom?" I was startled out of my thoughts by Axel shaking me. "I've been talking to you. Are you okay?"

I looked at him funny. That was an odd question. His father might not live past today and he was concerned about me?

"He'll be okay, Mom."

His hand was on my shoulder in a reassuring gesture. It was then I realized that Axel was almost a man. He stood by me, tall and strong, much like his father. He had been training with him and I only now noticed how much he was beginning to take on Chris's features. He was no longer the scared, timid kid that watched himself around Slasher. He was fierce and would one day be the warrior Chris was. I knew for certain that would be his path, especially after today.

I gripped onto his hand as he led me into the waiting room. Slowly, every person from Reed Security filtered into the hospital, coming to wait to find out what was going on with Chris. I couldn't stand all the people coming up to me with their reassuring thoughts and their pitying gazes. All I wanted was for everyone to leave me alone.

Hours passed as I waited for any scrap of news from the doctors, but we waited all afternoon and well into the night without any word, other than he was still in surgery. That could be seen two ways: one, that his body was surviving long enough to tolerate the surgery, or two, that there were complications and it was taking longer than expected. I couldn't dwell on that right now. I walked in circles around the waiting room, trying to keep everyone from coming up to me and trying to soothe me. When Ice walked up to me for the third time in the past hour, I turned on my heel and walked away. I realized that he was one of Chris's closest friends, but I wasn't in the right state of mind to deal with him.

A firm hand gripped me around the bicep and started dragging me down the hall. We walked down several halls and down a flight of stairs. I barely had time to register that it was Gabe as I was shoved into the women's locker room.

"What are you doing? We can't be in here."

"You look like shit."

Typical Gabe. Would he ever treat me as anything other than the enemy?

"Look, I'm not exactly worried about how I look right now. I just-"

"Do you want Chris to see you like that?" he snapped. He pulled a strap off his shoulder and I realized he had a backpack with him. "Here, you need to change out of those clothes. I talked with the nurses and they're going to let you use the locker room to clean up."

"I need to be back out there. The doctors are going to be coming out any minute now to tell us what's going on with Chris."

"You need to pull yourself together. Chris doesn't need to see you looking like a scene from *Carrie*."

"I hardly think that he'd care what I look like when he gets out of surgery."

"He'd worry about you instead of focusing on getting better," he snarled.

"Why are you still treating me like crap? What did I ever do to you? Have I not proven myself enough yet?" I shouted.

He grabbed me by both arms and shook me slightly. "I'm trying to get you to take care of yourself. You're a fucking mess and nobody is trying to put you back together. You know that Chris will be worried about you if he sees you all covered in blood. It's gonna stress him out and he doesn't need that. And you don't need to wear the reminder of what happened today anymore. You need to get in that fucking shower and wipe off his blood and get your head on straight. You've been pacing the fucking waiting room for hours and it's not helping you. But you can get cleaned up and stop reminding yourself every time that you look at your hands that you were at the scene of a murder."

I looked into his wide, fierce eyes and started to cry. I didn't mean to, but he was right. I was a complete mess and part of me didn't want to wipe away his blood because I was scared that it would wipe him away. Gabe pulled me against his chest and ran his large hand up and down my back as I cried against his massive frame. I gripped the back of his shirt and held on tightly as my body fell apart. It was all too much for the day. I wanted a do over on my life. I wanted to go back in time and have none of this happen. I just couldn't deal with anything else right now.

Gabe eased me back and looked at me in concern. "You're going to be okay. So will Chris. Now, go get cleaned up. I'm going to be right outside the door if you need me. Ice will let me know if he hears anything, okay?"

I nodded and sniffled as I wiped my nose. I could do this. I could shower and wipe away all the crap from today. I took the backpack from him and walked around the locker room until I found the shower. I stripped robotically out of my clothes and threw them right in the garbage. I didn't need to see them again. I turned on the water and started to wash away the blood and dirt from my body, but the more I washed, the more appeared. What was going on? I couldn't get it to come off.

A desperate cry tore from my throat when the blood continued to stain my skin. I poured more soap onto the cloth and scrubbed harder. "Come on!" I yelled as I washed harder. Tears were pouring down my face as I slid down the wall of the shower, unable to stand and look at the blood anymore. I cried into my hands until I felt the water shut off. I looked up in surprise to see Gabe standing in front of me with a towel. He quickly covered me and helped me to my feet. When my knees wobbled, he picked me up and carried me into the changing area.

"It's okay. I've got you," he murmured. He set me down on a bench and walked away, returning a few seconds later with another towel. He dried off my legs and arms and slipped the towel around my back. Opening the backpack, he pulled out underwear and a pair of yoga pants. He slid them onto my legs and I was surprised that it didn't feel intimate. He actually looked a little embarrassed to be helping me. That's when my brain finally kicked in and I stopped him before he had to slide them all the way up my legs.

"Thanks. Sorry, I'm okay now."

He nodded and stood up. "I'll be outside."

I quickly got dressed after that, embarrassed that I had gone into a full meltdown and had to be rescued by the one man that I thought completely hated me. I walked out with the empty backpack to see Gabe waiting for me in the hall. We silently walked up to the waiting area where everyone was still waiting. Did they all know what had just happened? It felt like everyone was watching me. My cheeks reddened when I thought of what Gabe had just done for me, but he just took a seat and nodded for me to sit down. I sat down beside him and ignored the worried looks.

It was about a half hour later when the doctor finally came out to talk to us. Apparently, surgery had been more difficult than antici-pated, but they were able to repair everything and he was in recovery. I wasn't allowed back to see him for another half hour that felt more like an entire day. I was anxious to see his face again.

When I finally made it to his room, Axel accompanied me, even though they told us to go one at a time. He had just as much right to be there as I did. When I walked in, I half expected for Chris to already be awake, which was silly because working in a hospital, I knew that people didn't just wake up right after surgery. He was pale with dark bruises under his eyes, but otherwise, just appeared to be sleeping.

I sat down beside him and held his hand, staring at his features. Hours passed and I was getting anxious for him to wake up. Axel had been staring out the window for a while now, just staring at the parking lot. I wished now more than ever that I had some hobby that could keep me busy, like crocheting or knitting. Anything to keep my hands and mind occupied until he woke up. I didn't have a book on me and I didn't want to turn on the TV. What if it disturbed him?

The nurse came in several times over the course of the next few hours to check on him and then informed us that visiting hours were over.

"I'm not leaving," I said urgently.

"Ma'am, we'll inform you when he wakes up, but right now, you need to leave."

"I'm pretty sure that family is allowed to stay."

"You aren't married," she said firmly.

"No, but he is the father of my child. I'm not leaving."

"Ma'am, if you don't leave-"

"She's staying."

I looked beyond the nurse to see Gabe standing in the hallway with his arms crossed over his chest. Ice, Jules, Cap, and Maggie were standing behind him with the same stern expressions on their faces. "We're his security detail and she's a part of that. They stay together until we're sure the threat is over."

When the nurse looked at everyone else and then back toward the nurses station, Gabe grinned and sent me a quick wink. I finally got it in that moment. Once I became a part of the Reed Security family, there was nothing that would keep any of them from looking after me. They weren't just here to support Chris, but also Axel and me.

The nurse huffed and walked away.

"Thank you."

Gabe nodded. "Is he awake yet?"

"No. It's been a few hours now. He should have woken up by now."

"Well, his body's been through a lot. I'm sure he's just taking it easy, trying to pull one over on all of us."

"Sure." I didn't really agree with his statement, but I knew he was trying to ease my worry, so I let it slide. "Do you want to go in?" I asked them.

"We'll wait until he's awake," Cap said before anyone else could answer.

As I looked around at Chris's family, I almost burst into tears, grateful that I had the support system of all his friends. I hadn't had anyone to look after me in years, and while I knew they were here for Chris, I also knew that they were here for me. As if sensing my distress, Gabe walked over to me and wrapped me in a hug before dragging me back into the room where he sat in the corner. Just knowing that it wasn't just Axel and I waiting took away some of the tension.

As the hours passed, I grew more and more anxious. The nurses started coming in more frequently and their hushed whispers were enough to make me feel like I was going insane. By the time the twenty-four hour mark came and went, I was a nervous wreck, snapping at the nurses every time they came in.

"Why isn't he awake yet? Something's wrong. I want the doctor in here now."

"Ma'am, his body has been through-"

"I'm a nurse. I don't need you to talk to me gently and give me a bunch of platitudes. I need to know what's wrong with him. Just tell me the truth!"

I was getting out of control. I could see it on the nurse's face and I could feel it in the erratic behavior I had started to display. I was truly losing my mind. If he didn't wake up, I was all alone again. Axel would move on with his life and make something of himself, but I would be left to deal with the fallout of losing the man I loved for a second time. I just couldn't do it. I couldn't stand here and wait for them to tell me that my life was essentially over. It was all too much.

Gabe's hands gripped my shoulders in support, but I feared also to hold me back from clawing this woman's eyes out. I was that close to losing it. I took a deep breath and tried to speak in a calm voice.

"Listen, I understand that you're not supposed to tell me anything without a doctor here. I know this, but please, try to understand that he's my whole life." My voice cracked and tears slipped down my face. I tried to pull myself together, but my body was done. I was breaking down. Her sad, pitying face just made everything worse. "Please," I whimpered. "Just tell me."

"Ali." It was faint, barely a whisper, but it echoed around the room like a shot. I spun around with blurry, tear-filled eyes and looked into Chris's dark, stormy eyes. He was awake. I rushed to his side, practically shoving Gabe out of the way to get to him. I gripped tightly to his hand, on the verge of crying hysterically when he squeezed mine back.

"You're awake," I cried. "I thought I'd lost you."

He struggled to lift his other hand and placed it against my wet cheek. His voice was rough, but there was a hint of teasing in it. "I told you I'd always come back to you."

Chapter Twenty-Eight

CHRIS

Three Years Later...

I was a fucking wreck. I was snapping at everyone that came within five feet of me and needed something. Everyone knew what was going on this week and I swear to God, they were all pushing my buttons just to see how long it took me to snap. I paced around the Reed Security building, holding my phone in my hand, waiting for the call that would forever change my son's life.

For the first two years after I was released from the hospital, Axel had been training with Reed Security. After everything that happened with Slasher, Axel was determined to join the military, but he didn't want to follow in my footsteps. He aimed higher. He wanted to be a fucking Navy SEAL. He trained with Knight every opportunity he had and was pushed way beyond his limits because Knight knew what it would take for him to make it through BUDs and then SEALs training. He had just completed his final week of training and I was waiting on his call to let me know if he made it or not. I think I was more nervous than his mother. I wanted this so badly for him that I could taste it.

"Chris."

"What?" I snapped as I turned around and stared at Gabe. The fucker had become like a surrogate brother to Ali and I couldn't shake the man. He was her shadow wherever she went. Half the time, he knew her work schedule better than I did. He was even in the room with her when we had our kid a few months ago. Ali was only eight months along, but she had gone into labor early and I was on a job. I was an hour late for the birth of our daughter, Elizabeth. Gabe had taken my place in the room and was now practically her second father. She was his little Lizzie and it pissed me off how close they were already.

Still, I couldn't be too hard on the man. He had gone from distrusting Ali to becoming her protector. After all that Ali had been through, I didn't mind another set of eyes always being on her. Especially when I couldn't always be there. If I had to be out of town, he was always at the house, watching over her or calling to check up on her. Any other man might consider that they were having an affair, but I knew better. I was the only man Ali ever looked at with those beautiful bedroom eyes. I would never have anything to worry about with her. Except maybe that Gabe would be buried right along next to us. That would be taking it too far.

"Dude, your wife is here with Lizzie. Chill the fuck out. She's having a rough day, so try not to be such an asshole," he growled.

My shitty attitude immediately morphed into concern at his words. I ran to the lobby where I knew she would be waiting and wrapped her in my arms when I saw the tears streaming down her face. "What is it? What happened?"

Her hiccuping sobs made a sharp pain rip through my chest. Something terrible had happened and I had no clue what it was or if I could even make it better, but I would do anything to try.

"I...tried on my jeans...this morning," she said between sobs.

"Okay?" I said, unsure where she was going with this.

"They didn't fit," she cried.

I rubbed my hands up and down her arms, trying to figure out what the hell I was supposed to say to that. "Well, you just had a baby, honey. The fat doesn't just go away."

"The fat?" she screeched. "Why would you automatically assume that my pants didn't fit because of the fat?"

"Because you just had a baby?" I said slowly.

"But why couldn't you assume that they didn't fit because I had lost so much weight?"

Ah. This was one of those trick questions that I learned about while she was pregnant. It ranked up there with *Do you think I'm eating too much?* Or *Do I look like I'm carrying twins?* I learned early on that there were certain questions that you just didn't answer. Unfortunately, I was distracted today and didn't really think about her statement until it was already too late. Time for some creative maneuvering.

"Honey, I know exactly where all the fat is on your delectable body and trust me, it's in all the right places. I love your curves and if you never lost the weight, I would be a happy man. But I want you to be happy with yourself. If you want to lose the weight, you go for it. If you need to go buy bigger pants because this beautiful body that gave me such a beautiful daughter has grown, then we'll go buy you a whole fucking new wardrobe. Either way, nothing's going to stop me from craving every inch of you any time I can have you."

I nipped at her earlobe and pressed my growing erection against her. I wasn't lying. I loved her curves and every inch of her body, no matter how much it had changed. Her breasts were bigger, her ass was bigger, and her hips had this perfect sway to them. Yeah, she still had a pouch from where she carried our daughter, but I didn't give a shit. That softness just reminded me of all she went through to give me a family. If I had to remind her every minute of every day how much I craved her, I would make it a priority.

"Chris," she sniffled. "You always know the perfect thing to say," she murmured. I had a secret weapon though. I didn't just come up with this genius on my own. Maggie had a running list of things that she wanted Cap to say to her stuck on the fridge. Any time I was over there, I looked at the list and studied any new entries. Call it research on the female mind. After all, a man had to take advantage where he could.

"Baby, I love you and I always will."

I pressed my lips to hers and gave her a slow, tantalizing kiss that I

felt all the way down in my groin. Shit. I had to stop this before I mauled her right here in the lobby. I should at least ask Gabe to watch Lizzie and take her to the training room. We could definitely have some fun there.

"Have you heard from Axel yet?" She asked against my chest.

"Not yet. I've been going fucking crazy, waiting for his call."

I heard Gabe's phone ring and saw him bend down to play with Lizzy as he answered. "Oh, hey, Axel. How's it going?"

My gaze swiveled to Gabe's and I glared at him. Did I mention that ever since he saved Ali's life, Gabe had also become somewhat of a hero to my son? Yeah, it didn't matter that I taught Axel how to use a gun and that had he not shot Slasher in the head, his mother could have still died. Nope, none of that mattered because Gabe had been the one to take a bullet for his mother. Well, in the vest. That shit didn't really count. He wasn't actually shot.

"No shit? That's fucking awesome. No, he's right here. Hold on."

Gabe grinned as he handed over his phone to me. I glared at him as I snatched the phone out of his hand. "Axel?"

"Hey, Dad. I'm in. I fucking did it!" he shouted.

A huge grin split my lips as I pulled Ali in close to me and squeezed the life out of her. "You earned it, kid." Moisture filled my eyes and a lump formed in my throat. I was fucking over the moon filled with pride at my kid. He had gone through fucking hell to make this happen. It was the one thing he wanted more than anything in the world. "So, now you're a SEAL."

"Yeah, well, I still have like thirty more weeks of training before I'll be deployed."

"I'm sure your mom will be happy to hear that."

"Dad, I couldn't have done it without your help. I don't know if I ever said it, but all you and everyone else did for me, you saved my fucking life. I'll never forget that."

I unwrapped my arm from around Ali and shoved my hand through my hair, pushing my cowboy hat off in the process. This kid was too much and everything I could ever ask for in a son. "I love you, kid."

"Love you too, Dad. And every time I'm deployed, I'm gonna be fighting for the same thing you gave me. Freedom. You're the reason I am who I am today."

Now I was fucking crying. This kid was shredding me and he didn't even know it. It felt like razors were cutting my throat as I tried to croak out some kind of response. I was so choked up, I couldn't say a fucking thing. Gabe snatched the phone from my hands and raised an eyebrow at me.

"What the fuck did you say to your old man? He's fucking crying over here."

Gabe looked up at me and gave me a chin lift. No doubt, he would fucking rag on me later for being such a pussy, but right now, he understood why I was so emotional.

"Yeah, I'll tell him to check his phone. Be good, kid. Here's your mom." Gabe handed the phone to Ali and shook his head. She moved across the room, gushing on the phone with her son. "He's been trying to call you all morning. He said your phone kept going to voicemail."

I pulled it out of my pocket and realized that it wasn't even on. Fuck, I had turned it off somehow. I turned it back on and saw that I had at least fifteen voicemails from Axel.

"I'm giving you one day," Gabe stressed. "One day to feel this and then I'm telling all those fuckers how you cried like a fucking baby because your kid became a SEAL."

"You know what?" I smirked. "I don't even fucking care."

"Care about what?" Ali asked as she stepped into my arms.

"He's making fun of me because I started crying when Axel was talking to me."

"Well, you know it does kind of take away the whole badass vibe you've got going. You're not going to cry on your next job, are you? I don't think people are going to be scared of you holding a gun and crying."

"As long as Axel isn't on the phone telling me that I saved his fucking life, we'll be good." I looked into her eyes and tried to convey how much I loved all that she had done for our son. "He's a great fucking kid, and I may have helped him become a man, but everything he is, all that's in his heart is because of you."

"Chris, I hate that we missed out on so much time together, but there's not a day that goes by that I'm not thankful to have such a wonderful man in my life. I couldn't have asked for a better, stronger role model for our son. I love you so much."

"I love you, too Ali," I whispered fiercely.

"Alright. Enough." Gabe crossed his arms over his chest, rolling his eyes in disgust. "You know, all you fucking women make us a bunch of pussies. I'm just saying," He yanked up his pants like he was trying to be more manly and puffed out his chest. "We're supposed to be protectors and fierce men who hold weapons and say shit like *don't fuck with me*. Then you walk in with your cute little baby girl and your kid calls and one of the most lethal men in this building is a fucking puddle of mush on the floor. I'm just saying, that shit has to stop. You're gonna ruin our reputations."

He walked away and I tugged Ali into me again. "What do you say we get Gabe to watch Elizabeth? It seems I have a reputation to uphold and I know just how to do that," I smirked at her.

ALSO BY GIULIA LAGOMARSINO

Thank you for reading Chris and Ali's story. There's still more to come further down the line, so keep reading. The Reed Security gang will be back in Lola's story!

Join my newsletter to get the most up-to-date information, along with new content in the Reed Security series.

https://giulialagomarsinoauthor.com/connect/

Join my Facebook reader group to find out more about my obsession with Dwayne Johnson!

https://www.facebook.com/groups/GiuliaLagomarsinobooks

Reading Order:

https://giulialagomarsinoauthor.com/reading-order/

To find the individual series, follow the links below:

For The Love Of A Good Woman series

Reed Security series

The Cortell Brothers

A Good Run Of Bad Luck

Made in the USA
Las Vegas, NV
06 November 2024

11208691R00152